GW00673652

# Hope for Everyone

## A Fresh Vision of the Afterlife

By

## David Bell and Dave Griffiths

Grosvenor House
Publishing Limited

All rights reserved
Copyright © David Bell and Dave Griffiths, 2024

The right of David Bell and Dave Griffiths to be identified as the
author of this work has been asserted in accordance with Section 78
of the Copyright, Designs and Patents Act 1988

The book cover is copyright to David Bell and Dave Griffiths

This book is published by
Grosvenor House Publishing Ltd
Link House
140 The Broadway, Tolworth, Surrey, KT6 7HT.
www.grosvenorhousepublishing.co.uk

This book is sold subject to the conditions that it shall not, by way of
trade or otherwise, be lent, resold, hired out or otherwise circulated
without the author's or publisher's prior consent in any form of
binding or cover other than that in which it is published and
without a similar condition including this condition being
imposed on the subsequent purchaser.

This book is a work of fiction. Any resemblance to
people or events, past or present, is purely coincidental.

A CIP record for this book
is available from the British Library

ISBN 978-1-80381-972-3
eBook ISBN 978-1-80381-973-0

# Dedication

To our families and close friends:
Thank you for your help,
understanding and support.

David Bell and Dave Griffiths

# Acknowledgements

As in our first book "Emerging from the Rubble", it is Dave Griffiths who has produced most of the storyline in this new work based on our regular discussions and joint insights. During the course of writing we have been privileged to be in contact with many others with similar beliefs through the wonders of social media and have benefitted from many relevant internet articles and books. We list these resources on our website www. loveaboveallthings.uk.

We would like to give special thanks to Mary Anketell for editing and proofreading our original draft. Working with Mary has been a wonderful experience, and she has greatly improved the readability and consistency of the chapters. In many places she has suggested alternative sections that capture our thoughts in ways that we struggled to express.

We are also grateful to the many friends who critiqued sections of this work during its development.

The cover was selected from the many designs offered by Matt Davies. We were fortunate to have found such a good illustrator.

# Preface

*"In our world full of strangers, estranged from their own past,*
*culture, and country, from their neighbours, friends, and family*
*and from their deepest self, we witness a painful search*
*for a hospitable place where life can be lived without*
*fear and where community can be found."*
Henri Nouwen

Working together, Dave Griffiths and I have had many conversations about the afterlife. We have each experienced the grief of losing loved ones and searched for inner peace about their future and ours. We have chosen to create this story to record our current thoughts in a format that we hope is both entertaining and informative.

We have described our vision through the experiences of four people from different backgrounds: a soldier killed in a war; a gang leader who dies after a life of crime; an African girl murdered by her captors; and a western housewife who dies surrounded by her family.

The ideas in this story are offered as suggestions for contemplation. Whilst we believe that it is possible, neither of us would claim that the future will transpire to be exactly as depicted. The story has many elements that will be familiar to those who know the Bible but can be enjoyed by all.

Dave and I were both raised within Christian families and live in the south of England. Whilst we now reject much that the church taught, we cannot but frame our thoughts using concepts from our upbringing and environment. We have come to recognise that aspects of all faiths and cultures can be helpful and that no doctrine or lifestyle should be considered as the final authority.

We do not have a definite view about what happens to a person immediately after death. We do, however, believe that at some point everyone will be resurrected into a new body. To simplify the flow of the story we have chosen to say that a person awakes from a sleep-like state when first given their new body.

In this book we frequently use the term *agape love*, which may be unfamiliar to some of our readers. *Agape* (pronounced *a-ga-pay*) is the Greek word used in the New Testament of the Bible to describe both God's love for people and the highest possible expression of love in human relationships. In our story *agape love* describes the love that Eternal Love (the creator, the ground of all being, God) has for everyone. It is actually very difficult to encapsulate the full meaning of such love in words. It may be helpful to think of it as being like a diamond with more facets than can be counted.

We hold that eventually everyone will love everyone and live an abundant life. If this is to be the future, we accept that the details of how each day of our new lives will be structured is a discussion that will remain ongoing until we each personally experience it. However we feel that the fresh vision presented in this story can bring hope to those with whom it strikes a chord.

This story is a sequel to our first book "Emerging from the Rubble". It continues the story of many of the characters introduced in that book. Readers of that book have often asked us what happened next. This book addresses that question and many more.

We are both convinced that after the period when Jesus returns to this earth (described in "Emerging from the Rubble") a New Earth will be created. We believe this is the destiny of all of mankind and have formed a view on how it might function. We suggest answers to such questions as: How will it be possible to live with those who have hurt others? Will there be money? What technology will be available? And how do immortal bodies recover from injury? We hope you find our suggestions at least worthy of consideration.

The objective has been to describe the structure of a future environment that would facilitate each individual reaching maturity without the use of coercion or diktat. Whilst using specific examples to make our points, the precise details of each storyline should not be considered a basis of a doctrine or moral position.

Now that we have envisioned and described a logical and practical way in which a harmonious life could be achieved for all, our minds are at peace. The future may not be exactly as we have portrayed it. But having constructed what we believe to be a feasible scenario, we have inner assurance that it will be possible for each and every human to eventually live an abundant life.

Our wish is that you may also achieve such inner peace.

David Bell and Dave Griffiths

12 July 2024

# Resurrections

Johan sensed light around him, like waking from a deep sleep to morning sunshine. Opening his eyes, he remained motionless. Slowly he began to feel his body. He touched his legs with his palms and turned his head from side to side. Was it a dream or had he really been travelling toward a light in a vast black space? The last thing he remembered with any certainty was blowing out a lantern in the dank dugout he shared with Wilhelm and two new recruits.

Looking around he saw that he was in a living room very similar to the one he had known in his childhood. It was light and airy with large windows overlooking a landscape of rolling hills. The sofa on which he was lying was so comfortable that he felt as though he was floating. Somehow, this place felt just like home, although he was sure he had never been there before.

To his right were folded clothes. Dry, soft clothes were a distant memory. He felt like a child getting into cosy pyjamas as he put them on.

Johan wondered if he had been injured. Was he in some sort of hospital? As he tried hard to remember anything about what had happened since snuffing out the lantern, he heard footsteps, and a door to his left opened. A face peered around the door.

"Johan," said the face, olive-skinned with thick dark wavy hair and a short beard. It was like an old friend greeting him with affection.

Johan smiled back, but with some puzzlement. The friendly face continued with a warm smile, "I know, it's confusing. Come with me, and all will become clear. All is well."

Johan followed the man through a short entrance hall into a kitchen.

This side of the house glowed with a welcoming hue that reminded Johan of firelight. Sitting at a wooden table was a figure that shimmered like a rainbow. Johan could clearly make out the being's shape and form but other features were hard to define.

The dark-haired man pulled out a chair from under the table and signalled Johan to take a seat.

"This is Ruach," he said.

The being's eyes seemed to take in the totality of Johan, both inside and out. Far from feeling self-conscious, Johan felt seen, welcomed and understood. The man placed a steaming mug on the table in front of him.

"Black coffee, no sugar."

Johan looked at the mug and then back at the man.

"That's how I like it," he said, bewildered.

"You're probably wondering where you are?"

Johan took a sip of the coffee. It was hot but didn't burn his mouth. He looked at the man and nodded, still trying to remember what had happened.

"My name is Jesus."

Johan nearly spat out the coffee he was savouring. Jesus and Ruach chuckled, and Johan laughed nervously with them as he composed himself.

"This is our home, and you are our guest," Jesus continued.

"Wh… why am I here?" stuttered Johan.

"Your time in the Previous Age has ended. In other words, you died."

"Dead?" Johan's eyes opened wide.

"It was very quick. You had no time to realise," Ruach reassured him.

"How?" asked Johan, trying to grasp what was happening.

"A shell hit your dugout. It killed you and three others," replied Ruach.

"What? I had no idea. So, wait, is this … is this it? Am I in Heaven?"

"Don't worry, all will become clear," said Jesus.

"This is our time to look at your existence so far – your experiences during the Previous Age, what you have learned and where we go from here," continued Ruach.

Johan took a deeper breath. "I see," he said. "So, if I died with the other three, why aren't they here too? Where's Wilhelm?"

"Everyone gets their own time with us," Jesus replied. "Every person has their own unique journey."

"So this is like an appraisal of my life? Wait! Isn't that what's called *Judgement Day*?"

"We think that sounds a little severe," said Jesus.

"I heard that God's judgement was supposed to be severe."

"Sometimes it can appear so," replied Ruach. "However, this is more like a discussion. Everything we do is because we love each person with unfailing *agape love*."

Johan thought for a moment. Questioning Jesus and Ruach seemed at once both strange and absolutely necessary. Desiring to know as much as possible, he continued.

"What does unfailing *agape love* mean?"

Jesus smiled and looked Johan in the eye. It was unnerving, yet somehow thrilling.

"It means the highest, purest type of love. Our love for people will not fail to seek the best for them. It comes in many forms to restore and reconcile creation."

This sounded rather idealistic to Johan, who had seen too much violence in his short existence to comprehend quite what Jesus meant.

"Ok, so if you love everyone, does everyone just go to Heaven?"

Jesus pulled out a chair and sat down at the table. "What do you mean by Heaven?"

"A place where good people go to be with God after they die," replied Johan.

"Well, that would not be our definition," said Jesus with a smile.

"What about Hell?" asked Johan nervously.

"Well, we don't have any *lakes of fire*, if that is what you are worried about."

That was actually what Johan was worried about, and he breathed a sigh of relief.

"Which brings us to you, Johan," said Ruach.

"Me?" whispered Johan. He bowed his head, suddenly feeling emotional. "I know what I am. I am a soldier - a man of war."

"That is not what defines you," said Jesus firmly. "You could not help where and when you were born. What matters is your heart."

Ruach nodded, "The circumstances you found yourself in were ugly, but your heart is beautiful. I saw you giving the last of your water to captive soldiers. I saw you hold your dying captain until he was gone, even though he belittled you every day."

Johan began to well up.

"But, but didn't you see all the times I failed? I couldn't save my captain, and I know our army did horrific things. I did things I am ashamed of."

"I saw," said Ruach tenderly. "But I know your heart hated that which was evil."

"But I swore an oath to the Fuhrer."

"You will get a chance to make new commitments." Jesus said, reaching across the table and placing a hand on Johan's wrist. Johan looked up, tears rolling down his cheeks.

"How can I live a better life? What must I learn to do?" he asked.

Ruach leaned in towards him, her presence somehow calming.

"We have a place for you. You will get to explore our *agape love* without the constraints of the Previous Age. How would you like to help care for some of our children?"

"Children? There are children here?"

"Yes, children who die in the Previous Age still get to grow up. They are placed with relatives who have been raised into this age."

"My sister!" gasped Johan.

Jesus and Ruach beamed as Johan realised that he was about to be reunited with his little sister, Gertrude, who had died when she was seven years old.

\*

Yuri opened his eyes and immediately jumped up. It wasn't unusual for Yuri to find himself in an alien environment. He must have blacked out, or been drugged and kidnapped. As soon as he had cast his eyes over the room, there was a knock at the door to his left. Yuri spun around, fists balled.

"Christ!" he yelled with surprise, alarmed that he might be joined by a stranger.

"That's right," chuckled Jesus.

"Huh?" replied Yuri, confused and coiled like a spring.

"Why don't you put your clothes on?" offered Jesus from behind the door.

Yuri didn't say anything, but his fists relaxed a little. To Yuri's right was a rail with some familiar-looking clothes hanging on it.

5

He grabbed the first things that came to hand and pulled them on roughly.

Striding over to the door, he jerked it open and saw a man leaning up against the wall just outside.

"Do you like your clothes?" Jesus asked.

Yuri stayed silent, feeling awkward. His eyes looked the man up and down and he wondered what this stranger wanted.

"Come through?" beckoned Jesus with an open arm, pointing across a hall to the kitchen.

"Where's the boss?" said Yuri curtly. "I want to see your boss."

"I don't have a boss," Jesus answered gently. "You can meet my friend though. She'll be along shortly."

"What do you want with me?" Yuri felt increasingly aware of how little he knew. If there was one thing he hated, it was not being in control.

"Come on through," repeated Jesus.

"You first," demanded Yuri.

Jesus nodded and held the door open.

Tentatively, Yuri stepped into the kitchen. His eyes furtively searched the room for anything he could use as a weapon, but there were no knives - not even a rolling pin.

Jesus gestured toward a seat that was pulled out from the wooden kitchen table. It was the kind of table Yuri had spent hours at, hunched over a deck of cards, chain-smoking Marlboro Reds and knocking back vodka.

"I'll stand," insisted Yuri. "Where is this friend of yours?"

"She'll be along in a minute," said Jesus, hardly able to contain an excited smile.

Jesus turned around and poured out a short drink. He slid the glass along the worktop towards Yuri.

"Here."

Yuri looked at the glass and, not wanting to give away any sign of weakness, slung the shot back and slammed the glass down on the worktop.

His eyes lit up and he stood up straight.

Jesus smiled. "We want you to feel welcome here."

The door at the back of the kitchen burst open and a shimmering being entered with a large German Shepherd dog.

Yuri gasped, "Gulag? It... it... can't be!"

The dog bounded across the room and began to smother Yuri, who had dropped to his knees.

"Gulag! You're alive!" Yuri laughed, shocked yet delighted.

He looked up at Jesus and the figure who stood next to him, still running his hands over Gulag as the dog repeatedly circled him, tail wagging furiously.

"How is this possible?" he asked, losing his defensiveness in the wonder of the moment.

"We raise and restore. It's what we do. Love endures forever and we know what this means for you both," Ruach replied, joy radiating from her face.

"Ok. You have my attention. What do you want?"

"The only thing we would like is for you to sit with us and talk for a while," Jesus replied.

Yuri rose from the floor and sat down in a chair with Gulag at his feet, gazing up at him devotedly.

"Just let us fill you in," said Jesus, sitting down at the table.

Ruach cut some bread and then joined them with offerings of butter and jam.

"Tuck in if you like."

Yuri's mouth watered but he defiantly ignored the food.

"Well, go on," he demanded.

Jesus began.

"This is Ruach."

Yuri took in the shimmering colours emanating from her form. She was unlike anything he'd ever seen, and although he wanted to stare at her, he lowered his gaze.

"We are here because we love you. We've been with you your whole life, and we are going to be discussing what you did and what was done to you. You have passed from the Previous Age, and we are responsible for you."

"Everything we say and do is for your ultimate good," added Ruach.

Yuri's face darkened.

"I'm *dead*? But I'm alive? But… " Yuri stopped, rendered speechless.

"You have passed over from the Previous Age, where you were conceived, born and began your journey as a human being. Your Previous Age body died of sudden heart failure after you were ambushed. Your life was full of violence - violence against you, and violence by your hand. However, the essence of who you are, your spirit, is greater than your body and the things you did. We are here to help you understand this." Jesus paused to allow this to sink in.

Yuri's eyes were locked on Jesus. He was listening but struggling to take in the fact that he was no longer living his life as he knew it.

"Everybody, including you, was made for loving relationships and deep connections with those around them. For reasons that we shall explore, you have not experienced this. We have ways to help you discover this wonderful way of living, but you'll have to learn to trust us."

"Trust you? I don't even know who you are?" Yuri yelled indignantly.

"You see Gulag?" asked Ruach.

Yuri's face softened at the sight of Gulag's adoring eyes staring back at him.

"We are the ones who give life. We are the ones with the creative means to restore all things and encourage reconciliation. All things that were born, lived and shared in our great gift of life, these things are being made new and encouraged to mature."

"You sound like you are playing God."

Jesus smiled. "That's an interesting expression."

"So, you are God?" snapped Yuri.

"Well, it depends on what you mean by God."

Yuri was stumped again for a second.

"Isn't God *almighty*? If you're saying I was evil, aren't I meant to be damned? I never believed in God anyway, but if this afterlife bullshit is actually real, shouldn't I be thrown into the flames or something like that?"

Ruach drew Yuri's attention.

"We aren't into torture. We are more interested in encouraging your journey into pure, unfailing love: *agape love*. That's what all of this is about."

"The only thing I ever loved was this dog!"

"And that's why we start with him," responded Ruach, warmly.

"If you're not ready to talk with us, you can wait with Gulag for as long as you need. Just head back into the living room."

Yuri hesitated. He was caught between two options, both of which left him feeling powerless and weakened. He was not used to this.

"No, I'll stay," he said abruptly.

"I'm glad," replied Jesus.

Yuri fixed his eyes on Jesus.

"How would you describe your life?" Jesus asked.

Yuri considered his response for a few seconds.

"I learned that the only way to survive was to be the top dog. If you gave me life, then why are you blaming me for trying to live it? You don't know anything. You don't know what it's like to be born poor and to be abused."

For the first time, Yuri saw Jesus' face turn more serious.

"Actually, I do. But this isn't about me. We aren't here to condemn you."

"So, if I'm guilty? Then give me what I deserve. If you're really God, then you can strike me, or torment me, or snuff me out! Yes, I had a shit life. Well done! Well done God for giving me a shit life." Yuri sarcastically clapped his hands in mock applause.

Jesus looked Yuri firmly in the eye.

"Yuri, I realise you..."

"Fuck off!" interrupted Yuri. "I'm done with this. Get me out of here."

Jesus nodded.

"Ok. You can go out of that door if you want to leave." Jesus pointed to the back door.

Yuri got up with Gulag following him.

"Fuck this!" he cursed as he strode out of the room, slamming the door behind him.

*

Fran was aware of the sound of her own breathing and opened her eyes. Looking around she found herself on a very comfortable sofa in a living room that felt somewhat familiar. Fran was immediately excited, but at once also embarrassed to find she was naked. Looking down at her body she was thrilled to see it was youthful again. With a great sense of relief, she saw a wardrobe with open doors across the room; it was full of clothes that looked like hers. She hurried over and got herself dressed.

Fran didn't have to know everything to guess that she wasn't in Hell and was therefore probably about to meet God. She rubbed her hands together, and as she did so, she noticed that all her liver spots had disappeared and her whole body was zinging with life. She was impressed with how real everything felt.

Fran tried to recollect her final memories. She remembered that she had skin cancer and had been surrounded by her children and her grandchildren in the hospital bed. She remembered the beeps of the machines keeping her sedated and the foreign nurses with their accents that she didn't like. However, she was pleased that she couldn't recall the actual moment of death.

Fran began to look around the room. It was simply furnished and illuminated with what she presumed was sunlight. Fran felt that maybe God's living room could be a little more impressive and wondered why she was on her own.

She noticed a door next to the sofa and couldn't help but open it. There was a moderately-sized entrance hall and another door with a frosted-glass panel. Whatever was behind that door glowed with a warm orange light.

Fran crossed the hall and strained to hear any noises that might give her a clue as to what lay behind it.

Without warning the door opened and a man with wavy black hair, olive skin and a short beard stood facing her. He smiled.

"Fran," said the man with a welcoming warmth.

"Yes. Hello," said Fran. "Who are you?"

"I'm Jesus," replied the man.

Fran couldn't prevent a perturbed look from crossing her face. "You're Jesus Christ?"

Jesus smiled.

11

"The *Son of God*? The *Lord*?" Fran continued, her voice high-pitched with surprise.

"Some might say that." Jesus seemed slightly amused.

"But you're so... you're so..."

Jesus stood smiling, waiting for Fran to finish.

"Not what you had in mind?" he eventually chuckled as Fran continued to search for the right words.

"Well, no, it's... I don't...," she stuttered.

"Come on in," invited Jesus, holding out an arm to keep the door open. Fran couldn't help but notice a large ugly scar on Jesus' wrist as she passed him and entered the kitchen.

"Francesca!" said a being, seated at the table, radiating an attractive glow.

"This is Ruach," explained Jesus.

"Who?" said Fran, curtly.

"You may have known me as '*the Holy Ghost*' or '*the Holy Spirit*'," said Ruach.

"Right! Ok! So I have the Son and the Holy Ghost," said Fran slowly. "Where is the Father?"

"Papa leaves this bit to us," replied Jesus.

"This bit?" questioned Fran.

"Yes, it's your... let's call it... *appraisal*. We're going to talk through your life in the Previous Age."

"Previous Age? Oh, Ok. I'm in Heaven though, right? This is the '*age to come*'?"

"It's one of them," replied Ruach.

"Here," said Jesus as he put a cream soda float in front of Fran.

She was delighted. "Goodness! I haven't had one of these since I was a child."

Fran took a sip and smacked her lips excitedly.

"So, I'm very pleased to be here in Heaven. I always knew I would be coming here. Is it true I get a mansion?"

Jesus looked back at Fran with a slightly furrowed brow.

"Slow down a bit, Fran," he said with an unsettling seriousness. "We have to talk about some things first."

"Why?" Fran said obstinately. "I believed in you and went to church every Sunday. I have always been a Christian. And now for my reward!"

Jesus took a seat next to Fran at the kitchen table.

"Fran, firstly you must understand that we love you. Love is above all. But, we desire that you come to fully choose *agape love*. This is our hope for everyone."

"Whatever do you mean? I loved my friends and my family as best I could. This is not what I expected from you, Jesus!" she said crossly. "You said there would be no condemnation for those in... well... *you*."

"What do you think that means?" asked Jesus, with a kindness in his eyes that irritated Fran.

"So, am I going to Heaven or not?" she demanded.

"Fran, you are now on the New Earth. It can feel like Heaven, or it can feel like what some might call Hell. Your attitude and desires will determine how you perceive things. You are the only one who can determine your openness to *agape love*," Ruach explained.

"That is not what I was told," said Fran, arms folded in a child-like sulk. "All that going to church for *this*?"

*

Adilah stirred, stretched out her arms above her head and yawned. A rush of endorphins made her feel good. Expecting it to wear off and be replaced with the usual aches, Adilah was surprised to feel a teeming joyful buzz pulsating through her body. She opened her eyes to find herself in a room with log walls. Golden light streamed through the windows and she could smell something cooking nearby. She sat up and found herself on a sofa.

Adilah didn't really mind where she was, because she immediately felt safe. She had not felt safe for such a long time. Maybe she had been given a new life as a rich person, she wondered. She reached up and touched her face. The injury that had marred her appearance had gone. Delighted, she reached up to where previously the wounds had robbed her of her hair. She laughed out loud as she ran her fingers through her hair and looked around for a mirror. She saw some beautiful dresses hanging on a rail. Realising her nakedness, she was pleased to get dressed. The clothes were exquisitely made and fitted her perfectly.

She heard a knock at the door to her left.

"Hello?" she called softly, nervous to meet anyone in this mysterious place.

"Hello Adilah," called back a voice. "May I come in?"

"Yes," answered Adilah politely, presuming the voice belonged to the owner of this home.

The door opened with a slight creak. A man peered around the door smiling and holding a hand mirror. Somehow, despite all she'd been through at the hands of men, she sensed this man was not a threat to her. There was a kindness in his eyes like nothing she had ever encountered before.

"Here," he offered her the mirror.

Adilah took it in her hands and shrieked out loud, clasping a hand to her mouth. Looking back at her was her reflection. She was clearly still Adilah, a young woman from West Africa, but her facial scars had completely gone.

"Uncle, I do not understand!" she gasped.

"Adilah, your time of healing has come. You are safe here."

"Where am I?"

"You are a guest in my house. Please, would you come and meet my friend."

Adilah didn't need to be convinced. She stood up, ready to follow Jesus. He led her across a short hall into a kitchen.

Adilah gasped.

"Oh, Friend! Is that really you?"

Ruach came across the room and the walls were ablaze with colours as she took Adilah in her arms. She wrapped her in a hug that felt like being held by the very source of love itself.

In the embrace, Adilah felt her consciousness expand past both her body and the room and begin to fill the surroundings of the house. In every direction, she felt a euphoric freedom emanate from her inner being.

Ruach began to gently loosen the cosmic hug and Adilah's consciousness gently retracted back to her body.

"Friend, I knew one day I would see you." Adilah's tears flowed freely.

Jesus stirred Adilah's favourite drink, deeply moved by the encounter.

"Friend, you were always with me and somehow ... *within* me. Even when I hurt the most, even as I was dying, you never left me. I couldn't see you, but I knew your voice, I knew your presence."

Ruach gently ran her hand down Adilah's cheek, wiping her tears away.

Adilah looked at Jesus.

"I beg your pardon, Uncle, but I don't know your name?"

"You can call me Jesus," he said, passing Adilah a glass of mixed fruit juice.

"Jesus? I thank you." Adilah slightly bowed her head as she accepted the drink.

"What has happened to me?" she asked, timidly.

"You died and we raised you," replied Jesus.

"But how? How is it you can you do this for me?"

"We have life to give. We do this for every single person. Everyone is special, a one off, and everyone is loved," added Ruach.

Adilah suddenly became anxious.

"Every person? The militia? Are they here too?"

"You are safe now," answered Jesus.

"Ok, but where am I?" asked Adilah, still unsure how safe she really was.

"You are on the New Earth. We are in the next age now. This is a time of deep healing for all. But Adilah, you know much of the ways of *agape love* already."

"*Agape love*?"

"Yes, my darling Adilah, the highest form of love," replied Ruach. "And we have prepared a place for you."

"I do not deserve this," whispered Adilah.

Ruach leaned slightly closer to her.

"You were always worthy of our love. The suffering you experienced in the Previous Age and the way your heart was so open have prepared you for what is to come."

# Yuri

Yuri tried to walk with his usual imposing attitude, but this was proving more challenging in this unfamiliar terrain. The path leading away from the house led into a land the like of which he had never seen before. Huge trees with thick trunks and dense branches stood proud across the undulating hills. Sounds of all kinds of animal life could be heard, hidden from view by lush green leaves. Gulag pricked up his ears, alert to his surroundings but not afraid.

Looking up, Yuri noticed the sky was awash with vivid hues in a sweeping gradient. Purple, pink, peach, orange, red - it was breathtaking. But he was a little unsettled by what appeared to be three suns in the sky. One seemed to be the sun as he knew it, but there were two other orbs that also illuminated the cosmos, too big to be stars and too bright to be planets, yet there they were.

Yuri and Gulag walked for a long time, and he began to feel a creeping sense of desperation. For most of his existence he had been surrounded by people who listened to everything he said. They feared him and he thrived off it. Every day he had all his wants taken care of. To be without human company in a strange land was a nightmare come true. He felt robbed of power, and it angered him.

Eventually, Yuri sat down on the grass at the side of the path, and Gulag nuzzled up beside him. The only sounds were the animals in the trees and a gentle breeze rippling through the long grass and leaves. Yuri looked at the sky and, for the briefest of moments, he forgot his anger as he took in all the colours. But almost immediately his anxiety returned. He stood up and looked back in the direction from which he'd come. He'd lost sight of the house a long time ago.

Scanning the horizon in the other direction, Yuri's heart jumped when he saw two figures on the crest of a hill. They were a good way off but close enough for him to see that they were dressed in white. One was clearly a big man, and the other also tall but more slender.

Yuri immediately began calculating how he could rob them. Surely travellers had money, and maybe food and water too? To his intense irritation, he realised that they were standing watching him.

Trying to appear as big as possible, Yuri began marching up the hill, his chest puffed out. The two figures in white simply watched him approach.

Yuri detested being looked down upon. Approaching from beneath them made him feel like a child and by now he was raging.

"Yuri!" one of the figures called out.

Hearing his name stopped Yuri in his tracks, a good hundred metres away from them.

"Who the fuck are you?" he demanded.

"Would you like some food?" asked one of them, a slim, willowy man with brown wavy hair to his shoulders and a short beard.

Yuri didn't know how to respond and remained silent.

The men simply turned around and began walking.

Perplexed, Yuri kept his distance but followed them, his curiosity overruling his pride.

As they came over the top of the hill, a forest lay out before them. As far as the eye could see, the thick green canopy was teeming with life. Birds were swooping back and forth and colourful apes could be seen swinging through the branches on the tree line.

Yuri took it in but soon realised that the strangers had not paused for the view and had disappeared into the trees.

"Hey!" he shouted and let gravity lead him heavy footed down the incline and into the cover of the forest.

The two men were peeling bark off a tree next to the path. Vapour rose from the trunk as they each pulled strips off it. Laying them on a large leaf, they handed Yuri a small stack of bark peelings as he approached.

The light steam coming off the bark strips smelt amazing, and the portions looked juicy and inviting. Yuri's mouth watered, but he couldn't shake off his paranoia.

"What are you giving me?" he asked again, looking at one of the men directly.

"I'm not sure it has a name as such," said the man calmly. "Would you like to try it?"

By now Yuri could not ignore how much he wanted to eat. Unable to resist, he picked up a strip between his thumb and forefinger and, not wanting to look weak, dangled the whole thing into his mouth. The morsel began to melt like butter and had a savoury flavour.

"Tastes like steak!" Yuri exclaimed. "What tree is this, to get bark that tastes like that?" he asked, taking another strip in his fingers. "It's hot as well!"

"See those orbs in the sky?" asked one of the men, glancing up at them. "They are between planets and suns. They're close enough to bring a new kind of light and energy to this earth," replied the man.

"New energy, new plants," added the other.

"There's new things in space?" asked Yuri, trying to understand.

"Yes," said the man. "It's a new earth, and there are new heavens."

Yuri had helped himself to the rest of the bark strips and shared them with Gulag. Feeling much better, he decided he needed more information.

"Who are you?" he asked, bluntly.

"This is Thomas, and my name is Bull," said the broader one with short, light brown hair. "Come, let's walk and talk. We have a long journey ahead of us."

"No." Yuri wasn't finished with his interrogation. "What do you mean? Tell me who you are and where we are going. I don't know you!"

"There's a place for you," said Thomas.

"A house?"

"Yes, a house for you within the community."

This was appealing to Yuri. Surely this meant that he would be with people he already knew, in which case he would find ways to dominate them. If there was one thing Yuri knew he could do, it was finding people's weaknesses and exploiting them.

*

*The sound of cracking ribs always gave Yuri a distinct feeling - a sickly satisfaction. He had crafted his ability to be such that he could strike a body blow and break ribs, leaving his victim choking for breath.*

*The city at night was his kingdom. He knew how to use gang culture and the offer of increasingly heavy drugs to lure young people into a twisted family of which he was the head of the household. Pushing people along a devastating pathway of addiction and dependency was a tried and tested technique by which Yuri created addicts who were easy to control.*

*Helena was fourteen when she appeared on the edge of Yuri's circle. Young, fatherless and eager to please, she was easy prey.*

Yuri had several men in their twenties trained to groom young girls for the sex trade. They knew how to conjure a sense of belonging and hook them on drugs.

Helena accepted all that she was offered and soon developed a dependency on heroin. Her handlers only gave her what she so craved if she serviced the men who came to their brothels. Pimping young women and selling drugs gave Yuri and his most loyal men a lavish lifestyle. It was easy to pay the police to turn a blind eye and avoid their quarters of the city.

Helena was ambitious. By the time she was seventeen she was regularly having sex with Yuri. He pulled her off the brothel work and had her installed in his penthouse as his personal sex slave. At first, Helena couldn't imagine a better life. She was able to wash whenever she liked and even had her own wardrobe for the clothes that Yuri enjoyed seeing her wear. For the first time in her life, she felt like she had something of her own. Yuri kept the purest heroin aside for her.

One evening, the heroin she took was unusually strong. She fell unconscious on the bed. When Yuri came to her for sex, she was unresponsive - unable to fulfil her only function in Yuri's world. Frayed by business that had gone badly that day, Yuri's temper snapped.

Helena's ribs broke easily as his fist smashed into her body. Weakened from years of malnutrition, her body began to convulse as she lost consciousness. Her shattered ribs had punctured her lungs and now she was drowning in her own blood.

Yuri held her by the neck against the wall while blood poured out of her mouth and nose. It ran down the back of his hand, thick and hot. Repulsed, he let go of her throat and she slumped to the floor. A soft gurgling sound came from her mouth as her frail body gave in and she died.

Yuri wasn't sure why thoughts of Helena had come to him now, walking through a forest following two strangers. She was neither the first nor the last person he had killed in his life. Her face seemed to float in his mind, eyes rolled back into her skull and her blue lips slack and motionless.

Suddenly Yuri felt sick. He stopped walking, turned to the side of the road and readied himself to vomit. Gulag had been following Yuri closely, and he stopped to remain near him. He let out a little wince, upset at seeing his master unwell.

Sensing Yuri had stopped walking, Bull and Thomas turned.

Yuri felt panic rise inside him. He desperately wanted to disappear, to be well and truly dead.

Breathing deeply to quell his nausea, he closed his eyes, but all he could see was Helena's lifeless face.

Yuri felt there was nowhere to hide.

Thomas turned to Bull. "Bad memories," he whispered. Bull nodded but didn't take his eyes off Yuri. Yuri locked his eyes back on Bull, trying desperately not to give any ground.

"You... you can fuck off now," he snarled.

Bull had learned by now that threatening behaviour and even violence went hand in hand with the task of trying to help people. Bull looked back into Yuri's eyes and stood his ground. Thomas stood with him, shoulder to shoulder.

"Yuri," Thomas said quietly but with resolve, "what have we done to wrong you?"

There was nothing aggressive about how Bull and Thomas were communicating, but it still felt to Yuri as though he was being taunted.

"Where is this community?" he asked curtly.

"It's some way yet," answered Bull. "We will show you."

Bull didn't wait for an answer. He and Thomas turned away and began walking. Yuri could tell they weren't looking to talk to him at this point, so he followed at a distance with Gulag by his side.

Yuri only interacted with Bull and Thomas when they stopped to eat. He was surprised to discover they treated him with no malice or hatred. They served him food and drink at various stops. At night they all climbed into certain trees that had hammock-style branches. They showed no fear of him, nor tried to control him, and Yuri could not understand why.

Now and then, Bull and Thomas would greet various people on the road, sometimes with a newly resurrected person walking with them. The terrain changed periodically, all familiar and yet new. The New Earth clearly had many of the same natural attributes as the old, with mountains, lakes, rivers, forests, meadows and heathland. Yuri grew curious as to why there were so few other people, and no cities to be seen.

After many days of walking, Bull and Thomas had led Yuri to a stark landscape. Bleached rock formations jutted up from the ground, shrouded by thick dark trees.

They came to a cliff edge and sprawled out beneath was a mass of grey concrete huts, laid out in rows. There were some larger buildings arranged around a square, with colourful flowers and bushes growing along and up the walls. Yuri could make out various figures walking about and a river on the far side of the camp with irrigation channels that were feeding what looked like allotments and vegetable patches.

"This is your new home," said Bull.

"This is one of many communities across the New Earth," Thomas explained. "I am sure you will quickly identify with many of its members."

A sudden thud came from behind Yuri that distracted him from the scene below. He turned and saw a huge creature, with wings like an eagle but a body like a lion.

"Cedric!" cried Thomas.

Bull turned to Yuri. "Cedric is a seraph. He's the guardian of the community."

Yuri tried not to look worried, but this strange creature was four times bigger than him.

"Come," Cedric said to Yuri with a voice deeper than any he'd ever heard.

Before Yuri could protest, Cedric was approaching him. Yuri hoped Gulag would defend him, but instead he was sitting calmly.

Breathless with anxiety, Yuri turned to Thomas.

"I suppose you will be keeping my dog?"

"No," said Thomas. "Gulag is a gift from Jesus. Let him be a reminder that you are loved."

Yuri was thankful but didn't voice it.

"Come!" said Cedric in a voice like thunder. He opened his huge wings and began to beat them.

Yuri gathered Gulag in his arms just as the seraph took hold of his waist and leapt over the side of the cliff. For a few seconds Cedric was in flight with Yuri and Gulag tucked close against his stomach. He landed, sending up a cloud of dust, and released Yuri and Gulag, who jumped down and began sniffing the ground.

Yuri could see Thomas and Bull observing from the cliff top, and in a final desperate act of defiance, he lifted both hands, fists balled, and slowly erected his middle fingers.

"Fuck you!" Yuri mouthed before turning away.

"I wonder how many jubilees it'll be before he finally learns the way of love," mused Thomas.

"A fair few I reckon," said Bull. "He's a proud soul in a community of proud souls."

"We'll be back soon to settle in with them," said Thomas. Living alongside these difficult men was one of the toughest assignments, but they knew there was much reward in the challenge.

Cedric had flown back up to the cliff top and had resumed his usual position watching over the camp from a comfortable nest. Bull and Thomas waved goodbye, and Cedric lifted a huge paw to his head in a salute.

"And now our meeting," Thomas reminded Bull as they set off back down the road.

# Fran

Jesus tried to make conversation, but Fran was still clearly upset with him. The two had left through the back door in the kitchen as it was time for Jesus to show Fran where she'd be living. Sensing her mood, Jesus kept quiet until she spoke again.

Fran stopped walking and waited for Jesus to turn to her.

"Look here," she said briskly. "Why wasn't I warned about all this? I find it entirely unfair that I was told that all I had to do was believe and I would be saved."

Jesus sat down on a nearby rock.

"Who says you won't be *saved*?" he asked.

"Well, this doesn't feel like salvation," snapped Fran. "What about 'For there is no condemnation for those in Christ Jesus'?"

"Do you feel condemned?" asked Jesus, sincerely.

"Actually I do!"

"Why don't you tell me what you were expecting?" asked Jesus.

Fran came closer to Jesus. She opened her mouth to answer him, but realised she didn't have anything to say that didn't sound like a cliché. Her face brightened as she remembered more Bible verses.

"Streets paved with gold... lots of angels... and people I know from my church."

"Well, all of that can be found here," responded Jesus. "Do you remember the bit about the New Earth?"

"Yes," replied Fran. "God said he would create a new heaven and a new earth."

"All of creation is being made new. And that includes each person."

"Right," said Fran, trying to show she could listen.

"But everyone starts at different points on the journey. We condemn no one; rather we encourage each person to become more Christlike."

"Like you, then?" said Fran with a touch of sarcasm.

"Our Father, I call him Papa, asked me to be like Him, to always show *agape love* and to demonstrate that he considers each person to be a cherished child. His desire is that all His children live in *agape love*. When they do, they will join me in God's household and live the abundant life we promised."

"Yes, so all Christians are anointed," insisted Fran.

"Well, not exactly. Some have knowledge in their head about the Bible, and they obey their religion with devotion; but they may never have known the anointing that comes from following me."

"But I did follow you!" exclaimed Fran, frustrated by the inference that she hadn't.

"What did that look like in your life?" asked Jesus.

"I worshipped you. I... I... I took the bread and wine. And I kept away from the horrible ungodly things in the world."

"You mean, you followed the Christian religion and cut yourself off from people who didn't fit your idea of what it means to be a good person?"

Jesus was telling the truth, but Fran felt increasingly angry with him.

"Did you 'love your enemies, and bless those who persecute you'? And did you 'not judge, unless you want to be judged'?"

Fran remembered how she had despised those who failed to match up to her expectations.

"I was trying to keep myself pure!" she burst out.

"And in so doing, you lost the heart of what I taught and how I lived."

Fran was at a crossroads. She could accept what Jesus was saying or she could try to defend herself. She wavered for a moment before her emotions boiled up again. Jesus was an easy target for her rage.

"It's alright for you!" she hissed. "You're God!"

Jesus simply nodded as though he understood her and said nothing. He waited for her to continue.

"You couldn't possibly get anything wrong!"

Jesus answered her calmly "Yet I was crucified."

Fran was unable to answer that. She remembered as a little girl looking up at the stained glass window in church. Most Sundays she would look at the face of Jesus on the cross and feel sad that he had died so painfully.

"I know," she said, calming down a little.

Jesus set off and looked back at Fran, inviting her to follow.

"Where are we going anyway?" asked Fran sullenly.

"There's a community waiting for you. It's where you'll live for the time being."

"The time being?" repeated Fran. "I thought this was eternity?"

"Time is different when you know you will not die. But time still exists. Seconds, minutes, hours all still work. We have the same measurements of time as the Previous Age; we're not trying to confuse anyone."

Fran wasn't really listening. She was still trying to process that this was really 'it', and that she would never die.

"So, I won't die? What if I jumped off a cliff?"

Jesus laughed. "Nearly everyone asks that. Your body is totally upgraded from your previous one. You will not age, and your body will recover from any damage. Your skin feels the same, but it will always repair itself. Your organs will always recover from injury. You'll just have to test what it can do, won't you? Remember, you've already died and been given a new body"

For the first time, a smile passed over Fran's face. She looked at her limbs and was very glad to feel so strong and healthy.

"So, I *am* in Heaven," she mused out loud.

Jesus turned and started along the path.

Fran walked just behind Jesus in order to avoid conversation. She was impatient to see where she would be living.

They crested the brow of a hill and, looking down, they could see a village. The houses were neat cottages and looked homely.

"Nearly there," he said.

Walking up from the village was a lady wearing a bright white trouser suit and a man sporting a white T-shirt and white flannels.

"Sylvia, hello!" called Jesus.

"Hello, Jesus!" she called out and waved.

"Jesus," cried Carlos with delight. "So good to see you!"

Soon they were close enough for introductions.

"This is Fran," said Jesus. "And Fran, this is Sylvia and Carlos. They will be with you in the community."

"Hello Fran. Welcome to your new home. Come, I'll show you around."

"Thank you both. I'll see you later," said Jesus, and he turned to Fran.

"Fran, this is a good community for you. Please remember this if it feels hard. Don't forget, we love you."

Fran nodded sullenly, feeling patronised. She didn't make eye-contact with Jesus, who put a hand on her shoulder before he began to walk back the way they'd come.

Fran was relieved he'd gone.

"How did you find your time with Jesus?" asked Sylvia as they headed towards the village.

"Not what I was expecting. Why is he so… condescending?" replied Fran.

"He *is* in charge here, you know," said Carlos cheerfully.

"Hmm," responded Fran indignantly.

They rounded a corner and Sylvia stopped next to a little house. It was made of stone and had wooden beams that could be seen supporting the walls. The roof was thatched, and Fran was rather pleased with the chocolate-box feel of the village.

They heard the sound of footsteps descending stairs in the small cottage next door and a key turning in the lock. The door opened a few inches and a face peered through the gap.

"Hello Imelda," said Sylvia. "This is Fran, your new neighbour."

The door opened a little wider and a stern face looked Fran up and down. Without saying a word, Imelda turned back to Sylvia.

"Really? Must she be so close? Can't she go somewhere else?"

"I'm afraid not. Come on, you've only just arrived yourself. I did tell you that there would be others."

Fran was feeling rejected and irritated by Imelda already.

"It's ok. I'll go somewhere else."

Sylvia turned to Fran. "I'm afraid that's not possible. This is the place reserved for you."

"Now look here," Fran said abruptly. "This is Heaven, isn't it? Surely we all get what we want?"

"I know it's perhaps not what you thought it would be, and yes, this is the New Earth, but you will have to put aside your images of Heaven from the Previous Age. Everyone outside the Eternal City is in a process. You included, Fran."

"Outside the City?"

Fran stopped short; a terrible realisation dawning.

She turned to Carlos with wide eyes filled with fear. "I thought only the ungodly were outside the City?" she gasped.

Fran's knees buckled and she fell to the ground.

"But... but... I'm resurrected! I'm in a new body! *I'm a bloody Christian!* Surely I'm meant to be in the City with the angels and saints and get to wear a crown?"

Sylvia sat down on the grass beside Fran. Imelda opened her door wide and looked at them with a smirk. Carlos stood some distance away, allowing the two women to talk.

"Ha!" scoffed Imelda. "Welcome to Hell."

Fran looked up at Imelda and glowered with rage.

Carlos turned and simply looked at Imelda.

"What? Surely I'm allowed to stand at the entrance of my own house?" she asked defiantly and folded her arms.

Carlos sighed.

"Hell?" said Fran, her voice trembling. "I can't be in *Hell*. Where is the fire? And the devils?"

"Those ideas about Hell were never the reality," said Sylvia. "The language of fire was always about a refining process, like when precious metal is smelted and purified. Here, outside the City, is where people are in the process of having the dross removed from their lives. This is where the learning and the growing happens."

"Ok! Ok!" said Fran, suddenly becoming animated, flapping her hands. "I'm sorry! I'm very sorry for all the bad things I did. I got some things wrong. I'm not perfect. I'm only human. I promise I won't do those things again."

"Pathetic," crowed Imelda from the doorway.

Sylvia looked at Fran. "I understand this is traumatic for you, but you can't just say the words and expect it to be the same as having gone through the process. The idea of just *saying* the right things shows that you still have much to learn."

Fran let out a slow and terrible groan of frustration.

Sylvia stood close to her.

"This isn't the end of your story, but it is the next chapter."

Fran pulled away from her and sat there, hugging her knees. Several minutes passed.

"Would you like to see your new home?" asked Sylvia, calmly.

Fran's face was stormy as she got up and marched into the cottage. Sylvia followed, but Carlos stayed outside to make sure they weren't disturbed.

# Johan

"We've been walking for so long now, and I don't feel even a bit tired!" Johan shook his head, overwhelmed.

"Your new body is much stronger," said Jesus.

"Yes, it's strange. Somehow even my emotions are stronger," observed Johan.

"There is much less distraction in this age. Without the aches and pains of a mortal body you will be able to observe your own soul more easily."

"Can you tell me more about the soul?" asked Johan.

"It is the central core of who you are. Within the soul the spirit essence that comes from God merges with your individual human essence."

"Why didn't we know about this in the previous life?"

"Many did, but many did not. Humans tend to take much less seriously the things that cannot be seen and measured. But the spirit is beyond measure." Jesus spoke with such clarity that it felt to Johan like his very words were alive. "The culture a person is born into also influences what they are able to observe and understand. For some, their culture blinds them, so they are limited in what they can accept about the unseen."

"I see," said Johan. "My father and mother were atheists. They thought religion was just a way to control people."

"Well, they weren't necessarily wrong. Religious practice can easily become corrupted by people thirsty for power and riches, and the weak things of the world can easily be trampled on by those with twisted desires."

"The weak things of the world?"

"Yes, in the same way as a young sapling is easily crushed underfoot, those new to trying to live a life of love can easily be trampled by strong but perverted characters. *Agape love* is characterised by kindness, joy, peace and self-control. These qualities come from a spirit that is greatly influenced by the cosmic parent of everything that exists. However, a mature understanding of *agape love* is required to exercise discernment and establish boundaries when necessary. Without this deeper insight into how love bears all things, those seeking to live in *agape love* can easily be abused and dominated by people with controlling tendencies."

Johan was now walking closely next to Jesus. He felt as if he was unlocking the secrets of the universe.

"Why must it be this way?"

Jesus looked at Johan with great affection, pleased to be asked such searching questions.

"The true nature of *agape love* was often misunderstood and miscommunicated in the Previous Age, and sometimes it was deliberately mistaught. Ruach always worked to encourage the full understanding and appreciation of *agape love* but could not override the desires of those not open to our message.

Here, in this age, it is easier for destructive ways to be recognised and rejected. Love will overcome hatred and evil - not by coercion or control, but by patience, forgiveness and mercy. When those with twisted and self-centred desires see clearly, they will turn away from their past way of life and learn to trust the love that is above all things. But this turning away can be a long and difficult process."

"So how will you treat the evil people in the world?"

"We treat everyone with love. We seek a genuine turning away from evil, so we introduce circumstances in which people are made to face the futility of evil and hatred. It's like a mirror. The longer they are made to look at their own reflection, the more they will see the ugliness of their evil desires."

"Will any resist forever?" asked Johan.

"I am confident that even the hardest of hearts will eventually soften. Every human soul was made for loving relationships. The Previous Age has made many forget this most basic and essential of desires. Our great work is to see the restoration, reconciliation and maturing of all creation, and that means every human soul. God will be all in all, but only when all conscious beings have willingly chosen to live in *agape love*."

Johan stopped walking. His mouth quivered and tears began to roll down his cheeks.

"I saw so much suffering. I thought that the evil and hatred in the world would overpower everything. I lost all hope. But now, being with you, I can see that all is not lost."

Jesus turned and looked at Johan, moved by the deep longing within Johan for all things to be made right.

"But my friend, you never lost all hope. Despite everything you saw, your heart remained set on goodness. You may have been one small candle, but you lit up your corner of the darkness. You did what you could to follow me."

"But, I didn't know you." Johan looked into Jesus' face, still weeping.

"Your circumstances meant you didn't have a fair picture of what knowing me meant. That is not your fault. However, our divine essence is *agape love*, and you did know this love. You sensed the guidance of Ruach, even in the most terrible dark days of war. We saw you. We knew you. You were never lost to us."

Johan took hesitant steps towards Jesus. Knowing what this meant, Jesus opened his arms wide. Johan collapsed into his arms and Jesus held him tight. The two stood in an embrace. Johan had never felt so loved, and Jesus felt Johan's deep gratitude and love returned to him.

"Thank you," said Johan in a choked voice.

"Thank *you*," Jesus replied in return.

They laughed, blowing out the emotion, and continued to walk together, allowing the power of the moment to linger.

\*

*Waking with a jolt, Johan sat up in his foxhole and tried his best to pull the blanket tighter around his freezing body. Keeping his arms against his chest he looked down at his wristwatch. It was 6.09am. He must have had about three hours sleep. Hunkered down with him to his right was Wilhelm, his closest friend in the company. Their shared body warmth had kept them alive another night. Their battalion had dug in, defending the town behind them from the advancing enemy. So far, the front had been quiet in their sector, but the sound of action had been creeping closer over the last two days. Plumes of smoke could be seen rising over the tree line as daylight slowly appeared.*

*Roused by Johan's stirring, Wilhelm wriggled slightly.*

*"Any water? I'm out," he asked, his eyes still closed.*

*Johan reached down. If you didn't sit on your water, it would be frozen solid in no time. He passed it to Wilhelm under the blanket. Despite being close friends, it wasn't unusual for Wilhelm to take advantage of Johan's good nature. Wilhelm was from a comfortable background and was used to having all his needs met.*

*Wilhelm finished off what was left of the water. Johan sighed, realising there was nothing left for him.*

Jesus noticed that Johan was lost in thought. He pushed some branches aside and held them open for Johan like a doorway. Johan was startled to see a plunge pool fed by a waterfall before him.

"Let's drink," suggested Jesus.

"How... how did you know...?" asked Johan.

Jesus whooped loudly and took a running jump, cannonballing into the pool. He emerged, shaking the water from his dark hair. Johan was more cautious.

"Try the water," said Jesus, swimming closer to the edge of the pool. He took a mouthful of the water and blew it high into the air like a fountain.

Johan stooped down and took a handful of the water in his hand and brought it to his lips. The water was warm to the touch and sweet to taste. It was the purest water he'd ever come across. Johan looked at Jesus and smiled. Jesus pushed out his hands, sending water splashing over Johan.

"Hey! That's it!" yelled Johan leaping into the water, sending a wave over Jesus. He took a huge mouthful of the water and swallowed it.

"What were you thinking about?" asked Jesus.

"My friend Wilhelm. I was just thinking about him. Seems like it was yesterday I was with him. Was it yesterday, or a lifetime ago? Maybe it was both."

"Ah yes, Wilhelm," replied Jesus knowingly.

"I loved him, but he was not a good man. He was selfish and could be cruel."

"Yes," said Jesus ambiguously.

"He died with me?"

"Yes, but remember, even if you die at the same time, you are raised to this age at different times," explained Jesus.

"Will I see him again?"

"When you are both ready. In the fullness of the ages, everyone will find one another. But for now, you have different paths to tread."

"I have my own path?" asked Johan.

"Yes, Johan. Come, it's time for you to see your new home."

The air was warm, and Johan and Jesus were dry again in no time.

"There's a couple I want you to meet," said Jesus.

Two people emerged from the trees. One was a shorter woman and the other a slight Asian man. Both had animated, excited expressions on their faces.

"Johan, this is Yvonne and Yan. They will bring you to your new community."

"Hi Johan!" said Yvonne with a broad grin.

Yan bowed toward Johan. Jesus ran around behind Yan, leapt onto his back and gave him an over-dramatic kiss on the cheek.

"I love this guy!" Jesus yelled.

Yan began charging around with Jesus on his back, giggling.

Yvonne laughed so loudly that it echoed through the forest.

"They always do this," she said breathlessly to Johan.

"Jump on, Yvonne" called Jesus as he passed her. Yvonne leapt like a cat onto Jesus' back and Yan groaned.

Johan stood back and watched a mass of humanity running around like a strange beast. He couldn't help but well up again at the sight.

'Well, I never expected the afterlife to be quite like this,' he thought to himself.

By now Jesus, Yan and Yvonne had collapsed into a heap of laughter on the ground. When they eventually untangled themselves, Jesus approached Johan.

"I'm going to have to say goodbye for now," he said. "I leave you with these two good folk. You're in great hands. They will show you your new home. I'll see you again in a while."

He held out his arms and Johan embraced him. He felt a knot of emotion in his throat as Jesus waved to him as he left the clearing.

"What a lovely man," he mused out loud.

"He's wonderful, isn't he?" replied Yan. "Not at all how most people expect him to be."

"Yeah, he's fun!" said Johan in a surprised tone.

"It makes sense that the one who created life knows how to enjoy it," chirped Yvonne.

Yvonne's observation made Johan think. "That makes sense. But… what of the bad things? Did he make those, too?"

"Desires can become twisted," said Yan. "But what we learn here is that the desires within our hearts can become untwisted and restored so that they are able to serve both us and other people."

"How does that happen?" asked Johan.

"Through a constant learning process. The more openly we engage with the process, the quicker we learn."

"It's a deep process though," Yvonne added. "Don't be surprised if you are shocked by how deep it goes."

Johan wondered what this idea of 'process' could mean for him. Maybe it was what Jesus meant by 'path'. The only time he'd felt he'd gone through anything like a process was when he trained to be a soldier.

The suns in the sky cast changing tones of light onto the wooded terrain. Johan followed Yvonne and Yan along the path through the forest, heading towards an unknown destination. Johan knew that he trusted these new friends, but a lingering anxiety flickered within him when he thought about the word 'process'. He hoped that it wouldn't be like boot camp all over again.

*

"Bravo, Gerty!"

Johan was crouched on the ground. He turned back to look at Yan and Yvonne. On the lawn before him, his little sister, Gertrude, was showing him how to hula-hoop. Their reunion had been more natural than Johan had dared hope. Gerty knew exactly who he was and had immediately run up to him, taking his hand to show him her rabbits.

"From her perspective, she last saw you a few days ago," explained Yan. "She went to sleep in the Previous Age and woke up here."

"She was raised just before you and had been told to expect you," added Yvonne.

"She died twelve years before me," said Johan. "She knew nothing of the war, thank God. She was only seven. I was thirteen at the time and I missed her every single day of my life."

"Now you will be with her as she grows up here on the New Earth. Everyone gets to be a child once," smiled Yan.

"When will our parents be here?" asked Johan.

"That's not for us to answer," replied Yvonne. "You will be together with all your loved ones at some point in the future. But the process must come to maturity, for both you and your parents. We don't know how or when this will happen for each person."

Johan stood up and clapped his hands. "You are so good at this!" he called to Gerty, who was laughing as she spun the hoop.

He turned to Yan and Yvonne.

"Our father. He… he had tendencies. You know, he liked other men. I saw him once, kissing another man in a forest. Will he be damned?"

"No one is ever damned, and it is not a sin to be homosexual," said Yan. "He may have to face a process for other aspects of his heart, but sexuality in and of itself doesn't conflict with knowing *agape love*. The culture he was born into may not have understood this, but that doesn't mean he was wrong to feel deeply for other men."

Johan nodded and released a breath charged with emotion.

"I think our mother always knew. She wasn't angry with him. I think she wished he could be free to express his love for this man without fear."

"I don't know where they are. They might not be raised yet, but you will both see them," Yan reassured him.

Johan nodded, pursing his lips, trying to keep from sobbing with relief at the prospect of seeing his parents again.

Gerty let the hoop fall to the ground, stepped over it and ran to Johan who squatted down to greet her.

"Come on, I want to show you something," she said, grabbing his hand with both of hers.

She led him excitedly into a wooden house. Through the open front door Johan could see bright bunting with letters for the words 'Welcome Johan' stitched onto the triangles.

"I made it with Yvonne last night!" enthused Gerty, bobbing up and down with glee.

"Oh, Gerty, I love it!"

Johan reached down and hitched his little sister up onto his hip.

"Come and see your room!" she exclaimed, clasping her brother's cheeks between her hands.

Johan looked at Yan and Yvonne briefly in turn as he and Gerty moved toward the stairs.

"We'll see you soon!" called Yvonne. "We'll leave you to settle in."

"There's nothing better than reunions with loved ones, is there?" said Yan as they set off down the path. "And speaking of loved ones, we need to get to the City for the meeting this evening."

# Adilah

"Come, I have something to show you." Jesus led Adilah out of the back door, round a corner and through a small garden. He held a gate open, and they entered a field with grass greener than Adilah had ever seen. There on the grass was a winged creature; Adilah felt a rising sense of panic as it lifted its head and looked at her.

Jesus approached the creature and put a hand on its head.

"Adilah, meet Cynthia. She's a seraph," he said with a smile.

Adilah tentatively approached the creature and, mimicking Jesus' action, stroked Cynthia's head.

"Hello Adilah." The seraph spoke with a deep but clear voice.

Taken aback but no longer afraid, Adilah laughed and looked at Jesus. He nodded, acknowledging Adilah's surprise at hearing a non-human creature speak.

"Are we to leave now?" asked Cynthia.

"Yes, let's go!" exclaimed Jesus with excitement.

Cynthia lowered herself to the ground and Jesus climbed onto her back, shuffling himself up to the base of her neck.

"Come on up," he invited Adilah, offering her his hand.

As Adilah climbed up, she noticed a large scar running up from Jesus' palm to his wrist. She couldn't stop herself from flinching. Where she came from, it was not unusual for people to have scars. Years of civil war had left many permanent reminders on the skin of her people.

"What happened to you?" she asked matter-of-factly.

Jesus looked at his scars as Adilah shuffled up behind him on Cynthia's back. He held up both arms, clearly displaying a mirror-image scar on the other arm.

"I was killed by the leaders of the country in which I lived."

"Killed? Why?" asked Adilah.

"They didn't like what I said and what I did. They saw me as a threat to the peace."

"Oh, I see. Did you lead an army?"

"No, I never spoke against the government. My followers were few and we were never violent."

"So why did they kill you?"

"The religious leaders thought I was disrespectful to God. They said I was a blasphemer and in league with demons."

"So, you were … rebellious?"

"No, I always said that we should love God and love each other. I followed the laws, but I said that the laws were about love and that all people were equally loved by God. They didn't like that."

"How did they kill you?"

"They nailed me to a wooden frame. I hung by my hands. The weight of my body tore my flesh. I bled a lot, and it was hard to breathe as I had to pull on my hands and push up on my nailed feet to get air. Eventually I lost the strength to breathe and I died."

Adilah had witnessed many horrors but had never heard of such a cruel death. The thought of it moved her deeply.

"I am sorry!" she exclaimed. "I am so sorry they did that to you."

Jesus turned around and smiled at Adilah with genuine thanks.

"Thank you. But you know, they didn't understand what they were doing. Very few people in the Previous Age understood the hurt they were causing. I had to die to show everyone that death is not the end. I had to die so I could come back to life."

"What do you mean?" asked Adilah.

"Well, I was given a special job to do. I had to go through death and all its horror to demonstrate that God overcomes death. Because so many did not believe that Papa would raise them up after death, I was made alive again to show them that he would."

Adilah was both awestruck and confused by what Jesus was saying.

"I heard that such suffering is a sign that God is not with you," she said.

"Yes, many have thought that way. We needed to show that God is *with* victims, not against. Hey, we are going to fly now! Let's go!" said Jesus in a loud voice, and Cynthia's wings began to beat, creating ripples in the grass. Gently they began to ascend.

Adilah looked around at the lush landscape that filled her vision. Trees, hills, lakes, distant mountains and all sorts of living creatures made up a patchwork quilt of beauty pulsating with life. It made the West African bushland she had known as a little girl seem like an arid desert in comparison.

Adilah felt safe even though she was high above the ground with a stranger and on the back of a talking winged beast. She was not used to being this close to a man without feeling threatened. Jesus was like no one she had ever previously encountered.

Adilah realised that Cynthia was descending and soon they were on the soft grass of a spacious woodland clearing.

Two people approached.

"Adilah, let me introduce you to my friends, Anne and Harmony."

"Hello Adilah. Welcome to the region of Beulah," said Anne.

Adilah smiled shyly. Meeting so many new people in one day was exciting but there had been a lot to take in. Anne had welcoming eyes, like Jesus – and Adilah felt immediately that she could be herself around her.

"Anne and Harmony will show you to your new community," said Jesus. "I must go now, but we will meet again."

Adilah was sad to see Jesus go and felt apprehensive about meeting more new people.

Harmony could see she was feeling uneasy. Motioning to Anne, Harmony sat down on the grass.

"We can just sit here for a while," she suggested in an accent Adilah recognised as American. "Let's just talk for a bit, if you want."

Adilah sat on the grass, legs crossed. Her hand found its way to her forehead again. Adilah was still getting used to not having scars. She smiled shyly at Harmony and Harmony smiled back, her curly blonde hair falling over her shoulders. Adilah liked Harmony immediately. She'd never met a white person before and had always been told to fear them, but this one felt safe – with the same peace about her as Anne and Jesus. Adilah was not afraid of silence, so the three women sat watching the birds feeding on the fruit high up in the trees around them.

*

*Squatting in the darkest corner of the hut, Adilah strained to hear what the men were saying the other side of the wall. They spoke in a different dialect, but she had been around them for years now and could follow most of what they said. It was nearly midnight and the men's voices could just be heard over the cicadas. Embers were now dying in the fireplace, and Adilah wished for more wood so she and her sister could keep warm. She looked at her sleeping sister. The West African nights could be so cold and Adilah had given her the only available blanket. She shuffled on her haunches closer to the fire, but then felt Friend draw her attention to a large log under a table near the doorway to the hut. Without hesitating, Adilah retrieved it. She had become used to Friend's* gentle guidance in her most desperate situations. Thanking Friend, she placed the log in the fireplace and blew gently, hoping it would catch the dying embers.

"Help me, please," she whispered and blew again. Her breath was enough to make the sparks leap into flame and catch the rough outer bark. Before long the log was burning and Adilah was warmed by its heat.

Stirring, her sister peeked over the blanket and smiled at Adilah. Adilah smiled back, grateful not to be alone. She and her sister had been the property of the militia since the day armed men had burnt their home village, killing their parents in another devastating episode of a long tribal war. Forced into slavery, every day they cooked food, cleaned weapons and sometimes had to give their bodies to the higher-ranking men. Adilah was the oldest and she had become the mother figure. Her younger sister was called 'Mama' by the men as she had lost two babies to miscarriages. Her real name was Eshe and she was the one they usually chose for forced sex.

Eshe had gone back to sleep in the glow of the fire. She looked so peaceful there in the orange light, but the moment of quiet calm was shattered when one of the militia men approached. Reaching down, he grabbed Eshe by the hair and pulled her up. Her eyes were full of terror at being so violently awoken, and before Adilah had a chance to think, she had flung her arms around Eshe to try to protect her and prevent her from being raped. The man pushed Adilah to the ground.

"You should know better! You should know!" he raged, kicking Adilah in the ribs. "How dare you!"

The man grasped Adilah's shirt and lifted her, dropping her on to the open fire, his boot on the back of her skull. Adilah screamed as the searing pain coursed through her body. Eshe cried out in horror as Adilah's hair caught fire.

Adilah didn't know how long she was in the flames. When the man eventually released his foot, she pushed herself away from

*the fire, clawing at her face and head. She fell back onto the floor*
*of the hut and passed out.*

*

Adilah couldn't find words to explain the peace and joy that settled upon her. She sat in silence - a golden silence that seemed to work its way through her skin and into her bones. Her new friends sat with her, no one needing to force conversation. Eventually Adilah noticed that the colours of the sky were changing. She wanted to ask where they would sleep but felt it would be rude to ask. Harmony pre-empted the question.

"You must be wondering where you'll be staying, honey?" she said gently.

Adilah nodded.

"Come with me and I will show you."

"You go with Harmony," said Anne. "I have to leave but I'll see you soon, ok?"

Adilah waved a hand and followed Harmony along a path that led down a slight incline into a woodland. After a few minutes they emerged into a large clearing with eight round log cabins equally spaced around its circumference.

"This is a safe place. It's only for women," said Harmony.

Adilah nodded, feeling relieved that there would be no men here.

"This is where I stay," continued Harmony, touching the outside wall of the cabin to her left.

"And this one is just for you." Harmony touched the cabin immediately to her right.

Adilah was relieved that her new friend would be so close. She followed as Harmony came round to the front door of the cabin.

"This place has been prepared for you. It is yours alone."

Adilah was overcome with the realisation that everything was so different now. For the first time, she had her own living space.

"You have clothing in the bedroom, food and drink in the kitchen. Anything else you need, ask me and we will see what can be done."

Adilah swayed her body in a dance of pure delight. She reached out, took Harmony's right hand in both of hers and raised it to her forehead as she bowed.

"Oh sweetie, please don't thank me. All of this is a gift. Now you must come and meet your other neighbour."

Harmony knocked on the door of a cabin to the right of Adilah's. She turned to Adilah and formed an 'o' shape with her mouth. Adilah looked back at her, puzzled.

As the door to the cabin opened, Adilah gasped and cried out with surprise.

Eshe came flying out of the door and into Adilah's arms. The two sisters began to leap about, laughing and crying.

"You both enjoy some time together! I'm going to cook some food for us all." Harmony called out as she headed into her cabin.

Their shared meal bubbled over with the joy of reunion, but soon it was time for Harmony to take her leave. Emerging from the woods she found Anne standing with a small herd of deer, stroking one on its nose.

"Meeting time!" she called out to her.

# Meeting in the Eternal City

Jesus' meetings were like happy family gatherings. Each group was composed of a unique blend of characters and Jesus enjoyed the connection he had with each of them.

Thomas' group was made up of those who had spent the last period of the Previous Age growing together in a particular community and helping it come to know unfailing love. The start of that period had been named the Great Suffering as many people had suffered and died in the calamities that occurred, most of which were the direct result of the imbalances caused in the natural environment by human activity. God had asked Jesus to return and, with the help of the resurrected saints, to set about healing the earth.

The saints Thomas, Anne, Harmony and Yan had been raised when Jesus returned and they had willingly offered to help him show the way of unfailing love on the old earth. They had been sent to a community where they demonstrated *agape love* to all they met. Four members of that community - Bull, Sylvia, Yvonne and Carlos - had grown to become Christlike, first through experiencing the love shown by the resurrected saints, and then by growing in their relationship with Ruach. These four had become mature enough to be resurrected directly into the Eternal City when the old earth and the Previous Age came to its final end. They were overjoyed to find they had been grouped together to help some of those placed in communities on the New Earth.

Jesus now set about explaining the next steps to the group. He loved to debrief over food that he had prepared.

"Absolutely delicious," said Yan, putting his bowl down.

Jesus smiled across the table. Not everyone loved his concoctions; they were adventurous in the extreme, as Jesus enjoyed creating new blends of flavours and textures. But he always had some safe bets in reserve, just in case he could see his friends struggling with his experiments.

"You always have been brave with my food!" laughed Jesus.

Harmony grimaced and pushed what was left in her bowl around with a fork.

"Here you are, Harmony."

Jesus took the lid off a pot, revealing a vegetable casserole that was rather more predictable. He winked and Harmony chuckled as she filled her bowl with the steaming stew.

"Thank you for welcoming each person into their community," said Jesus, looking around at his friends. "We've only raised a small number so far. Only another one hundred billion to go!"

There was laughter at the sheer enormity of the number who were yet to be raised and inhabit the New Earth. Everyone who had ever been conceived - from aborted and miscarried foetuses to the oldest people to have lived in the Previous Age - each was to be brought to the New Earth to either immediately serve with Jesus from the Eternal City or to mature in a community before gaining admittance there.

As they ate, Jesus shared about the challenges that lay ahead.

"The environment selected for an individual depends on how their desires have been shaped by their experiences in the Previous Age. Within their communities everyone will have the opportunity to mature and learn the ways of *agape love*. Not all processes will be the same; some will be more challenging than others. Every fifty years the populations of each community will be rearranged. These jubilee periods will help the overall process in ways that I will explain later."

The team were all leaning in over the table as Jesus continued.

"You're all ready for this. You were chosen because you have matured to truly follow me, in mind and spirit. I know you still make mistakes, but you have come to understand that all situations can be resolved with patience and forgiveness. You are willing to show *agape love*, because you know that God's love for you is unfailing.

You will be beacons of *agape love* in each community, ready to assist members if they ask for help. Your presence will help even the most stubborn of individuals to understand Papa's heart. We will keep showing everyone *agape love* for as long as it takes for people to be reconciled. I must warn you that the work ahead will have difficult moments, but remember that you are able to access your dwelling places here in the City whenever you need time away from your community."

"Jesus, can I ask you something?" said Yvonne. "If you wanted to, could you shorten the process and make it easier for everyone to understand and demonstrate *agape love*?"

"The honest answer is no. During my first time on earth, I couldn't bring even my twelve closest friends to a point of total trust and understanding. But that's ok. The truest, deepest works of the heart require time and a process of learning. There is no quick fix for the human will. In fact, it is not about will power."

"So what could people have done before you returned to the earth in the Previous Age?" asked Yvonne.

"Ruach did her best to encourage people to listen to her and follow her guidance. If more people had followed her promptings, the suffering that came upon the earth would have been greatly reduced. Many strived to control their actions, but they didn't realise that perfection of character is not the goal. *Agape love* is the destination that everyone is moving towards, and it can accommodate failure and mistakes. It's the great safety net that will allow all of humanity to exist in peace and safety once everyone is living within its flow."

51

As Yvonne considered this, it raised a new question.

"So absolute perfection is not the ultimate goal?"

All the team were listening intently as Yvonne voiced some of the questions that many of them had been carrying. Jesus took a deep breath, looking at the bread he held in his fingers.

"It really depends how you define 'perfection'. *Agape love* makes all things work. All things will eventually become good, but not everything will be perfect - people won't stop making mistakes, being irritating or causing upsets and misunderstandings. People are too complex for that. Remember, all of you experienced suffering at the hands of others, long after you chose to follow me. What made the suffering bearable for you was knowing and trusting that it was not the ultimate truth or power in the situation. Rather, you came to know that *agape love* is the highest power and that if you hold to it all things will be well in due time. That's why you're all here. You all came to see that *agape love* is the ultimate divine good and you did not compromise your trust and belief to accommodate upset, hatred or revenge."

Now it was Bull's turn to speak up. "So there will still be upset and hurt one hundred million years from now?"

"In relationships, it's impossible to never upset each other, but when all things are reconciled to Papa God and I hand over the New Earth to him, everyone will be rooted in unfailing love. Upset and hurt will happen, but the remedy will be quickly applied."

Bull understood what Jesus was saying but had no idea how it might be achieved.

"Things will become clearer as the age plays out. *Agape love* is the reason all things exist. It is the ultimate, deepest meaning in every atom and fibre of creation and in due time it will succeed."

"The Eternal City is a place where *agape love* already flows unhindered," added Thomas. "This is the place where we can come and receive all that we need to be encouraged in our work and to just... *be.* Don't forget, this is where the living water is, and the leaves on the trees are for the healing of the nations."

"Where are those trees?" asked Sylvia.

"The trees are by the River of Living Water," replied Jesus. "They have real leaves and produce much fruit. Those trees and their leaves have been used as a metaphor for the library of material we have built up recording the experiences of individuals in the Previous Age. The descriptions of those experiences will often be helpful in warning people about the potential consequences of pursuing a particular course of action. Soon a few people from every group in the history of humankind will be represented here. Those who heard Ruach's voice and accepted her invitation to follow the way of *agape love* will be formed into teams and, like you, will have a place here in the City, as well as assignments spread out across the New Earth."

As Thomas' team had been busy settling people into the communities, it hadn't been possible for Jesus to fully explain his plans before this meeting. Each member was still in awe of the New Earth, so they were glad to now have the opportunity to ask him their questions.

"In the ages to come, you are going to have plenty of questions," laughed Jesus. "It takes time to figure all this out. I can only tell you what I see Papa doing and what I know from our communication. One day I'll hand the New Earth over to him; all things will accept him as their Father and creation will finally be grounded and saturated in *agape love.*"

Jesus' voice trembled with emotion as he continued. "I cannot tell you the beauty I've seen. No words can possibly describe it. Every inspired work of art, be it a painting, dance, music, book or film, all of it is reaching for what is to come. The crescendo at the completion of this symphony will be beyond what any eye has seen or ear has heard."

Jesus began to weep gently, tears running down his face and into his short black beard. He let them flow.

"The wonder and the beauty of it all! I was there when Papa spoke it into existence. But that was just the start. When I hand it over, it will be complete, and everything will be restored and reconciled. *Agape love* will not have failed anyone or anything. Thank you, my friends, for believing and for reaching beyond your own understanding and your pain. Thank you for trusting me and for joining me in our Father's work."

A silence descended on the table. Each team member was lost in the wonder of Jesus' words. For a few precious moments, each one could see and feel the crescendo Jesus described as if they could take it in their hands and eat it like the food before them. Following Jesus was hard at times, but at junctures like this it was more than worth every struggle, every hurt and every minute spent outside a personal comfort zone.

Everyone joined in the washing up after the meal. Jesus always insisted on having his hands in the suds, while the others wiped things dry and put them away. It was a time for telling stories, cracking jokes and some enjoyed playfully whipping each other with rolled-up tea towels.

"I've been so looking forward to some time here," grinned Yvonne excitedly to Carlos. "The beds are so comfy, and the views are spectacular from every single room."

"Have you ever walked by the River of Living Water in the cool of the evening?" Thomas asked Yvonne. "Light hits the golden streets, and everything glows in a perfect amber hue. Maybe we can go down there now?"

Jesus turned away from the sink and nodded, "Go ahead. Get down to the riverside before the light changes. We're all done here."

Thomas and his team bade Jesus goodbye as they quickly gathered themselves and stepped outside onto the golden streets.

"I guess some things weren't metaphors then?" mused Harmony to Yan as they set off at a brisk pace towards the river.

Yan laughed, "No I guess not! We have golden streets, there is a river of living water lined with trees, and there are those huge gateways. It seems that the visions depicted in the Book of Revelation really did foretell of this place."

Harmony and Yan came from a similar time period in history and could relate easily despite coming from different sides of the planet. For a team of people from across the centuries, the eight of them had developed a remarkably good understanding of each other through their many years together.

The sky seemed to roar into a new phase of luminescence as the heavenly bodies moved in their orbits. The city around them was beginning to throb with warm golden light as the pavements reflected the changing colours. In various windows and doorways of the dwelling places people began to appear and stood in wonder, enjoying the spectacle unfolding before their eyes.

The River of Living Water seemed to dance and sway as the friends looked out. It was a wide river, but the other side was clearly visible. Small groups of people were gathered on its banks; some dangled their legs in the water, while a couple were drinking from their cupped hands and splashing each other.

"Every summer evening in my hometown was pointing towards this," sighed Harmony. "We used to say it was like heaven on earth when the sun set over the delta and the kids would swim and play."

"It was the same for us," said Anne. "We would keep cool by playing in the Jordan. There were places where you could jump in and some where it was deep enough to dive. We used to say it was 'like heaven' too."

"Seems like all the good things we knew were just whetting our appetite for this," said Carlos as he gazed out over the stunning vista before him.

The golden streets began to mellow as the intensity of the moment wore off. The sound of laughter and conversation could be heard throughout the city as people began to settle in for the night. The colours in the sky continued to wax and wane, continually changing the reflections on the streets of the Eternal City.

Thomas' team made their way back from the riverside to their dwellings for the night. Everyone had their own room and went to bed full of gratitude for all they had heard and seen.

*

Sleep was different in the City. Peace hugged each sleeper close, and the pure bliss of complete safety meant that all dreams were sweet.

In the morning it was time for the group of friends to move back out to the communities to which they had been assigned. There would be no more additions to these communities, as the first jubilee period was about to officially begin.

Each pondered what new experiences awaited them as they bade each other goodbye and set out.

Anne and Harmony were to return to the settlements in the woodlands in Beulah.

"Why do you think we get to be so close to the City?" asked Anne.

Harmony thought for a few seconds. "I think it's because those who were victims of much abuse in the Previous Age are often humble of heart and open to love. I think Jesus wants them to know they are close to him."

Anne nodded in agreement. "These people have certainly been traumatised and their lives have been so full of suffering. It will be good for them to be in a safe environment and to know they are loved. It will need much care and attention to bring out their true identity - not as victims but as beloved children of God."

Anne's settlement was a ten-minute walk away from Harmony's. It also had eight cabins surrounding a small communal space.

"I'll see you tomorrow." Anne waved Harmony farewell as she headed off to her clearing.

*

On the side of a valley further into the woodlands was the kindergarten where Yvonne and Yan were helping newly reunited families. When babies and children had died in the previous age, they were reunited with resurrected family members and grew up in small communities.

Yan cast an attentive eye over the dwellings as they entered the village.

"I like how children are reunited with relatives," he said to Yvonne. "Stillborn children can grow up in a family, as they would have done had they lived."

Yvonne was a bundle of energy and fun. She was enthusiastically waving and pulling faces at some of the children as they watched from their windows. Some ran cheering from open front doors, approaching Yvonne expectantly.

She turned and smiled at Yan as several small children pulled at her arms.

Yan was a wise and calming influence and was a good friend to adult family members such as Johan. The village was situated on a hillside with slides and swings and other play equipment built into almost every nook and cranny. The wooden houses were all different colours and there were views out across the treetops. In the distance, the huge radiant walls of the Eternal City could be seen.

"Yan, you must come for some tea and cakes," called Johan from his balcony. "I want to thank you for all your help yesterday."

Yan looked up and saluted Johan. "Ok! I'll come in an hour or so."

Yan loved to sit and talk with people. He would listen more than he spoke, but when he did speak, it was with wisdom and consideration.

"You get real tea, while I have make-believe tea parties sipping air from tiny wooden cups!" laughed Yvonne.

"You wouldn't change it even if you could," replied Yan with a chuckle.

"True!" called Yvonne as she was dragged by a mob of giggling children towards their hamlet of Wendy houses.

*

Carlos and Sylvia entered their village, a picturesque settlement of small thatched cottages.

"Off you go to your end then!" said Sylvia, jokingly pushing Carlos' shoulder.

The women lived at one end of the village and the men at the other.

Carlos smiled ruefully. "I know exactly how today will go. I'll see a few solitary men trudging around, hands in pockets. Or there'll be a small group huddled together complaining how they have been wronged and plotting ways to gain the upper hand. None of them will even look at me."

"Well at least you get a quiet life," replied Sylvia. "I can already envisage the women outside my door complaining that she said this and they said that and so-and-so always does whatever… Ugh, it's exhausting! This would be such a beautiful place to live if it wasn't for all the gossip, griping and envy."

Carlos nodded sympathetically. They were both relieved that they didn't have to get too involved most of the time, so there were still plenty of opportunities for them to enjoy the New Earth.

*

"Always grateful for the lift!" said Bull to Cedric as they soared over the terrain below them.

Thomas held out his arms, getting a thrill from letting go of Cedric's back. The air around him felt increasingly arid as they approached their destination.

The settlement where they had left Yuri would be their home for the coming jubilee period. Thomas and Bull had been through enough to feel both excitement and trepidation about the challenges ahead.

"This will certainly be no picnic," said Bull.

"True," replied Thomas, arms still outstretched. "There are going to be some difficult days ahead."

The jubilee period would be regularly interspersed with time back in the Eternal City, but they would have to live among these hardened and violent men for many years.

"I'll be watching," said Cedric in his deep resonant voice.

Knowing that the giant seraph would be watching over them was a great comfort to Bull and Thomas. Jesus wouldn't have asked them to suffer without providing them with a clear sign of his presence and ultimate authority. Cedric was a reminder that everything would be working towards the reconciliation of all things.

"Hold on," warned Cedric as he began his descent. Swooping low to land at the edge of the gorge, Bull and Thomas knew they'd have to climb down from Cedric's back and be delivered in the same way as everyone else.

Cedric reached out a giant arm and gathered the two men to his chest. He took off again and dived down into the camp. After touching down, he released his passengers, nodded to them and flew off towards his nest on the cliff top.

# Adilah: Past Injustices

Harmony knocked on the final door. She'd been to each hut and gently called to the woman inside. Leaving a steaming mug of hot cocoa or coffee on the windowsill of each cabin was one way she enjoyed serving the community.

Some were nervously accepted and silently brought inside; others sat on the windowsill until they grew cold. Only Eshe, Adilah's sister, would come out and sit with Harmony to drink. Together they would usually admire the birds and animals that could be seen in the trees surrounding the camp.

"Where are you from?" asked Eshe one morning as the sun drew the dew from the grass.

Harmony hadn't thought about the Previous Age for a long time. She smiled wistfully.

"I'm from a country that was known as the United States of America. I grew up in a little town where everyone knew each other."

"Yes, I heard of America. What animals did you have there?" asked Eshe.

"Horses, lots of cows in the fields and many people had dogs. How about you?"

"I come from a small village outside the big city. There were many animals in the land - elephant, giraffe, rhino, hippo. I loved them all, but the elephants could be a nuisance and spoil the crops."

Harmony knew that Eshe must have experienced great suffering at some time in her life. However, she had refrained from asking, preferring to wait for Eshe to talk if she wanted to.

"Did you ever have a pet dog?" she asked Eshe.

"No, there were many chickens and goats in the village, but we didn't have dogs. I don't like dogs. Only the militia had them."

"The militia?" asked Harmony gently.

"There was a war between the tribes in my country. The militia would attack villages and take whatever they wanted."

Eshe was speaking without emotion, but Harmony detected a sadness in her eyes.

"Did you ever see them?" she asked.

"Oh yes. They came to my village when I was only twelve and took me, my sister, some other girls and some boys. They killed the elders and our parents with machetes and fire."

Harmony turned towards Eshe to show that she had her attention and was listening. Sensing it was safe to speak, Eshe continued.

"We were taken away by the militia. If we tried to run, we were hunted and brought back."

Eshe looked down.

"They made me so dirty."

"Those men, they didn't take your value from you. You are loved and precious. Jesus has brought us here so we can recover from all we have experienced."

"The things I saw. They are still in my mind. I am so scared they will find me here." Eshe's voice trembled slightly.

"Let me show you something," said Harmony.

She led Eshe through the woods until they came to a tree with a trunk five times thicker than the others. Steps had been built around the trunk, with a rope for use as a handrail. They climbed

61

up the steps until they came to a wooden platform which was supported by sturdy branches. Here there were some wooden chairs bathed in dappled sunlight. Through a gap in the foliage, countless treetops spread out to the horizon where distant hills appeared in shades of purple.

"You can see out over the woodlands to the hills beyond," said Harmony. "All of this is protected by seraphs like Cynthia, who brought us here to our camp. Jesus will never let anyone come here who should not be here. The New Earth is divided, for now, into different regions, each with its own community. The people in each community are in a process of healing and restoration that is specific to their experience and character."

Eshe nodded and then pointed to smoke drifting over the treetops from the east. "What is that?" she asked.

"It's smoke from Anne's camp. She's our friend. The women in her community are lovely, just like you. When you're ready, you can get to know them. Everyone in this region of Beulah has been chosen to be here, not too far from the Eternal City."

The two women lingered, sharing the quietness together, until Harmony suggested it was time to head back.

Eshe loved her home. It felt so safe and quiet, and the animals around her were a joy to watch. She surveyed the camp happily, feeling more secure after talking to Harmony.

*

One evening Eshe approached Harmony, who was sweeping out her cabin. The crickets were playing in their night-time orchestra and a delicate mist was rising from the grass. Animal calls echoed from the trees and the rays from the sky orbs were dimmed in their silent dance above the New Earth.

"I'd like to meet the other women who live with your friend Anne one day. Maybe we could sing with them?" suggested Eshe.

"Like a choir? What a beautiful idea!" replied Harmony with delight. "I'll suggest it to Anne and see what she thinks. Maybe we could invite the women who are interested to come and hear you and Adilah sing for them, and you could teach them some songs?"

Eshe nodded as she pondered this. "Yes, I would like that very much," she replied with a gentle smile.

"Do you feel you have everything you need?" asked Harmony, taking the opportunity while Eshe felt relaxed and open to conversation.

"Oh yes, I am very happy with my home. I am so pleased to have so many things that I can use, but..."

"Go on," encouraged Harmony.

"I would very much like to make myself some more clothes and some for the other women too. Do you think we could get some material and some needles and thread?"

"I will talk to the angels. They can get things like that. The City is full of inventive people making all sorts of things for others to use."

"Really? I'd love to meet them one day."

Harmony was pleased to hear this, as Eshe could be so timid around other people.

"I'm sure you will. Can you imagine being in a new place?" she asked.

"If there are angels to protect me, then yes I can," Eshe replied.

"Well, there are many angels there doing all sorts of important things. In the City, you won't need protection from anyone or anything. Only people whose lives are in tune with *agape love* are allowed to go there."

"Ok, it sounds as though I will not need protecting. But maybe I will need reassurance. New places are so scary for me."

Harmony pondered on this distinction into the evening.

\*

"Do you think people will feel daunted and overwhelmed by the Eternal City when they first go there?" Harmony asked Anne when they met later that night.

"I think it may take some getting used to," she replied.

"I guess so. Maybe one thousand years of learning how to live by *agape love* meant that we had no fears when we finally got there."

Anne nodded in agreement. "I'm sure that when the time is right, it will be the same for Eshe and for everyone else."

The two friends bade each other goodnight and retired to their respective camps. Each group was arranged in the same way with a circle of cabins facing inwards. The women could choose whether to go in and out through their front or back doors. In the centre of the circle the communal campfire was often smouldering as it was used every day for cooking and heating water. There were benches made from logs and thick-set tables where the women could make things, prepare food and enjoy each other's company.

*

A few weeks later Harmony placed a steaming mug of cocoa on Adilah's windowsill and was about to continue to the next cabin when she heard the door open. Turning, she was delighted to see Adilah standing there.

"Thank you," Adilah said quietly and picked up the mug. Without saying anything more, she gracefully crossed the wooden porch and stood next to Harmony.

"You're welcome," replied Harmony with a warm smile, slightly surprised by this response after weeks of watching the cocoa go cold.

"Shall I come with you?" offered Adilah.

Harmony nodded and continued towards the next cabin.

"This one is black coffee," said Harmony, motioning with her head toward a mug on the far side of the tray. "Could you put it on the windowsill for me?"

Adilah did so, still holding her own mug in one hand, and returned to Harmony's side.

"The last one is for Eshe. She usually joins me."

Eshe saw them coming and skipped out of her cabin, her long colourful dress that she had made herself flowing behind her.

"Good morning, Adilah!" Eshe beamed at her sister. "Let's go up to the tree house."

"Come and see," Harmony invited Adilah warmly.

The three women sipped from their mugs as they walked to the tree house, balancing them carefully as they climbed the steps to the viewing platform.

Settling into their chairs, the women gazed out over the forest. Birds swooped and wheeled above the canopy and all kinds of animals could be heard in the trees below.

Adilah looked at Eshe and Harmony, noting how peaceful and contented they seemed with their warm morning drinks. She felt a wave of envy well up within her.

Noticing her stare, Eshe asked, "Are you ok, Adilah?"

Adilah looked at the wooden floor for a few moments before replying.

"How do you have this peace, Eshe? There are days when I still feel frightened and want to hide. You come from the same place as me, yet you can just sit here contentedly drinking your coffee."

Eshe was surprised by what felt like an accusation.

Harmony put her mug of cocoa down on the floor and folded her hands on her lap, which encouraged Adilah to continue.

"And you are always so happy!" said Adilah, looking directly at Harmony. "You have never suffered like me. Your American life was comfortable. You had money and food and never had to work."

65

"I see why you think that," Harmony said gently. "I am from a rich and powerful nation in the Previous Age. I know this afforded me many privileges."

Adilah burned a little hotter inside.

"That's right. The West never helped us. Our civil war was not something white people cared about. We were forgotten and left to suffer. Eshe, why are you not angry like me? Have you forgotten where you come from?"

The painful memories of those terrible times and seeing her sister in such distress brought tears to Eshe's eyes.

"Adilah, you know that Harmony left America to help people. Why are you angry with her?"

But Adilah refused to be pacified.

"I'm not just angry with her but with all the so-called good people who did nothing to help us. Remember how they raped and killed so many of us? Remember how they turned our brothers into soldiers and forced us from our homes?"

Eshe was becoming distraught and turned away, sobbing.

"And don't look at me with such pity," Adilah said indignantly to Harmony.

Harmony didn't defend herself and lowered her eyes.

Adilah began to pace the floor.

"You both look so peaceful and calm. I want to be like that too. But inside I feel... so many things. I feel like a pot that is boiling over."

Adilah's face displayed the intensity of her feelings.

"I still dream that the men are on top of me," she said with a trembling voice. "I still see the flames of the fire that burned me. All the hot cocoa in the world cannot take those memories away."

Harmony sat still, but her eyes were filling with tears.

"I know they will come to this place," continued Adilah. "They will find us. If they are raised from the dead, they will find us and make us their property again. Jesus should keep them dead!" Her voice was now raised. "Or torture them like they tortured us! Is he not the judge? Are they not guilty?"

Eshe turned to Harmony, trauma etched on her face. "Yes, he should keep them dead. If they stay dead, they will truly never find us."

Harmony could sense their rising panic and could understand their anxiety.

"I hear you," she said supportively.

Eshe stood up and drew close to Adilah's side.

"Or maybe it would be better if *we* had stayed dead?" she said, desperately. "Harmony, tell us. What can really stop those men finding us here?"

"What if the men who hurt you were kept away until they no longer had any hate or wickedness in them?" asked Harmony, careful to keep her voice calm and reassuring.

Adilah and Eshe looked at one another for a second.

"But how can this be?" asked Eshe.

"Jesus determines who is in each community and prevents the communities from mixing. He is making everyone new. Every single person is going through a process designed to help them live in *agape love*. Think of it like this - in a way, those men you knew won't exist anymore, because what made them bad will be healed within them."

Adilah and Eshe were now listening intently.

"Let me tell you about a man called Saul. He was very aggressive in his religious beliefs and hurt people who disagreed with him. He even looked on and approved when they were killed by angry mobs. Jesus came to him one day and Saul's heart began to change in a big way - so much so that his name was changed to

Paul. So, in a way, Saul was destroyed and Paul was the new and healed version of the man. The same divine essence lived in both, but the person after the encounter was very different to the original."

"But will they be changed as quickly as that?" asked Adilah.

"It's unlikely, but you never know. Saul was obviously ready to accept who Jesus wanted him to be. He changed a lot in a few years, and some who come into communities on the New Earth are able to do the same. However, most people take a long time to learn all they need and let go of their harmful twisted desires. But everyone will get there eventually. Papa God's *agape love* never fails. Every person is important to Papa God, and he knows when they are ready for complete reconciliation."

Adilah suddenly seemed tired. Looking a little deflated, she sat down cross-legged on the wooden deck.

After several minutes of reflective silence, Adilah spoke again.

"I wish I could see Jesus again. When we first met, I felt safe and he answered some of my questions. But I have many more questions now."

"That's ok. It's quite normal," Harmony reassured her. "Maybe you could write your questions down?"

Adilah looked upset again. "See, there it is! We never learned to read or write. We were not educated like you in the West."

Harmony was disappointed in herself for not thinking. She hadn't meant to hurt Adilah and quickly apologised. "Adilah, I am sorry. I should have thought before I spoke. I shouldn't have assumed."

Adilah looked at Harmony and for the first time in the conversation there was a look of dignity in her eyes.

"I am not ashamed that I am uneducated. I do not know the things they teach in schools, but I can cook, and I can sew, and I can dress any wound you show me."

Eshe nodded, feeling affirmed and dignified by Adilah's words.

Harmony gave thanks that her thoughtless comment had resulted in Adilah recognising her abilities and her worth.

"Please forgive me. I want to learn more about your lives. I don't want to presume anything."

"It's ok," said Eshe. "You're a good person, Harmony."

Harmony was grateful for the reconciliation. The three women sat in silence gazing out over the treetops.

# Johan: New Desires

Yvonne threw up her hands in mock dismay as thirteen children swarmed towards her from their schoolhouse. It was time for them to play outside and they desperately wanted to play 'stuck in the mud' with Yvonne. As they surrounded her, she couldn't help but grin as they started to organise themselves for their game.

Yvonne remembered her own childhood, just before the Great Suffering. She and other children her age had been taught this same game by a kindly older lady who had been killed when the looting started, along with many others in her town. Yvonne wondered when she would be raised and where she would be placed. But now a boy was pulling her by the hand and Yvonne snapped out of her memories.

"Look at them playing," said Johan from the ladder that reached up to where Yan was arranging new straw on a thatched roof. "They will never know war, or hunger and abuse. Doesn't that make you wonder?"

Yan paused his work and looked down on the playground.

"But they will need to learn to love one another," replied Yan. "And that can only be learned through relationships and everything that goes along with them."

Johan looked up at Yan, wiping sweat from his brow.

"Yes, but doesn't it make you wonder why we had to suffer so much before coming here? I don't understand why God couldn't just make it all like this in the first place."

Sensing Johan's need to talk, Yan settled himself on the roof near the ladder.

"The Previous Ages were a time of multiplication of the species on the earth, and the desires we had were designed to ensure that the population increased. These desires were essential to produce great diversity and ensure that each person and creature was a unique individual. But the desires to procreate and protect ourselves, our families and our communities could become twisted and be used in the wrong way. That's what caused much of the pain and suffering that you and many others experienced. Now that God has brought that time to an end, the desires in our resurrected bodies are of a different nature. We do not need to procreate or protect our own interests as we once did."

"So is that why I've felt no desire for sex since coming here?" asked Johan, relieved to be able to ask Yan about a matter that had been troubling him.

"Yes, on the New Earth our resurrected bodies do not drive us toward sex anymore."

"Can I tell you something?" asked Johan quietly, glancing around to check nobody was within earshot.

"When I was a soldier, I went into the city..."

Yan nodded.

"My comrades and I..., well, we went to a house." Johan eyes were fixed on the ground.

"There were girls there. And I had never... you know... I went along with it. We all did. I paid the girl and.... I felt sick afterwards. Not because of her, but because it felt so cheap and meaningless. I think about her sometimes."

"Johan, thank you for telling me. The way you felt shows that you were open to your conscience. Did you learn anything else?"

Johan held tight to the rungs of the ladder and avoided Yan's eyes as he took a deep breath and continued.

"I wanted to be with someone, I guess. I wanted human touch - one that wasn't violent. I wanted a woman's touch. But I was just one in a long line of soldiers and she touched me because I paid her. At that moment it felt good, but afterwards I felt I had degraded what human touch really means. If we had been in love and just the two of us, it would have been so different."

"I understand," said Yan quietly. "It is a hard thing to recognise, but you have seen clearly how this was not the right place to fulfil your natural desires. It was loving relationships and real feelings that made sex so enjoyable and fulfilling in the Previous Age."

"Yes, and I am sorry for it," said Johan, looking back into Yan's face.

"Listen, Johan. This is part of the process. Our experiences help us learn and recognise what is good. When we see clearly, we can face up to our regrets and we can let them go. We are all loved, and nothing we did is held against us. God keeps no records of such things."

"But when he sees me, doesn't he see the things I've done?"

"He does not bring them to mind, but he is aware of the influence they have on your heart. He understands how they have affected you, but our intrinsic value is not in what we did or didn't do. God's love is so special that we have a special word for it - *agape.* It's hard to describe in words, but this divine love heals, restores, reconciles and redeems all who embrace it. When we come to realise that we are held in *agape love*, we change - sometimes quickly, more often slowly. It depends how open our heart is. *Agape love* comes to us in many ways and forms. It doesn't demand to be worshipped but always seeks to gently nurture us."

Yan reached down and put an arm around Johan's shoulder as he digested these words.

*

Snack time meant a generous mix of fruit and nuts and Eric sidled up to Yvonne to enjoy his portion.

"Yvonne?" asked Eric, squinting up at her. "Gerty's big brother, Johan. He's nice, but... he seems sad sometimes. He plays with Gerty, but he never joins in the games with us."

Yvonne smiled down at Eric and ruffled his hair.

"You know what?" she said. "Some of the grown-ups have seen some awful things in the Previous Age. Do you remember, we learned about that in school? Most of you kids don't remember much about the Previous Age, because you came here when you were so young. But the grown-ups still think about what happened and often struggle to understand it."

"He seems jealous of you, Yvonne."

"That's very perceptive of you. What makes you think that?"

"I sometimes see him watching you when you play with us. When you laugh with us, I see his face. He stares at you looking a little cross."

"So why do you think he might be jealous, Eric?"

Eric took another handful of nuts and berries, chewing them thoughtfully. Before finishing his mouthful, he looked back up at Yvonne.

"He wants to laugh like you do."

"Ok, so why do you think he doesn't?"

Eric put his bowl down. "I think he is still sad about what he saw before."

"Why do you think that might stop him having fun with us now?"

"Well, maybe he is thinking that the past is more real than where we are now?"

Yvonne was startled by Eric's simple but profound insights. Looking up, she could see Johan and Yan thatching the roof of one of the houses nestled on the hillside.

"So, Eric, what do you think would help Johan?"

"If he could believe that everything will be made right, then the hurt of the Previous Age might go away."

"Will everything be ok here?"

"Well, Jesus and all his friends like you are helping everyone find the love inside them that can make life better for everyone."

Yvonne was delighted with how much Eric understood. He had died in infancy on a cotton plantation in the late nineteenth century. His parents had been slaves.

"What do you remember about your time in the Previous Age?" asked Yvonne.

Eric furrowed his brow.

"Not very much. Men on horses. I was scared of them because they beat us. And I remember singing together with my family, and Mumma and Papa swinging me as I held their hands."

"It's so good that you can be with your Mumma and Papa again."

"Yes! Jesus resurrected them so that we can all be here together."

Eric stood up and smiled at Yvonne.

"Can I go now?" he asked sweetly.

"Of course you can. Thank you for the good chat."

Eric skipped over to Gerty and sat down to join in comparing the animals they'd seen that day.

\*

"Not like that," said Johan. "Like *this*." He dug deep into the stack of straw and twisted the fork, pulling out an impressive amount.

Eric pushed in his fork and lifted out a tuft which promptly fell apart and floated off in the breeze.

"No! You must twist the fork! Twist the fork!" Johan was now yelling. "All this spare straw needs sorting out."

Eric waited for Johan to attack the stack of straw again before turning to Gerty.

"Why is he so bossy? Is he always like this?"

Gerty checked her brother wasn't watching and then nodded. "He sometimes shouts at home as well."

Johan turned back to the two children. "Try again, then!" he ordered.

Eric dug in his fork, twisted it and successfully hoisted a golden clump of straw into the air.

"Ok," said Johan. "Now spread it like I did."

Doing his best to lower his straw to the ground, Eric held the fork in a horizontal position while Gerty instinctively helped him by removing the straw with her hands.

"No, Gerty! Leave him alone. How will Eric learn if you help him?"

Gerty sighed and stepped back. Eric spread the straw as he had been told and looked back at Johan, searching for approval.

"Ok," said Johan. "And again."

"So, what makes him so angry and why does he shout so much?" Eric asked Gerty as they walked home together, once Johan had called the work day over.

Gerty thought for a minute. "I think it's because he was in the army. War broke out when he was only fifteen and he wanted to be like the other boys in our village who signed up for the infantry. His training was very tough, but it taught him how to fight. Maybe he thinks that all teaching should be like his army training."

"We had angry men like him where I grew up. They shouted at us from horses and had whips. I hated them."

"Do you hate Johan?" asked Gerty.

"No, I don't hate him. I have seen him be kind to people too. I think it's just when he is doing things for the village he feels he needs to shout and be bossy. I like him when he isn't shouting."

"Ok, I won't say *you* said anything, but I will try and talk to him later."

Eric was thankful for Gerty's courage and her willingness to confront her big brother.

*

"How do you think Eric did today?" asked Gerty over the table.

Johan looked up from his plate, knife and fork in hand.

"He did fine. He's a hard worker."

"I think he is too, but... it was his first time today and you were really hard on him."

Johan looked startled. "Was I?" He sat back in his chair, recalling the events of the afternoon.

"You are such a kind person," Gerty reassured him. "But Eric felt a little sad about how you were angry with him."

Johan sat forward again, and Gerty was pleased that he seemed to be listening.

"I guess I never thought about it. I'm glad you've said something. I don't want to discourage Eric. I just want everyone to do a good job. I think maybe I shout at him because that's how I was taught in the army."

"I thought so," said Gerty. "I remember watching you on parade in the town square. The man shouting at you all frightened me."

Johan smiled through sad eyes.

"He was shouting at us to help us learn how to stay alive. He was shouting to make us into better soldiers."

"But everyone is safe here, aren't they?" replied Gerty. "And we have time to learn."

"I guess you're right. Still, we need to have focus and discipline."

Afterwards, Gerty thought about what her brother had said but decided that she didn't completely agree with him.

As the weeks passed, Eric steadily improved in his thatching skills and joined Johan and several other men and women roofing new structures around the village.

One lunchtime, Eric was sitting with Gerty and Johan enjoying some of the fresh bread made at the bakery that morning.

"You're dropping crumbs everywhere," Johan remarked impatiently as Eric tucked into his currant bun.

Eric glanced up, embarrassed, but no longer surprised by his brusque manner. Brushing the crumbs from his shirt, he summoned up the courage to speak, "But Johan, we are outside."

Johan was not used to Eric talking back. Johan cleared his throat, got up and walked away.

"He's always telling me off!" said Eric indignantly.

"I know," acknowledged Gerty. "I did try to speak to him about it, but he doesn't seem to realise that he is harder on you than on anyone else."

"Yoo-hoo," called Yvonne, calling from across the field

Eric and Gerty waved back.

Eric jumped up as he recognised his father, Ebo, walking with Yvonne. "Come and see our roof!"

"Oh, it's spectacular!" marvelled Ebo. "Great job, son, and well done Gerty, too. Did you do this one yourselves?"

"Johan did help a little," admitted Eric, just as Johan rounded the corner of the building having heard voices.

Ebo greeted him with a broad smile. "Johan, I see you are teaching these young ones very well."

Johan did not return the greeting.

Noticing the awkwardness between the two men, Yvonne was quick to add, "I think you're all doing a great job."

"And what are you doing today?" Johan asked, directing his question to Yvonne.

"We're looking at some fields to the west. They are ready for more crops to be planted, and we have received a shipment of seeds. Ebo is going to head up the cultivation project."

"You will be in charge, Pa?" asked Eric, with pride in his voice.

"I guess I will be," said Ebo. "But it's a team effort."

"Yes," added Johan. "A team effort."

"What is it with him?" asked Ebo, as he and Yvonne continued back to the village hall.

A familiar and warm feeling came over Yvonne. She knew it was Ruach. A picture formed itself in her mind. She saw Johan as a boy, wearing the uniform of a Nazi soldier. Before him a children's book lay open with grotesque racist illustrations on its pages. In that moment Yvonne understood how Johan was still influenced by the racist culture that had shaped him from an impressionable age.

Ebo knew the answer to his question. Although he tried to quell his anger, part of him was seething that even here on the New Earth he still faced prejudice. He didn't want to voice his suspicions and create problems in the village. For the most part he and his family felt welcomed and accepted.

Yvonne sensed Ebo's mood. "Some folk still have so much to work through."

"Well, I guess that's just fine. And what about you, Yvonne? What do you have to work through?"

Yvonne was surprised by the sarcasm in Ebo's tone. "I would like to tell you, but I don't want to give you defensive answers."

Ebo was stopped short. He shook his head and turning to face Yvonne, he saw empathy in her eyes.

"Oh, I am sorry."

He shook his head again. "Yvonne, I am sorry. I'm not asking you to make everything right, but I have to tell you, I am feeling angry."

"I know," said Yvonne. "I hear you."

The two sat and talked, Ebo shared his frustrations. When the conversation reached a plateau, Yvonne reached down and took Ebo's hands.

"Come, let's go and see the seed delivery."

*

Johan woke with the birdsong as he did every morning. His village, surrounded by pine forest, was shrouded in a delicate pink mist. Though he had now been living there for three years, the peaceful atmosphere that reigned each day was still striking. Johan enjoyed his job, which had evolved from thatching into general building maintenance.

When he woke, he loved to get out of bed and do one hundred press-ups, feeling his body's natural strength. This was part of his normal routine, but today was a special day. It was three years to the day since he had been reunited with his sister.

Gerty was now ten years old, counting from her birth in the Previous Age and including her years after resurrection. She benefitted from having grown up mostly on the New Earth and possessed a wisdom that constantly surprised Johan.

On awakening, Gerty laughed with delight to see the special cake that Johan had made her sitting proudly on the kitchen table.

"It's our three-year rebirthday!" he announced.

"It doesn't feel that long at all!"

"That's true. Time here is so different."

"What are you doing today?" asked Gerty, demolishing a large slice of cake.

"Varnishing the wheel at the mill. How about you?"

"We're continuing our experiments with crossbreeding tomato plants at school. Eric has some really interesting new ideas to try."

"Is that right?" said Johan.

"You always do that!"

"Do what?"

"Be sarcastic when I mention Eric! Why can't you just accept him?"

Johan felt sad that he had disappointed Gerty, but he couldn't deny that he still had negative feelings about Eric and his family.

"Ok. It's our special day today and I want to show you that I'm listening."

There was a polite knock at the door, and when Johan swung it open, there stood Yan with a backpack full for the day of work ahead.

"Varnishing day!" Yan announced.

"Right," said Johan. "Let's go."

Gerty came to the door and waved them off on their way to the river. The village was bustling into life with people setting off for work, and the narrow streets were filled with the sound of friendly chatter as people stopped to greet their neighbours.

"Hello, you two!" called a familiar voice to their right.

Yvonne was carefully descending a steep path with a wheelbarrow full of fresh compost. She had spent several hours the previous evening in deep meditation thinking about Johan's past and was pleased to see him.

"Hi Johan, shall we get some lunch together sometime this week?"

Johan was a little taken by surprise, but he felt a great affection for Yvonne and was pleased to be asked.

"Yes, I'd like that very much. What about tomorrow?"

"I'll come and find you at the mill at midday."

"Ok, right..." Johan suddenly felt a little self-conscious and was unable to finish his sentence.

"See you both soon!" chirped Yvonne as she headed off in the direction of the plant nursery.

Yan slapped Johan on the back. "You ok?" he chuckled.

"Yes, it's just... I haven't been asked to spend any time with her before."

"Ah, she's great. You'll get along very well."

Soon the two men were happily coating the wheel at the watermill with varnish made from tree sap. Some of the bakery team arrived to fetch freshly ground flour from the mill and several conversations were struck up between the various working parties.

Further up the river a group were partly damming the flow of the water to create a swifter current. The sound of people singing together drifted back downstream. The day was warm, but a gentle breeze kept the air fresh. The work was hard, but everyone enjoyed the physical activity and the power of their resurrection bodies.

# Fran: A Lost Opportunity

Fran awoke to birdsong not far from her bedroom window. Though she would never have admitted it to any of her neighbours, she loved her new living space and was exceedingly pleased with how beautiful her village was. Days started peacefully with the natural world around the village slowly stirring, and as the morning wore on the members of the community began their activities.

But this morning Fran's sense of contentment was short-lived as she groaned, remembering that she was nearly out of water. This meant a trip to the wellspring and interaction with people.

"Why couldn't they have put in decent plumbing?" she thought to herself as she procrastinated in bed. "Surely 'heaven' could have taken on the best of human technology from the Previous Age!"

Mulling these thoughts, Fran dressed and went downstairs. She and her husband had always taken it in turns to get up and make the early morning pot of tea on the gas stove at home. Keith and Fran had shared their lives for twenty-three years before her death. Keith was a steady man, who worked hard at his job on the railway. He liked watching football, seaside holidays, fish and chip suppers on a Friday and the occasional flutter on the horses. Typical of many young people in Britain in the early 1960s, they had met at the local dance hall and dated for six months before getting engaged. They were married in the local church within the year and soon started a family. Fran had enjoyed their simple life together, and Keith's hard work meant their family had never wanted for anything.

But life was different now. Making tea needed water, and water had to be fetched. You also needed wood for the stove to heat the water, so wood had to be gathered. There was plenty of wood to be found, and Fran didn't have to go far to collect it. There were particular trees that seemed to drop perfectly sized twigs and branches specifically for human use. The whole process of making tea thus entailed regular interaction with the land and its natural resources, which were varied and plentiful. Fruit trees, berry bushes and root vegetables grew in abundance and were larger and more nutritious than in the Previous Age. Mushrooms, edible bark and delicious tree saps, similar to maple syrup, added to the variety of food that was freely available for everyone across the New Earth. Hunger and lack were things of the past.

However, food still needed to be harvested and prepared. In the Previous Age, Fran had only needed to go to the shops to buy everything they needed. This she had done every few days, enjoying the opportunity to catch up with all the latest gossip from the various shopkeepers and acquaintances she would meet on the local high street. But here on the New Earth, Fran was irritated by the need to gather what she needed. She felt it was a rather primitive and unrefined way to live.

Fran peeked through her net curtains. Her view took in the village green and several of the cottages on the other side. As on most mornings, she noted the twitching curtains in the window of the cottage directly opposite and was irritated that someone else was observing her and the neighbourhood. Fran tutted and went into the kitchen.

"Damn!" she cursed under her breath, realising that the fire in the wood burner had gone out and the water in her kettle was tepid. She put some twigs on the embers, hoping they would catch alight.

"Oh, for crying out loud!" she wailed, as the last glow in the embers faded. Glancing through her kitchen window she was infuriated to see Imelda watching her from over the hedge.

Fran marched through the back door and up to her side of the boundary.

"Morning, Fran," smirked Imelda. "How're things?"

"Fine, thank you," snapped Fran defiantly. "But my fire has gone out."

"Oh, I'm so sorry for you! Want a splint from mine?"

"That would be... thank you," she said briskly.

"Come around the front," invited Imelda.

As Fran approached Imelda's door, it opened and her breath was taken away by the sight of a beautiful full-length coat hanging proudly on the banister at the bottom of the stairs. It was made of sumptuous purple cloth with bright golden buttons and was just like the ones she had seen wealthy women wear about town when she was a teenager. Imelda was pleased to see Fran's reaction. She held the splint close, making Fran come nearer to take it.

"Thank you," she said, forcing a smile, before hurrying back to her cottage.

Imelda closed her door, satisfied with the exchange.

Fran felt so flustered that it took her four attempts to light the kindling from the splint. She seethed as she stood and watched the flames spread in the wood burner.

"How the hell did she get that?" she whispered to herself as she leant against the kitchen wall waiting for the kettle to boil.

Next door, Imelda gazed lovingly at the coat. She had drawn the design herself and then shown it to her neighbour, Dawn, who had been happy to show off her needlework skills.

\*

Dawn's finger stung from a pin prick.

"Oh, poor you!" cried Imelda as Dawn hurried to the bathroom to wash off the blood before it stained the silk garment in her hands.

While she was gone, Imelda's eyes remained fixed on the dress that was beginning to take shape.

Dawn sat back down and continued to sew the hem she was working on.

"I really need this dress finished in the next hour. Do you think that's possible?"

"Forgive me, Imelda," said Dawn meekly. "I'm so clumsy when I'm working this fast."

Imelda raised her eyebrows. "Well, I guess you are doing your best," she said with a note of exasperation and returned to her daydream. She couldn't wait to see the look on Fran's face when she would open the door to her later that evening wearing her new creation.

Making things brought Dawn satisfaction and she had always been talented with a needle and thread. Like all the women in the village, she had been born in the second half of the twentieth century in the Previous Age, and she had run a successful dressmaking business in Birmingham, England. Dawn's heart was generous, but she had a tendency to store up bitterness and grudges. She was happy to demonstrate her skills by working with Imelda but was beginning to feel frustrated with Imelda's self-centredness.

"You know, maybe some of the other girls would like some new clothes too?" suggested Dawn, trying not to sound too assertive, as she wanted to remain in Imelda's good books.

"Yes, all in good time. There might well be a chance to make a lot of..." Imelda stopped. "Hang on. What do we make here, if we can't make money?"

"Well, when I was running my own business, there were times when we traded things rather than getting paid. I had quite a good deal going with a gardener. In exchange for dressmaking and repairs, she would spend a few hours doing jobs in my garden."

"Well, yes, obviously we could do some swaps."

Dawn sighed quietly. Imelda seemed to have the knack of making her feel small and of little consequence.

"But how would we split things?" she ventured.

"No need to worry about that now. We can decide nearer the time. Now come on, I want to try this on so you can make adjustments before I go. Then you can start on this blouse design I've come up with. I think you'll agree I've excelled myself this time."

"Yes, Imelda," said Dawn as she continued with her sewing, pushing down her growing resentment.

*

Fran tried desperately not to look at Imelda's dress as she stepped inside her neighbour's cottage. Imelda took the bunch of herbs Fran had brought with her from her garden.

"These will do I suppose."

Fran hardly heard her, trying to look anywhere but at her neighbour.

"So, a new and rather ravishing dress!" cried Imelda, striking a pose.

"Well, yes," replied Fran with fake nonchalance. "It's..." she deliberately paused, "... very nice."

Imelda could sense Fran was struggling to hide her envy, and so she kept pushing.

"Of course it's all silk, you know. And New Earth silk feels just sublime. You can't imagine until you've tried it. I feel like I've been raised all over again!"

Fran pursed her lips and cocked her head to one side, trying to unnerve Imelda with a critical eye.

Imelda wasn't deterred.

"And actually, I'm soon going to be a wealthy woman. It won't be much longer until I can upgrade to a much nicer neighbourhood."

Fran saw her chance to catch Imelda out.

"Haven't you heard? That's not at all how things work here."

Imelda was determined not to reveal any cracks in her veneer of confidence.

"Oh, is it that right? And who did you hear that from? Jesus Christ himself?"

Determined to gain the upper hand, Fran lied. "Actually, yes, he said so himself when I was raised. He said that there's no way out of our community. Didn't he explain that to you?"

"He never said that. You're lying!"

"I am not and you can't prove it."

Having reached an impasse, Imelda changed tack.

"In any case, I will be rich as soon as we open our clothes shop."

"*We*?" asked Fran. "Who is '*we*'?"

"Oh, just me and my workforce," Imelda exaggerated.

"Exactly who though?" pressed Fran.

"All will become clear when we open for business. Let's get those herbs in the dough, and we'll have herb bread ready in no time."

Fran followed Imelda to the kitchen, comforting herself with scathing thoughts of the preposterousness of Imelda wearing such a fine dress just to bake bread.

"Well, I was more of a miniskirt girl myself," sighed Fran, slightly wistfully.

"Oh, really? When were you alive in the Previous Age?" For the first time, Imelda showed genuine interest.

"The 1960s," replied Fran. "Well, that's when I was a teenager anyway."

"Well how about that? Same for me!"

"And I'm guessing that's a Liverpudlian accent," said Fran with a tentative smile.

Imelda snorted with laughter, "Yes, and I'm glad you didn't say *Scouse*! How do you know the difference?"

Fran looked back at Imelda with a knowing look.

"Two words," she said with a cheeky grin.

"The Beatles!" shouted the two women at the same time, laughing.

"Well, Liverpool was the centre of the universe for a time, wasn't it?" said Imelda.

"I was a London girl," said Fran, "and all we wanted to do was go up to Liverpool and see the Cavern Club... and Penny Lane."

"I didn't live far from Penny Lane. In the early days we'd sometimes see the Fabs just walking around. My dad knew Paul's dad!"

"I wonder where they are now? Do you think they've been raised yet?" said Fran with all the enthusiasm of a teenage fan.

"Oh, that's a good point!" exclaimed Imelda. "I wonder if John still thinks he's more popular than Jesus?"

"Oh gosh, yes! That certainly makes for an interesting encounter. And what about that song of his, 'Imagine there's no heaven... no hell below us.'

Imelda looked thoughtfully at the dough she was kneading. "You know, heaven and hell are sort of redundant concepts here, aren't they?"

"Peace and love," smiled Fran, holding up two fingers on each hand.

Imelda smiled but caught herself.

"Pass me the salt?" she asked in a flat tone, the joy now gone from her face, as she began to knead the dough with more force.

Fran was disappointed to see Imelda shut down the conversation and wondered what had caused the sudden change. She passed the salt.

"Well, I must be off now... things I need to do."

Alone in the kitchen, Imelda's face flushed a little with embarrassment. Part of her wanted to run after Fran to apologise and rebuild the connection, but as she considered it, the moment passed and self-consciousness regained control.

Imelda continued kneading the dough, but in her mind she was imagining where The Beatles might be on the New Earth and hoping that they might not be too far from each other.

# Yuri: Dog Eat Dog

Thomas and Bull scanned the community. Men were standing about, staring at them. Some stood with their arms folded, while others held rocks in their hands that they had been using to improve their dwellings. The camp was silent other than the distant sound of the waterfall gushing on the far side of the gorge.

"Come on," whispered Thomas to Bull and started off towards a simple stone hut that was to be their dwelling.

"Let's see what we can gather. It'll be cold at night," suggested Bull.

Bull began to wander around the base of the wooded cliffs that lined the ravine looking for branches and sticks. After several minutes he had a decent armful to bring back to their quarters.

Bull felt a clip on his heel and before he had time to react, he was sprawled out in the dirt, his sticks and branches strewn on the ground. He tried to get to his feet but, with some shock, realised that a foot was pressing down between his shoulders.

He tried to look around but could only crane his neck so far. His assailant's features were blotted out by the bright sunlight behind him. The man put all his weight on Bull's upper back, forcing the air out of his lungs. Bull groaned helplessly.

Stepping forward the man scooped up the wood and headed off, leaving Bull winded and in pain. Noticing staring eyes from nearby huts, Bull returned to the edge of the camp without a word and began searching for more branches. He returned with only a meagre offering and found Thomas gently encouraging smoke from a tiny pile of sticks and dry leaves. Thomas noticed the scratches on Bull's face and the dirt on his clothes.

He dumped his sticks next to the circle of stone that acted as a fireplace and sat down.

Thomas came and sat close to Bull and put his hand on his shoulder.

"It was the surprise. I didn't see him coming," said Bull.

"It won't always be like this," Thomas smiled at his friend.

Bull thought back to the time spent with Jesus in the Eternal City and the exhilaration he had felt as Jesus described what was to come.

"One day... one day all will be well," said Thomas.

Bull pulled himself upright, looked at Thomas and nodded.

The flames were now flickering in the fireplace. Bull closed his eyes and enjoyed the warmth.

*

Thomas woke with a start. Shouting could be heard echoing off stone walls and heavy footsteps thudded past his window. He opened the door a crack and peered out into the half-light. Unable to see anything, he crept outside. Several blocks away, flames were shooting up into the sky.

Thomas returned and put his hand on Bull's shoulder, gently shaking him awake.

"Something's happening."

Bull followed Thomas outside.

"Should we go and take a closer look?" he asked, seeing the flames.

"Ok, but let's keep in the shadows. We aren't here to intervene and prevent the consequences of people's actions playing out."

The two friends quietly made their way toward the fire.

"Looks like someone will be without a hut," whispered Bull.

There was more shouting close by and the sound of breaking glass.

"Over there," said Thomas pointing to where three men were brawling in the dirt on the pathway. They could see other men looking on from the windows of their huts.

The words the men were shouting were hard to make out, but suddenly a fourth man emerged from behind a hut. Before anyone had time to react, he brought a large rock crashing down on the head of one of the men on the ground. The other two scrambled away as the victim lay motionless, a pool of dark blood spreading across the dirt. The assailant raised the rock above his head again and this time threw it down onto the victim's back. Thomas and Bull remained concealed in the shadows as the figure disappeared back into the darkness.

Rushing over, Bull lifted the rock from the man's back. He was unconscious and bleeding badly from an open gash on the top of his head.

"Let's get him to our hut," said Thomas.

Laying him carefully on Thomas' bed, Bull fetched water and tore cloth from a shirt drying near the wood burner in the corner.

After he had gently cleaned the blood away from the man's face and neck, the man's eyes began to flicker.

Thomas sat down on the bed, next to the man.

"He's starting to come round."

The man opened his eyes and looked first at Thomas and then up at Bull who had finished wiping his forehead clean.

"The wound has closed," reported Bull to Thomas.

"Yes. There'll be a scar and bruising, but only for a day or so."

The man's eyes widened as he realised he was in someone else's hut. "What do you want?" he asked in a quiet, husky voice.

"Nothing. You're safe," replied Bull.

"You've been hurt, but you'll be fine soon," Thomas reassured him.

The man looked at Thomas with a deadpan stare.

"Who are you?"

"My name is Thomas, and this is my friend, Bull."

"Friend?" said the man sardonically. "No one has friends here."

Thomas smiled. "Bull has been my friend for a very long time."

The man looked unconvinced.

"This is our hut," Bull explained.

"You share?"

"Yes."

"No one shares!" The man groaned as he attempted to sit up. "We just take what we can."

"Not everyone," said Thomas. "We are here together."

"Who attacked me?" asked the man.

"We don't know," answered Bull truthfully. "Do you have any ideas?"

"It's been madness since I got here. Every man against everyone else. All trying to be top dog by whatever means."

"What's your name?" asked Thomas

"Oliver." He reached up to feel his wound and winced with pain.

"It'll be tender for a while yet," said Bull, "but your body will heal quickly."

"Why are you helping me?" asked Oliver, as he lay back on the bed. "What do you want?"

Thomas stood up and pulled over a wooden chair from near the wood burner.

"We don't need anything. Can we do anything else for you?" asked Thomas, taking a seat next to Bull.

"No one helps each other here!" Oliver said, staring up at the ceiling. "This shithole is an endless dogfight. And I'm no different."

"How so?" asked Bull.

"I've been hoarding fuel. I just take it from anyone I see with it. If I can, I will."

Oliver continued to stare up at the ceiling, not looking at Thomas or Bull.

Bull turned to Thomas and raised an eyebrow.

"Do you kick their heels to take them down?" asked Bull.

Oliver breathed out slowly through his nose, resisting the urge to look at Bull.

Suddenly he sat upright, scrambled off the bed, ripped open the door and disappeared.

Bull and Thomas looked at each other in surprise at the speed of Oliver's recovery and his exit.

"He'll be ok," said Thomas, closing the door.

*

The next morning dawned bright but an acrid smell hung in the air as Thomas and Bull went to inspect the burnt hut. The roof had fallen in and everything inside was reduced to ashes. As they made their way to the wellspring to collect water, they noticed small groups of five or six men gathered here and there. Some appeared to be arguing with hand gestures flying.

"Talking to one another for a change," said Bull.

"A positive step, I think," said Thomas in a quiet voice.

Heading back to their dwelling with two large pails of water, they heard a voice shout out behind them.

"You!"

They turned and saw Oliver coming towards them.

"A meeting. Tonight. Main square. Be there!"

With no further explanation, Oliver turned and headed off in the opposite direction.

"No mention of last night," remarked Bull. "Maybe he's embarrassed?"

"He approached us, which is progress," said Thomas. "And so is a meeting. I wonder how this will go?"

*

Arriving at the square, Thomas and Bull were greeted by an unusual sight. Men were working together arranging chairs into rows in a semi-circle. As more people arrived, the seats soon filled up. Hardly anyone spoke; most stared at the ground or into the distance, trying to avoid eye contact.

As the trickle of new arrivals came to an end, a man stood up, flanked by two others, their arms folded.

"Listen to me," began the man in the middle with an authoritative voice. "My name is Owl. Thank you for coming tonight."

His words were met with steely silence.

"A dwelling was burned down last night. I don't care what grudges you hold against each other, but we need order, not anarchy. If you'll listen to me, I will tell you how..."

"Who the hell are you?" shouted someone near the back.

"In the Previous Age I was chief of police and I led a community of survivors for many years after the Great Suffering. If any of you think you are better qualified, then let's hear it now."

A man stood up.

"It's Yuri," whispered Bull.

"Eastern Europe was once mine. There's nothing you can teach me."

"Eastern Europe was the minor league!" yelled another, standing to his feet. "We knew how to control governments in South America. If you want a leader to run things around here, you'd better listen to me!"

"This is a bragging competition," said Thomas under his breath. "Let's go."

Thomas and Bull slipped away down a path leading from the square just as a roar began to swell. The sound of chairs being smashed and men shouting echoed through the grid of dwellings.

\*

Many of the men had bloodied and bruised faces the following morning, and all of them kept their eyes fixed to the ground as they passed by to collect water and wood.

After a few days the groups of muttering men began to reappear at various places around the settlement.

"Another meeting. You two had better be there," Oliver called out to them later one afternoon.

This time a different figure stepped up to the front and called for quiet, as some of the men seated in their rows were already quarrelling with their neighbours and making threats.

"Now, gentlemen, let's see if we can be civil this time, shall we?" He was well-spoken with an upper-class British accent. "It's clear that chaos is tiresome and childish, and I for one believe we are capable of civility and decent public discourse. Now, I suggest we all turn to the chaps either side of us and jolly well shake hands?"

The man stepped towards the front row and offered his hand to one of the men seated there. However, noise had begun to erupt from the far side of the semi-circle. One man had pulled another into a head-butt, leaving him on his knees with blood pouring from his nose. Another had come up from behind and smashed a chair over another man's head in the back row. In no time at all, the crowd was once again engulfed in hand-to-hand violence.

Thomas and Bull stole away again as the square was engulfed in another night of brawling.

This pattern persisted at the next three attempts to hold a meeting. Men would turn up ready to exact revenge on those who had offended them at the previous gathering. A lust for violence and a desire for 'justice' brought most of the men back for more, although injuries kept some away. For most, the brawling had become a brutal game.

And then it ceased.

The following two days were unusually quiet in the camp with hardly anyone venturing out of their dwelling.

Thomas and Bull made their way to a small grove of trees near the waterfall. Here it was cool and shady, and birds sang joyfully from the higher branches of the trees. It was the time of day when the light from the heavens was at its richest and Thomas and Bull had each brought a blanket to create a comfortable place to sit.

When they had first arrived at the community, the two men had set aside time every few days to meditate, but they had soon felt the need to do this daily once they had experienced the violence and chaos of the settlement, which was more intense and stressful than anything they had experienced in the Previous Age. It was through meditating that they were able to obtain comfort and guidance. Some days the time spent in silence was short, while other days they sat for hours. Often after meditating they would discuss important issues together and were frequently encouraged at how similar their thoughts were.

After some time in silence, Thomas turned to Bull.

"I feel that we should meditate in the square just before the next meeting."

Bull nodded in agreement. "I had been feeling we should demonstrate something of this to the community too."

*

Next morning they observed once again the now familiar scene of huddled men deep in discussion, and later in the day they noticed Oliver rapping on the door of a nearby dwelling with some force. The door opened just a little. Oliver motioned with his hands toward the square and, although his words were out of earshot, it was clear he was spreading news of another meeting.

"Let's go early this evening and have our time of meditation before the meeting starts," suggested Thomas.

By the time men began to gather in the square, Bull and Thomas had already spent a while seated in contemplation on their blankets in a corner of the square where a huge elm tree created a shady spot.

"Odd way to take a nap," said Oliver quizzically as he passed by. "What the hell are you doing?"

Bull and Thomas remained quiet.

"Anyway, it's time for the meeting." With that Oliver strode over to the rows of chairs and took a seat, fidgeting a little as he waited to see who else would turn up.

"Shall we stay a little longer?" suggested Bull.

They heard a sudden thud and were showered in dust as a large round stone landed just in front of them. Looking around, they saw Yuri smirking as he headed towards the crowd.

Thomas stood up. Bull followed suit and they took their places near the middle of the semi-circle of seats, next to a makeshift aisle.

The atmosphere was uneasy with a different group of men standing at the front.

"Right, for everyone's sake, let's do things differently tonight," one appealed to the crowd, a note of desperation in his voice.

"We been thinking and we've already talked with some of you," said another.

"We've proved we can fight," said the first, "but apart from that we have achieved nothing."

"So let's agree something here and now," said the other man. "It's clear we've been grouped together because we're all a match for each other. We're all used to running things, and we're all strong."

A man in the seats stood to his feet.

"I reckon you're right. None of us is going to stand aside and see someone else come out on top. Fighting is pointless."

"So, what do we want to do?" said the first man.

Owl stood up. "We need order. We need structure. We need to organise. I can do that."

"It isn't about us here at the front," said the second man. "We just wanted to say that we can't keep on with this endless fighting. Owl, if you want to organise things, we aren't going to argue."

"Right," said Owl. "I just ask for some trust. I don't know you, and you don't know me, but things can improve here, if you can let me try."

Bull stood up. "I know you, Owl."

Owl turned to see who was speaking and visibly bristled when he saw Bull.

"I think you'd be good at organising," said Bull confidently. "But maybe it would be good to select members for the first committee at random to create trust."

Bull sat down, pleased that he had been able to speak to Owl with kindness after all that had passed between them in the Previous Age.

Owl turned back to the men at the front.

"Ok. Names out of a hat," he said decisively. "It's the only fair way to create the first committee."

"He's gone with your suggestion," whispered Thomas, surprised.

"Ok, meeting adjourned. We will reconvene tomorrow and draw names," announced one of the men at the front.

"Progress," said Thomas to Bull with a hopeful smile.

# Experiencing the Eternal City

"Good morning."

Thomas lifted his head from his pillow to see an angel bringing in a bowl full of steaming porridge and a glass of fruit juice. He never knew what would arrive each day, but breakfast was always delicious.

The angel gently placed the food on the table near the balcony. The doors had remained open all night allowing the sweetly fragrant breeze to waft over Thomas as he slept. As usual the sky was dancing with colours, decorating the walls of the bedroom with a slowly evolving kaleidoscope of orange, yellow and delicate pink.

The angel stood for a second, looking at Thomas.

"I'm sorry, but are you Thomas, the apostle?" asked the angel.

"I understand that's what some call me," replied Thomas, sitting up.

"Oh goodness! I'm sorry, it's just such a pleasure to meet you."

The angel's embarrassment surprised Thomas.

"We frequently talked about you when Jesus was first on the Old Earth. We admired your integrity."

"Really?"

"Well, many of us thought you were a good example of someone who said how they really felt about things. Someone who didn't just go along with everyone else. I think it took some guts to say you weren't sure until you had proof. Anyway, I must be going. Pleased to have met you."

It wasn't unusual to talk with angels in the Eternal City. They brought food and clothes to those who were staying for respite from their work in the communities beyond the City's borders. Thomas and Carlos were back for a week to recuperate and to take further lessons in the history and languages of the Previous Age.

After Thomas had enjoyed his breakfast, there was a knock at the door, and another angel appeared carrying a set of clothes.

"These are for you. We heard you have long been an admirer of the denim Carlos wears."

Thomas couldn't hide his pleasure when the angel held up a beautiful denim jacket and a pair of jeans.

"These have been made especially for you. Oh, and we thought this white T-shirt would look good with them."

"Thank you!" Thomas exclaimed with genuine gratitude.

He pulled the T-shirt over his head and stepped into the jeans. Putting on the jacket, he went over to the mirror hanging on the wall. Turning to his left and then his right, he admired the perfect fit and ruffled his thick black hair.

"Oh, *very* twentieth century!" declared the angel with amusement.

"I really like the look and I've never had clothes like this before. Do you think I look 'cool'?"

"*Very*," said the angel. "It's funny, one of the few differences between us angels and you humans is your constant creativity in how to dress."

Thomas held up his hand.

"High five?" he asked, with a cheeky grin.

The angel laughed and clapped his hand against Thomas' making a pleasing sound.

The angel left Thomas, who was feeling very pleased with his gifts. There were constant surprises in the Eternal City, as there were so many ways in which Jesus showed people they were loved and appreciated.

Thomas strode down the hall and found Carlos' door open.

"Wow, look at you!" exclaimed Carlos.

"I've always liked denim," said Thomas.

"Have you got your talents with you?"

"Yes, I've put them in my back pocket," said Thomas patting the seat of his new jeans. "Let's go and see what the market has to offer."

"Can you explain the talent system for me? I'm not sure that I've totally grasped it," asked Carlos.

"Jesus set up the talent exchange system within the Eternal City. Whenever a person works for a community or on an article to sell in the market they earn ten talents an hour. The rate is the same whatever work a person does. If someone happens to amass a lot of talents, they aren't considered to be wealthy in the way they would have been in the Previous Age, as everyone here knows it's just a mechanism for ensuring everyone is rewarded for what they do. We are given talents to use when we arrive in the City."

"Does that kind of system operate within any of the communities?" asked Carlos.

"Some have tried, but it soon ran into the problems of inflation and disparity that created such hardship in the Previous Age. The talent system in the Eternal City only works because everyone is honest, everyone trusts everyone else, everyone considers themselves to be equal and everyone works to the best of their ability."

"So there's no inflation in the Eternal City?"

"No, the rate will be the same in a million years."

They arrived at the market in the fresh morning air, savouring the buzz of activity as people engaged in the commerce of the City. Many inhabitants had come to understand that they had a unique skill they could use to contribute to the economy. No two stalls were the same, and everything that was for sale had been made with care and pride. Such markets could be found in squares and greens across the vast landscape of the Eternal City. Gone was the heavy mass production that had so taxed the Earth's resources in the Previous Age, and instead hundreds of artisans and chefs had been able to open shops and trade.

"One of the things that went so wrong in the Previous Age," remarked Carlos, "was that people never thought they had 'enough'. We consumed goods until many of the Earth's resources were exhausted."

"It grew worse as the Previous Age wore on," said Thomas. "Even in my time the rich and powerful withheld food in order to control the population. The very poor could scratch out an existence through harvesting what they could in the wild, but if there was a drought or a flood, many suffered terribly from hunger and lack of shelter."

The two men took their time looking through the many market stalls that lined the town square, where the facades of the Baroque-style buildings shone radiantly in the morning light. Stallholders chatted to one another over hot drinks and swapped stories of how they had developed their skills. Beautiful woven cloths and printed fabrics swayed in the breeze as they hung on ornate wooden frames, and food stalls filled the air with all kinds of tantalising aromas. Some folk worked away at their craft behind their stalls as they patiently awaited customers. They were pleased to receive many compliments, as the citizens of the Eternal City appreciated and respected people's handiwork, even if it wasn't to their personal taste.

"It's funny how I might not 'get' a piece of sculpture as a work of art, but I can still really enjoy it as a product of someone else's imagination and skill," mused Carlos.

"Yes, I know what you mean. *Agape love* doesn't mean that we all have the same taste, opinion or vision," agreed Thomas.

"What do you mean by *vision*?"

"Well, all art is someone saying '*This is what I see.*' And it's that artistic vision that makes a person create that sculpture, write that story, compose that song..."

"And we don't all see things exactly the same way, do we?"

"And that's what surprised me for a while," continued Thomas. "I'd imagined 'heaven' as somewhere where everyone always agreed on everything."

"I know what you mean. I was the same. But now we know the important thing is not *if* we disagree, but *how*."

Thomas chuckled.

The two friends took their time as they made their way around the market square, chatting to the vendors as they went. Each had a fascinating story of their life and what had led them to their current occupation.

"I never enjoyed 'shopping' until now," reminisced Carlos. "As a boy I would always groan when my mother dragged me around the stores. Then the Great Suffering came, and I would daydream of shops full of food and clothes, all brand new and available for me and my family to buy."

"I hear that before the Great Suffering you had more available to you than any other generation."

"Yes, we took it for granted that almost everything and anything was available as long as you had enough money to buy it. Then droughts, floods, superstorms and plagues began to disrupt all aspects of the supply chain. People began to riot and ransack shops within a few days of the fuel running out."

Thomas and Carlos stopped at a stall manned by a Latino gentleman with long brown hair tied back into a ponytail that flowed down onto his lap. He sat behind his table of wares, concentrating on his hammer and chisel as he slowly chipped away small shavings of wood. Thomas and Carlos quietly observed him, amazed at the process. A sculpture of a barn owl about three feet tall was emerging on the plinth, its feathers carved in minute detail.

The woodworker noticed Thomas and Carlos and put down his tools. Patting his hands on his overalls, he came over to greet them.

"Hello friends," he smiled.

"That is a beautiful piece of work," enthused Carlos. "I've never seen a carving so lifelike!"

"Thank you, I've been working on this one for several months now. As you can see, it's a bit bigger than my usual range."

Thomas picked up a wooden horse standing on its hind legs in an impressive stance.

"How many talents for this one?" he asked respectfully.

"Hmm," the woodworker said thoughtfully. "Forty, please."

Thomas took out the folded talents from his jeans pocket. Each talent was not much to look at - just a plain piece of cream-coloured parchment with the numeral '1', '10' or '50' on both sides.

Thomas counted out forty talents and handed them to the man.

"This object will give me great pleasure," said Thomas. "Where did you learn to create such beautiful things?"

"I lost my life in a cloth factory in the Previous Age. My friend got caught in the machinery and I was killed when I tried to save him. When I was raised, Jesus gave me some tools and I set about learning to whittle."

The three men chatted a little longer, before Thomas and Carlos moved on to the next stand, and then the next, taking their time to appreciate the range of products on display.

"No two markets will ever be the same, will they?" remarked Carlos.

"You're right," replied Thomas. "Nothing is mass produced here. Every single person in the Eternal City is discovering and refining their individual skills, each contributing to the amazing range of things on offer. And that reminds me, we should get to our classes."

"I have Hindi. What about you?" asked Carlos.

"I'm finishing my Russian classes today. I'll be able to serve the community I'm in a little more insightfully when I can navigate the nuances of the Russian worldview using their own language."

"A drink afterwards?" suggested Carlos.

*

Thomas arrived at the café and saw Carlos leaning back in his chair, his hands behind his head and legs stretched out in front of him, eyes closed.

Thomas grinned mischievously and with a frond from the mimosa tree at the café entrance crept silently up behind his friend. Stifling his mirth, he gently tickled Carlos' forehead and nose as though an insect was looking for a place to settle.

Carlos furrowed his brow for a split second before bolting upright and hastily brushing his hands over his face.

Thomas burst into laughter, making Carlos jump up and spin around.

"Hey!" he exclaimed, so loudly that everyone in the café looked up, but he soon dissolved into laughter at the expression of mock innocence on Thomas' face.

"Little trickster! I've not often seen this side of you."

"I know. It's this place. It brings out the fun side of me. It helps me realise I am often so serious. But here," Thomas took a deep breath, "I feel so free."

Carlos resumed his relaxed position with a happy sigh.

"I know exactly what you mean. In the Previous Age we couldn't imagine how wonderful this place would be."

After they had finished their iced coffees, a sprightly south-east Asian lady came out from the café with the name badge 'Mai' on her apron.

"Another drink?" she suggested, collecting up their glasses. "Enjoy the coffee?"

"Loved it!" replied Carlos, without hesitation.

Thomas looked at her and grimaced slightly.

"Well, I can see you didn't love it," she said with a smile.

"I'm sorry. It just wasn't what I'm used to," said Thomas.

"No problem. If you tell me what you'd like, I'll make it for you. I won't charge."

Thomas drummed his fingers on the table for a couple of seconds, and then his face lit up.

"Well Mai, do you have any *calda* like we had in Palestine at the beginning of the first century in the Previous Age?"

"Oh, no one has asked for that since Jesus was here about two months ago. Yes, we can do that for you. Jesus showed me how to make it."

"Thank you so much. That will suit me much better than the bitter drinks that my friend likes" said Thomas, pointing at Carlos with his thumb.

"It shouldn't take long, just a few minutes."

"No problem. It's lovely here in the evening light. We're thinking of going on to the comedy club around the corner later. Do you know anything about it?" asked Thomas.

"I haven't been, but people say it's great. I've been meaning to see something there."

"Come along with us?" asked Carlos.

"I'd love to," beamed Mai. "I'll be finished in an hour if you don't mind waiting for me."

"If we help you clean up, will that mean you can finish earlier?"

"It would," she replied with a grateful smile.

After Thomas had enjoyed the *calda*, the three new friends chatted about their journeys in the Previous Age as they cleared up the café in preparation for closing time.

Mai finished wiping up the wet crockery on the draining board, while Thomas swept the floor and Carlos put chairs on tables. Soon their tasks were done, and Mai closed the door to the café.

"I still love it that I don't ever have to lock up!" she exclaimed as they walked away.

"It took me a little while to get used to not having to think about protecting myself or keeping an eye on my belongings," agreed Carlos.

"I've been in a very challenging community, where people steal and have no respect for each other's property," added Thomas. "But here there are no locks and that seems perfectly natural."

Carlos looked out across the square. "And everywhere is so clean," he marvelled.

"Well, firstly there is very little in the way of waste, but secondly, everyone contributes to the tasks needed to keep the place clean," explained Mai. "Each week someone draws up a list of what needs to be done - including cleaning and maintaining our toilets - and then people put their name against one or more of the tasks. No one wants the place to be spoiled, so everyone is willing to play their part. In that way, the city virtually takes care of itself."

"And what about all the leisure activities that go on here?" asked Thomas.

"There are some people who really enjoy organising those kinds of things. They usually have a strong passion or interest in something. So that's why there are choirs, orchestras, all kinds of sports, plays, walking trips - almost anything you can imagine that people like to do."

"So, if I wanted to go and explore a certain part of the Eternal City, or maybe look for butterflies or birds, how would I organise that?" asked Carlos.

"It's as straightforward as putting up some notices in the cafés and restaurants, and there are community notice boards in the market squares. Or you can just talk to people and invite them along. Decide a time and place to meet and then you head off and do it. It works really well, as organisers do it for their own enjoyment and, equally, for the enrichment of others. If only two people show up, they have as much fun as if there are twenty. In fact, some of my favourite times have been when there have only been a few people. I enjoy volleyball and we meet by a lake each week to play. If there are only a couple of us, we might throw the ball around for a bit and then decide to do something else."

The three continued chatting as they turned a corner onto a main street lined with more shops, cafés and restaurants. After a few minutes they came to a doorway with stairs that led up to a large room with a stage at one end and a thick maroon curtain forming a backdrop. People were already seated at tables, chatting and waiting for the performance to begin.

Mai went to the bar and paid her talents for some beers, bringing them back to the table just as the curtains were being pulled over the windows. Candlelight gave the room a warm and welcoming glow and a cheer went up as a black woman with spiky hair took to the stage.

The next couple of hours were filled with performers taking their turn to tell jokes and funny stories. The humour ranged from slapstick to relatable, observational sketches and the surreal. It was clear that none of the performers had been comedians in the Previous Age but that they had since discovered a love of making people laugh. The audience was supportive and before long they were well and truly over any initial nerves.

"So, sleeping in a bear's cave isn't the best way to spend your birthday!" concluded one comic before giving a small bow to friendly cheering and applause.

"Wow, that guy was funny!" said Carlos, dabbing his eyes.

"I don't think I quite got it," said Mai, "but I had a great time watching you laugh so much!"

"Another beer anyone?" asked Carlos.

The trio decided to have one more before heading home. Carlos was carrying the tray from the bar to the table when a man stood up and backed into him, sending one of the beers crashing to the floor. People turned to look and smiled empathetically.

"I'm so sorry," said the man, embarrassed. "I didn't see you. My fault. Let me buy you another."

"No problem," replied Carlos with a grin. "These things happen."

"Don't worry," said the lady behind the bar as she poured another beer. "We've got this. It was an accident."

"That's very kind but at least you can allow me to help clear up the mess. Throw me a cloth," said the man.

As he set to work with a cloth and the lady from the bar joined him with a dustpan and brush, Carlos scouted out any shards that had fallen further afield. Within a few minutes the mess had been cleaned up and Carlos returned to Mai and Thomas.

"There was a time I couldn't have had just a couple of beers," said Carlos. "In the Previous Age I'd drink to try and have a good time and forget about other things. But I'd always drink too much and an accident like that would have made me really angry. When I drank I'd sometimes get violent, releasing all the anger that built up in me. I can't believe how different I am now. It feels so good to know I can stop when I know I've had enough."

"It's great to see how everyone can enjoy alcohol without taking it too far," agreed Mai. "Self-control is one of the things that mark people's lives here in the City. And kindness too. No one ever wants to leave another person to do all the work. Sometimes the way people bend over backwards to help each other is almost as comical as the acts tonight!"

The three finished their drinks and walked back to their accommodation, bidding Mai goodbye at her café.

"We will never stop learning from all the people we meet," said Thomas.

"Every person here has an amazing story and their lives reflect God's character in so many ways." replied Carlos. "And there is never a dull moment."

Carlos gave Thomas a hug. "Sleep well, and I'll be thinking of you as you rejoin Bull back in your community."

"Thank you. You'll be pleased to see Sylvia back at your village - please pass on my greetings."

The two friends parted with a little sadness at the prospect of not seeing one another for a while. The Eternal City had given them an exciting and memorable break, providing them with rest and new language skills. They'd gained new friends but now it was time to resume their lives back in their communities.

# Johan: Questions and Revelations

There was something about Yvonne's love of life that gave Johan the freedom to be himself. From their first meetings he had been aware that his fondness for her was very different from the way he had thought about women in the Previous Age. Spending time with Yvonne did not send the blood rushing to his head as it would have done back then, and he marvelled at how he could enjoy their friendship without the need for any mind games or strategy aimed at moving it towards a sexual encounter.

However, along with this freedom, he also noticed other more confusing emotions coming to the surface. Recently Johan had been thinking a lot about his mother.

Johan's mother had been tall for women in her country, and she had been strong. She had raised Johan almost singlehandedly, as his father had been a busy doctor and was often away from home. Johan had deeply respected both his parents but had yearned for more affection. As a boy, he had longed for physical touch, but had felt ashamed to admit this. He recalled with some discomfort the one time he had hugged his mother; it had been a stunted and somewhat awkward moment on the day he had left for the frontline. He had wanted to be held tight in his mother's arms, but by then he had grown as tall as her and their embrace had lasted only a second. He had left that morning on the train with a deep regret in his heart, and had not seen her since that day.

113

Yvonne and Johan had arranged to meet for lunch, and Yvonne arrived at the mill with a picnic. Johan loved listening to Yvonne and he marvelled at how she was fascinated by every tree, flower, animal, child and grown person she came across. She seemed to have insight about everything in the world around her. It was a relief that he did not need to talk too much; enough to just listen and enjoy the food.

Yvonne spoke with unforced enthusiasm. She was delighted to be able to spend time with Johan. He intrigued her. She perceived that there was much going on under the calm surface that he presented.

Yvonne had lived during the time of the Great Suffering, in the Previous Age. She had been raised by a small group of women who had banded together to face the challenge of bringing up their children with their partners gone. Many children at that time grew up without male role models because most of the men had left to try and find work to provide for their families. The mother figures she had known were brave and resilient. Starvation and disease was rife across the world as supplies of food and clean water became increasingly scarce.

Only those with a strong will to live and the ability to cooperate found a way through. In the aftermath of the worst years, Yvonne's family had been able to set up a farmstead where, despite much hardship, they farmed livestock and basic crops successfully. It was during this time that Yvonne had met Thomas, Yan, Anne and Harmony and had been able to help them relocate their community.

Yvonne loved to be around men, having had little male company when growing up. She had come to think of Yan and Thomas as older brothers after all they had been through together. She had known sexual desire in the Previous Age but had never had the opportunity to explore it. Here on the New Earth, it was one less thing to think about and her life did not feel lacking without it.

"Tell me more about your life in the Previous Age," asked Johan as they finished their picnic.

"I met Thomas and the others when I was very young. I grew up around them, I guess. After we had established our community, the focus became more and more on learning the ways of unfailing love. Thomas called it *agape love*. It's a love that is divine. We learnt how to make choices so that our lives were immersed in it. But it was a process, and that takes time."

"Did everyone learn to live that way in your community?"

"To varying degrees. I embraced *agape love* along with a man called Carlos, another called Bull and a lady named Sylvia. We were so changed that we were able to fully trust Papa God when it came to the end."

"The end of the millennium period?"

"The end of the entire Previous Age. The end of the Old Earth."

"I have heard people speak about that. What did you see?" asked Johan, listening intently.

"I remember the fire," said Yvonne, opening her arms wide. "All-consuming fire. The wall of fire was higher than any mountain. It didn't burn things; it totally vaporised everything in its path. When the people saw it approaching, they cried out in sheer terror. Carlos, Sylvia, Bull and I, we watched, but we knew it was Papa God's hand of mercy. We stood together and our hearts were ready to transition."

"Transition? Do you mean die?"

"Yes, but we knew we were going to be raised. Thomas, Anne, Harmony and Yan had gone through it already and had told us what would happen. We trusted them, so we knew that Papa would receive our spirits and raise us to new bodies and that death was by no means the end. I won't say I wasn't daunted by the wall of fire. The worst part was when it got really, really close and you knew there was no way out. I admit it was terrifying, but at the same time exciting because we trusted Papa together. I stood arm in arm with my brothers and sisters, and we allowed it to take our breath and our bodies. It was over very quickly. We felt no pain at all. It was exhilarating!"

"But what about the other people in your community? The ones who hadn't learnt *agape love* to the extent that you and your friends had. Do you know what has become of them?"

"At some point they will be raised and brought to a community where they can begin the next phase. Just like all of us. Most of them had already learned a lot, so it won't take long for them to progress to the Eternal City. I'm sure of that."

"I wonder how long it will take me," said Johan with an air of sadness. "I didn't have any time to prepare. As you know, I was killed by an explosion. Didn't even hear it coming. I fell asleep in my dug-out with my friends and I remember dreaming that I was in a vast black space heading toward a beautiful light. And then I woke up in Jesus' house."

"Yes, that happens when our spirit is released from our old, mortal body and we are heading toward our new body. Memories of such occurrences were called 'near-death experiences' in the Previous Age and they helped people believe that we are more than our physical bodies. As for how long it will take you to get to the City, I don't have the answer to that question. But I know that the only way anyone can really enjoy the City is to be completely ready. If we aren't given over completely to the ways of *agape love*, it will ask too much of us."

"That's interesting," said Johan, slightly raising an eyebrow. "It's almost like you're saying that it's a good thing I'm *not* in the City yet."

"To be honest, yes. It would be very hard for anyone to enter the City unless they were ready. Following Jesus means having a heart that is always able to choose *agape love*, and that might look like hardship and suffering through any other lens."

Suddenly Johan felt a deep sense of peace. He looked around at the meadow where they were seated and at the river gurgling past and realised that this was exactly where he should be.

Yvonne could sense Johan's thoughts.

"You are in the best place for you, right at this moment," she reassured him.

"I believe so," said Johan, looking her in the eye. "For the first time I really think I believe so. It's all a gift, isn't it?"

"It certainly is," she replied with a smile.

*

Each day Johan was grateful to be with his little sister, Gerty, who was now growing into a young woman. However, he couldn't shake off thoughts about his parents and wondered if they too might have been raised and how long it would be before he saw them again. His friendships and work in the community gave him a great sense of satisfaction and enjoyment, but he longed to see his mother and father.

Walking with Yan one evening, he decided to bring it up in conversation.

"We all need to discover who we are within ourselves for the time being," explained Yan, "so that when we do get to meet our parents and other family members we are able to relate without the often broken identities that were forged in the Previous Age."

"But I loved my parents, and I'm sure there was nothing broken about my relationship with them."

"Even so, I think that they are finding out who they are away from being a parent, a wife, a husband, a son, a daughter…"

"What about Gerty?"

"When she is fully grown, she will spend some time away from you, establishing who she is apart from being your sister. We are each wonderfully unique, and Papa wants us to really know, understand and accept who we are. However, we are also part of families and communities. Many of the problems in the Previous Age stemmed from unhealthy dependence and attachments caused by desires that we sought to fulfil in the wrong way. We have to be free of those, so that we can relate to each other in the best way possible. If you think about Jesus, Ruach and Papa God, they are distinct but also one. They relate perfectly with each other, but they always retain their individual identities."

Johan listened. What Yan was saying made sense, but it didn't ease his longing to be with his family.

"Your love for your family is a beautiful thing, and I'm sure that your parents feel the same about you. But our longings must be tempered by our growth as an individual."

"What about you, Yan? Don't you want to see your family?"

"Yes, I do. But I am sure this will happen when it is the perfect time for all of us. When I see them, they will be ready, I will be ready, and we will come together in the most complete and wonderful way. All the healing that must happen will have taken place, because we will have let go of all that hinders and restricts. It will be a true and lasting reconciliation."

"But don't you sometimes get tired of longing?"

"I am human, so of course my feelings and emotions are with me each day. But I exercise my 'trust muscles' and have done so for many centuries! That's how I stay strong in my faith that all will be well. You see, for a long time I believed and trusted Jesus before I had even met him. But when the day came and I met him face to face, my faith and all my longings were rewarded in that very moment. I know now that there are stages and seasons and ages, and that all things are working together to bring about an environment of *agape love*."

"I guess I am still immature in many ways," said Johan.

"You are growing all the time, every day. Take heart, my friend! The Jesus-like part of you is being revealed and the same is happening within every human being. Each one of us will be fully formed when we stop resisting him and give up trying to find our identity in other things."

"But what if people don't want to be like Jesus?"

"Then they are free to resist, but every path they turn down will eventually lead them back to Jesus. He is the beginning and the end of all things. Trying not to be like Jesus is like fighting your own breathing."

"But surely many people will reject these ideas?"

"Yes, but that's because they don't yet understand the 'science' of God. Everything was made *by* love and *for* love. It is the very foundation of the universe. When we reject these ideas, it's because we haven't accepted the basis on which everything stands. All resistance is just a detour on an inevitable path, because love is the metaphysical reality that sustains all things. Denying love is like denying you exist. The purpose of this age is to bring people into an understanding and experience of *agape love* - within themselves, with their neighbour, and with God."

Johan was quietly trying to piece together Yan's explanation. Jesus was real; that was for sure. But he struggled to get his mind around the idea that the humble man who had welcomed him to the New Earth was also God in bodily form and the walking, talking logic of all reality. It was more than he could comprehend.

"It's going to take a while to get used to these things," Yan encouraged him. "You don't have to work it all out now. We have all the time we need to grow in our sense of wonder and awe at the whole amazing story, and there will always be more mystery to explore."

"For some reason, right now," began Johan, "I just feel incredibly grateful to be alive."

"That's wonderful!" exclaimed Yan with delight. "That's what thinking about this does. It fills us with gratitude, so that gradually we find that we aren't longing for what is *not* but are joyful and thankful for what *is*."

\*

Johan felt more at peace after each conversation with Yan and Yvonne. They had a gift for knowing how to explain things in a way that helped him to understand.

Johan's new passion for learning was leading to some surprising new revelations. He realised that he could absorb new knowledge far more easily than in the Previous Age. He enjoyed using his mental faculties and, alongside Yvonne, had begun to help the children in the school, grateful to be reacquainted with maths and science and relieved that resurrected brains weren't as forgetful or easily distracted as when he had been a child.

"Language interests me," said Johan, as he chatted with his two friends after the school day had come to a close. "I liked English at school, and here on the New Earth I speak it fluently as though I were speaking my native German. However, there must be many other languages here as well?"

"Yes, of course," agreed Yvonne. "Every tribe and tongue are present on the New Earth. For now, we are in an English-speaking community, but there are many other communities that use different languages. We will all be able to learn other languages over the course of the ages here, and our brains will learn faster and more easily than in the Previous Age. That way, we get to learn about many other cultures and different ways of thinking."

"So we might become able to speak every language eventually?"

"It's hard to imagine, but yes, that might be possible in the ages to come. And I wouldn't be surprised if a new common language didn't evolve as well."

"This brings up another question," said Johan. "Where are we? I mean, I know we are on the New Earth, and in many ways it's a similar planet to the Old Earth, but whereabouts on the New Earth are we living?"

"The New Earth is much bigger than the Old Earth and has completely different continents," explained Yan. "The climate has been upgraded, and the ecosystems are able to thrive in new ways. The land is literally a different shape, so no one can say, 'This was China,' or 'This is England,' or anything like that."

"God had many objectives when he created the New Earth, and one of them was to mould a new landscape so that the New Earth could support God's purposes for this age," added Yvonne.

Johan smiled. "Well, if the old has gone and the new is here, it means that there is a whole new world to explore. I like the idea of that!"

"Yes," said Yan, "a day will come when all the New Earth will be accessible to everyone. But for now, we must live where our communities are situated, and we cannot go beyond the boundaries that have been set for us."

Johan was satisfied with this explanation. He knew that he could trust Yan and Yvonne. He felt confident in the timing of everything, and for now was perfectly happy to be living within his community.

*

Harvest on the New Earth was very different to the backbreaking work in the fields in late summer that Johan had experienced in the Previous Age. The constant energy from the three "suns" meant that fruit and vegetables could be harvested throughout the year, but certain crops required the whole community to work together to gather them into the communal storehouses.

Johan found it easy to work alongside most of the villagers, but being placed in a team with Ebo, his wife, Jemila, and their son, Eric, caused him to clam up inside. For some reason his tongue become tied and his words dried up when he was around them. The only times he felt able to speak were to correct or reprimand them when some aspect of their work failed to come up to his high standards.

Out in the fields Gerty could do little but look on in quiet frustration at her brother's critical attitude. It was clear he was still struggling with something that prevented him from relating with his usual good humour to Ebo and his family, so back at home in the warmth and familiarity of their dinner table, Gerty once again raised the subject.

"You still seem different around Eric's family. Why are you always so negative when you talk to them?"

Johan looked at his sister. Her face was not angry, but full of an innocence and sadness that disarmed his defensiveness. Johan stared into space for a few moments. He gently put down his cutlery and finished chewing his mouthful. Dabbing the corners of his mouth with a napkin, Johan's shoulders drooped.

"Are you alright?" asked Gerty. "I didn't mean to upset you."

"I've just realised something," her brother replied in a hushed voice. "When I was growing up... and when I was in the army... we were told over and over again that we were the 'master race'. We were told that everyone else was inferior."

"What do you mean?"

"I'm so glad you don't remember," he said, pushing his plate away. "We were taught that people of other races - Jews, Asians, people with black skin like Eric and his family - were less than human."

Gerty looked at her brother intently, unable to fully comprehend what he was saying.

"Oh, Gerty, I'm so ashamed. I think there's still something left in my heart from what I was told, and that's why I treat Eric's family that way."

"But that's not like you," she reassured him. "Your best friend is Yan, and he's Asian, isn't he?"

"That's true," said Johan, encouraged by her observation. "And maybe it means that I can be free of the things I was taught in the past. Give me some time, Gerty, and I'll see if I can work out the rest too."

*

A new awareness had dawned for Johan. Over the next few weeks, he observed his interactions with Eric and his family and noticed how his feelings swung between prideful stubbornness and disgust at his own prejudice. Little by little, he showed more kindness toward Eric, using encouraging words rather than critical ones. It felt hard to start with, but Johan was pleased at how Eric flourished under his improved guidance.

"Great job, young man," Johan enthused, examining Eric's thatching.

Eric beamed with pride, and Johan felt a glow of satisfaction as he saw the effect of his words on Eric's confidence. After lunch as they resumed work on the roof. Eric struggled to tie the correct knot with the thatching thread that was used to keep the straw in place on the rafters.

Johan frowned and Eric's head drooped in anticipation of harsh words. But at that moment when those words were on the tip of his tongue, a rush of determination coursed through Johan; his frown melted, and a broad smile spread across his face. He gently placed his hand on the boy's shoulder and, crouching down to his height, felt a surge of love towards both Eric and himself.

"Hey, you're doing great. Let's give it another try."

The glow inside Johan was obvious to everyone around him that afternoon, and they enjoyed their day's work all the more.

At the supper table that evening, Gerty noticed that Johan seemed more relaxed and had an even better appetite than usual.

"You look happy. Did anything special happen today?"

"Well, you know I have been paying close attention to my attitudes? Today everything was going well with Eric, but then he got something wrong. Awful words crossed my mind, but I realised where they came from. I don't want to think that way anymore, so I threw those thoughts out and chose to affirm and encourage Eric instead. As soon as I'd done that, I felt so good. I'm not my thoughts or my background; I am my choices. I am what I do. I can choose love and goodness."

Gerty was overjoyed. "That is so powerful. You're right. Sometimes we can't help our thoughts but we can choose what we do with them. I am so proud of you!"

Johan blushed a little. "I am proud of myself too, and I think it's ok to say that. But I know what I need to do. I need to speak to Eric and his family."

After clearing away the supper things, Johan and Gerty walked in the quiet of the evening along the path that led to Eric's home. Johan looked at his sister, who nodded her support, as he took a deep breath and knocked on the door.

The door was opened by Jemila, and behind her they could see Ebo in the kitchen wiping his hands on a cloth.

"Hello Johan," she said brightly, "Hello Gerty. How lovely to see you both. Won't you come in?"

"Come in, come in," echoed Ebo, waving to them as his son emerged from upstairs.

"Thank you, but I don't feel I can until I have said what I need to say." Johan looked at the family gathered in their entrance hall. "I am here to apologise."

"First of all, Eric, I want you to know that I should never have shouted at you the way I used to. I was not patient or kind, and you didn't deserve to be treated like that. You are a hard-working, intelligent, trustworthy young man, and I did not... "

Before Johan could say anything else, Eric flung his arms around Johan. Johan put his arms around Eric and felt the healing of the embrace wash through him.

"And I need to apologise to your parents too. Ebo and Jemila, I was told so many lies when I was a child about people of other races. I am so sorry. I don't ever want to think that way again."

Ebo reached out his hand and grasped Johan's. "Come on in, my friend."

Johan bowed respectfully and he and Gerty took their seats around the family table while Ebo filled their glasses with fruit juice.

"You know," said Ebo, "I have to say something, too. We were taken by people with white skin like yours. We were treated like animals and put in chains." Ebo sat down and held Jemila's hand.

"I need you to know that Jemila and I died in an uprising. We hated our masters and their people. One day we fought back, but they were too strong and they beat us to death. So when we came here and had to live with white people, we also struggled with what we felt inside."

Jemila looked searchingly at Johan and was moved to see tears trickling down his face.

"We found that people here expected us to be compliant because we are black. Jesus warned us when we were raised that many people expect black people to forgive quickly. But then we met Yvonne and she was so different to all the white people we had known in our time. It was the first step towards us changing our minds. What I am saying is, we have had to work on our attitudes as well."

Ebo reached across the table and took Johan's trembling hand in his. "I accept your apology. Will you accept mine?"

Johan squeezed Ebo's hand and looked at each person around the table in turn. "Yes, and I renounce every lie I ever believed about all people not being equal."

"And we renounce all hatred against white people," declared Ebo quietly.

Eric and Gerty understood the solemnity of the moment but could not restrain their beaming smiles. Jemila laughed to see their expressions.

"Isn't it good to know that these little ones will never know the burdens of the Previous Age?"

"Everything is right now, isn't it?" asked Gerty.

"Yes," said Ebo firmly. "We are learning. Step by step, we are learning how to treat everyone as our brothers and sisters in this wonderful new world."

# Fran: Anger Is Good

Fran walked purposefully through the village hoping to hear some new gossip. She spotted Kelly, her neighbour from across the green. Fran quickly approached her but was frustrated when she disappeared into Imelda's cabin. Not wanting to face Imelda, she walked on.

"Well, look who's here. Come on in." Imelda greeted her visitor in a slightly condescending tone.

"Hello Imelda," replied Kelly, shyly.

"You've never yet got yourself one of our outfits, have you?" said Imelda, her hands clasped together as she looked Kelly up and down.

"That's because you've always sold out before I could afford anything," replied Kelly, meekly.

"Well, here you are, and all the new clothes are right in front of you. Why don't you choose something, and I'm sure we can come to some arrangement."

Kelly walked around the shop floor admiring the results of Dawn's needlework based on Imelda's designs.

"How about this one?" she asked, holding up a pleated skirt.

"Ah yes, I can see you wearing that around the village," Imelda gushed with well-rehearsed enthusiasm. "So, what can you give me for it?"

Somewhere at the back of the shop Dawn cleared her throat and corrected her loudly. "What can you give *us* for it?"

"Well... I think I have a full box of walnuts you can have."

Imelda tilted her head and grimaced.

"Walnuts? My dear girl, I don't want your walnuts. Try again."

"I could copy out my recipe book for you?"

Imelda looked unimpressed and shook her head.

"Hmm, that doesn't work either. I would like..."

She clicked her fingers and her eyes lit up.

"We would like you to grow rose bushes from cuttings of your pink rose and then plant and tend them in each of our gardens."

"Roses for two gardens?" winced Kelly. "No, Imelda, that's too much work."

"Fine," snapped Imelda and snatched the skirt back from Kelly.

Kelly turned and walked out of the shop, her cheeks burning.

"That horrible old cow!" she thought as she walked down the main street of the village. "Why must life be so unfair?"

Kelly had long believed that life was against her. After her divorce in her mid-forties, she had devoted all her time and energy to her daughter, Clare. When Clare was just nineteen she had been killed by a drunken driver on a country road. The loss of her only child had torn a hole in Kelly's soul. There was not a day in her life that she didn't cry out with longing for her daughter. The only thing that could dull the hatred she felt for the driver was her addiction to painkillers. She had come to believe that God didn't care about her and had died of a stroke in her early seventies.

Kelly had been welcomed by Jesus when she was raised three years previously. But however much she had wanted to like him, her resentment toward God still lingered.

Kelly found herself wondering every day why she couldn't be reunited with Clare. This only served to fuel her distrust of God. She couldn't understand why Jesus referred to God as 'Papa'. That sounded far too familiar, smug even. To Kelly, God was at best a negligent father and at worst an abusive bully. However, Kelly felt lonely and desperately tried to find ways to connect with the other women in her village, but none of them wanted to hear about the hardship she had experienced. Everyone seemed wrapped up in their own concerns.

Lost in her thoughts, she didn't hear Sylvia's greeting from further down the path and was annoyed to suddenly find her standing in front of her.

"How are you today, Kelly?" asked Sylvia in her usual warm and genuine way.

Kelly clenched her teeth.

"Same as ever, Sylvia. I'm tired of being pissed off and I'm pissed off because I'm tired. Life is one long fucking nightmare. I hate it here and I hate everyone here. Honestly, I'd rather just be dead."

Sylvia wasn't surprised by Kelly's words. Kelly was one of the few women in the village who allowed herself to be so bluntly honest.

"Come for a meal," said Sylvia firmly. "This evening?"

Kelly agreed, as it would be a chance to let Sylvia and Carlos have both barrels of her anger and resentment.

"Ok, but you don't know what you're letting yourself in for!"

"Come anyway," Sylvia replied.

*

Kelly lingered outside the front door for a few minutes, trying to collect her thoughts. When she knocked, Sylvia opened the door and greeted her warmly. Kelly returned the greeting but with none of the warmth.

"Try this," said Carlos, handing her a glass. "Freshly squeezed apple juice."

Sylvia led the way into the garden area that was bursting with colour and fragrance. The three sat at a wooden table and each took a moment to take in the sights, smells and sounds of a garden that was truly humming with activity.

"I've wondered for a while about how you're doing," began Sylvia, getting straight to the point.

Kelly folded her hands.

"Well, I can tell you it's not what I'd hoped for," she began. "I wanted to not exist, be properly punished or go somewhere blissful. But this? This is worse than any of those."

Carlos sat forward and Sylvia nodded silently.

"So, yeah, not great at all. I want to leave this stupid village. It's full of stuck-up selfish bitches!"

"You say you want 'proper punishment'?" asked Sylvia.

"I think I probably belong somewhere a little hotter. I'm not exactly an angel. I hate God for the shitty life he gave me. I hate him for taking my daughter from me. And I hate him for all the suffering that existed in the Previous Age. Tell me, what's the point of it all? Why create us to suffer, die, and then find there's even more suffering on the 'other side'?"

Sylvia and Carlos continued to listen.

"Oh, for fuck's sake!" she exclaimed. "Have you really got nothing but silence for me?"

"Actually, we understand your anger," said Carlos.

Kelly was surprised and sat back, her mouth slightly open.

"Yes," added Sylvia. "Your anger is good. It's sacred in its own way."

"What do you mean?"

"Your anger comes from an instinct deep within you. An instinct that pain, loss and suffering aren't the way existence should be," said Carlos.

"Your anger tells you that there must be another way... a better way," said Sylvia.

"Maybe, but why doesn't an 'all-powerful' God stop these bad things from happening?" protested Kelly.

"God doesn't micromanage everything," said Carlos.

"Yes, life is not controlled by God. In that sense, God isn't 'all-powerful'. Choices are ours to make. Some choices we make are for good, and some are not," explained Sylvia. "This is because we have agency over what we do in our lives."

"But I didn't choose for some bastard to drive into my daughter at eighty miles per hour. And I didn't choose to become addicted to painkillers. These things just happened to me." Kelly's voice was now fraught.

"I understand," said Carlos. "But that man chose to drink and drive that night. The fault lies with him. Chaos exists, without a doubt it does, and frequently bad choices create it. But it's *in* chaos that we can see how love invites us to create a new way."

"But I couldn't see anything," sobbed Kelly, who by now was quivering as she wept. "I had no strength to choose anything. I was desperate. I was powerless."

"That's where we need help," Sylvia said, compassionately. "And we all need help."

"Well, you tell me who was there to help me?"

"You suffered terribly," said Sylvia quietly.

"We are not here to tell you how you should feel or how you should understand your Previous Age experiences," said Carlos. "Only you can come to terms with what has happened, and you have all the time you need to get there."

"That's right," agreed Sylvia. "It took Carlos and I centuries to get to a point where we could understand and respond to what we were learning. And we are here to walk alongside you as you grow in your understanding too."

"Pass me the salad," said Kelly, changing the subject. She wiped her face with her sleeve and didn't look at Sylvia or Carlos.

The conversation turned to gardens, what was growing where and what was starting to appear. Carlos sensitively supported the conversation while attending to the practical aspects of the meal, leaving Sylvia free to stay by Kelly's side.

Kelly began to regret her outburst, and by the time she was leaving to go home, she had resolved to say something.

"Look, I hope I didn't offend you with what I said."

Sylvia waved her hands in the air. "Not at all. This is a safe place. You need - we all need - to be heard and understood."

Kelly smiled awkwardly, still unsure whether Sylvia was just being polite.

"We both needed many, many hours of being heard and understood. You are not alone. In fact, you never need to be alone here. We are always ready to listen and to share our stories with you," Carlos added.

"Thank you," replied Kelly simply and stepped out of the door.

"That was good," sighed Sylvia to Carlos as they put the dinner plates away. "She needed to voice her true feelings. It's something we all need to do."

"It's interesting how some people assume we will be offended on Papa's behalf."

"Yes," replied Sylvia. "As if Papa needed defending! Papa has seen and understood our feelings before we've even worked out what they are."

"When we identify our true feelings and express them, it feels like a burden is lifted," said Carlos, thoughtfully. "When we realise Papa is never angry with us for what we feel and think, we can let it all out and begin to process it."

"I was so angry at God for all the times I was abused," reflected Sylvia. "Not that I realised I was angry at God. I thought I was just angry at life."

"You had every reason to be angry," said Carlos. "You knew what was happening to you was wrong and that you didn't deserve it. My problem was that I was numb and didn't really feel anything for a long time."

"You had to learn to feel again and to allow your emotions to flow. After the Great Suffering, many of us who survived became hardened and callous inside because of what we experienced."

Carlos and Sylvia sat down, both feeling deeply for the people around them.

"One day, we will all be completely free," smiled Sylvia. "Everyone will know the truth of who they are and how good Papa is, and everyone will be able to love their neighbour."

"We mustn't forget that the process is happening," agreed Carlos. "Little by little, every day, people are learning and growing and moving towards more freedom. The God who allowed all things will redeem all things."

\*

Kelly tried to avoid Imelda. It made her feel worse about herself when she saw how busy and fulfilled Imelda and Dawn appeared with their clothing enterprise. She also tried to stay away from Fran, whose garden produce was clearly doing much better than hers. Fran, however, always made a beeline for Kelly to try to persuade her to let her help cultivate her strawberry plants in return for a healthy share of the crop.

"Come on, Kelly," called out Fran, when she next caught sight of her. "Stop being so wasteful. You know that you have the only strawberry plants in the whole village. In the whole of this world for all we know! Let me come and help you get the best out of them."

"I don't care," snapped Kelly. "They're mine and besides, I am no gardener - never have been."

"That's why I am offering. I just want to help," retorted Fran, her frustration rising at Kelly's resistance.

"You know what, Fran? Mind your own business!"

They had by now reached the end of the path and Fran watched as Kelly marched off to her cottage.

"Arsehole!" exclaimed Kelly, slamming her front door shut. She made her way to the kitchen and looked out of her back window. A handful of juicy strawberries hung on one of the plants, shining in the bright daylight. Kelly went outside and without hesitation stamped on them until nothing was left but a jammy pulp mingled with dark soil.

"There you go, Fran," she muttered.

Kelly looked down at the crushed plant. Something about the sight broke through her anger and filled her with a deep sadness. After she had lost her daughter, owning her actions was something that she had avoided. An increasing recklessness had taken hold of her, and she had used her grief and anger to excuse her behaviour.

It was a familiar cycle: anger leading to sadness, and then a defiant justification of her actions, all within a matter of moments. But this time the sadness lingered all day. That evening, Kelly came to the painful realisation that she was feeling regret, not only for her destruction of the strawberries but also, much to her irritation, for her interaction with Fran as well.

*

"I know what she's doing," complained Kelly, as she sat once again at the dinner table with Sylvia and Carlos. "She's trying to get her hands on a cutting so she can plant strawberries in her own garden. She's a scheming little snake!"

"Ok, but can I ask you something?" said Sylvia.

Kelly rolled her eyes. "Oh, here we go! Here comes the holy suggestion."

"I'm not telling you to do anything. You know that's not how this works. What I want to ask is this. What would happen if you gave her a cutting?"

"Well, then I'd play right into her hands!"

"Ok. But what is the worst that can happen?"

Kelly gathered her ammunition.

"She would always have one over on me. She'd be the one who would bring the strawberries to the market and she'd get all the glory for them."

"Ok," said Carlos. "We hear your concern. But I guess we would make the gentle observation that you already have the capability to grow the strawberries and bring them to the market, but you're choosing not to."

Kelly stared at her plate for a moment and then looked back up at Carlos.

"But I can't grow anything. I never was a gardener."

"Maybe in the Previous Age you weren't. But here on the New Earth everything grows really easily, so it doesn't need nearly as much work to produce healthy, tasty crops. You *could* pick those strawberries and swap them, but something seems to be holding you back. Are you sure it's just that you don't feel you have 'green fingers'?"

Kelly groaned. "Why do I keep coming here?"

"Maybe deep down you enjoy it," replied Sylvia with a smile.

Kelly by now could not repress a wry grin. She secretly felt a strange pleasure in being challenged, and that was why she kept coming back. There was something about their mealtimes together that made her feel that she was making some sort of progress. When she had spent time with Jesus after being raised, she had initially been buoyed up by his evident interest and care for her. She had felt ready to grow and embrace her new life, but this had soon been quashed by being placed in a community with other women who only seemed to want to antagonise each other. But in the past few days she had begun to feel her confidence slowly returning. It was the feeling that she could grow and change, and that maybe her experience of life right now was not going to be forever.

Sylvia sensed it was a good moment to encourage Kelly.

"You're doing well to keep coming back here. I know it's not comfortable to be challenged, but you are listening and open to what we have to say. This is the way that seeds of change are planted."

There was a hint of lightness and a new sense of purpose in Kelly's response.

"Speaking of seeds, I think I might be planting some soon."

# Exploring the Eternal City

The fire crackled as the friends sat in a circle around it. The orange glow lit up contented faces, rosy with mulled cider. A large pan near the flames was keeping the cider warm.

Sylvia and Yvonne listened intently as each person took it in turns to tell their story. Those gathered there would not have been considered 'great' in any way in the Previous Age. Tolu had still been a child when she began taking care of several members of her family who had lost their sight, but she had done so with such an unwavering selflessness that Ruach had seen and rewarded her with access to the Eternal City. Greg had checked up on every elderly person in his village for years until he was attacked and beaten up one evening for the contents of his wallet. He had died several days later in his local hospital. Now spending time in the City, the group had all signed up for a hike in one of the mountainous regions and had been enjoying the breathtaking views and each other's company for the past three days.

"I had never even thought about whether dinosaurs would be here on the New Earth," said Greg, after the stories had given way to observations about the Eternal City. "I mean, it makes sense, but to see them in the flesh today was such a surprise."

"Yes, you certainly jumped out of your skin when you saw that sleeping Tyrannosaurus," laughed Yvonne, "but so did I!"

"And the way it was all curled up with a Diplodocus - that certainly wouldn't have happened in the Previous Age," said Greg. "I loved dinosaurs as a kid and I thought I knew all about them."

"That's what the Eternal City is like," said Sylvia. "I find the most surprising things happen here that would have been impossible before."

"The whole place is built on trust," said Tolu. "That's my observation. Nothing here happens without trust."

"Trust and respect," added Greg. "This is life where all insecurity has been replaced with trust and respect. All living things honour one another. It changes everything."

"And yet nothing loses its distinctiveness, does it?" continued Tolu. "We aren't all swallowed up into one mass, where we lose what makes us... us?"

"Unity in diversity," said Yvonne.

By now the sky was as dark as it could get on the New Earth. The four friends took a pause from their discussion to gaze up into the sky as they continued to be warmed by the fire.

"Those stars," said Greg, after several minutes of reverent silence.

"Yeah," said Yvonne, also lost in wonder.

"Do you think we'll get to explore the universe?" asked Tolu. "What's it all *doing* up there, anyway?"

Greg chuckled at the awesome nature of the question. "I don't know exactly, but it's reminding me that I am very small."

"Sometimes in the Previous Age, I would feel so small and insignificant, but then when I began looking after my relatives, I realised that I was very important to them and that I could make a difference in people's lives," said Tolu. "Then I felt at one with the whole universe."

"I know what you mean," said Greg. "When showing love became important to me, I didn't feel so lost in the sea of existence. I felt like I belonged as I got to know the people around me. Helping them gave me such a sense of purpose and meaning. The only time I felt like my life had no meaning was when I was a young man."

"Ah yes," said Sylvia. "You were saying how you went to work in the city and made lots of money, just like your dad."

"I made heaps of money and lost even more. By the time I was thirty I was miserable. I was divorced and convinced that all women wanted was my money. When I gave it all up and became a postman in the middle of nowhere, that's when I started to notice the human needs around me."

"Wealth can blind people to other's needs, can't it?" said Yvonne.

"Money can cause a feeling of entitlement," agreed Greg. "That's why I love the talent system here in the Eternal City. It's just another way we can honour each other. There are no banks, because no one needs to protect their money or save it up for a rainy day."

"When you look at people in the various communities here on the New Earth," said Tolu, "it's easy to see how misguided their ideas are. I'm living and serving in a village of voodoo witch-doctors. But I can see how they've inherited their beliefs as they never had any experience of an alternative culture around them."

"So how are they responding to their new circumstances?" asked Yvonne.

"Well, they are struggling to make sense of the world without their previous paradigms and are having great difficulty letting go of the traditions they had always known. That's understandable. However, they do have an attitude of wanting to help others. So much of what we used to call 'evil' was just people's misplaced ways of trying to do good things."

"Creeds certainly don't get you into the Eternal City," added Yvonne. "Some people have to give up their beliefs in the god or gods of their old understanding before they can begin to learn about the true nature of love."

"They might even have to give up certain ideas of who Jesus is," said Sylvia. "The name of Jesus that was thrown around where I was brought up often bore little resemblance to the actual man and what he taught."

"But I have to say that even though I've met him," said Greg thoughtfully, "I am still no expert on him and his teachings. I was a very lapsed Catholic in the Previous Age. Imagine my shock when Jesus said my faith was enough, and that my heart was in the right place. When I was raised and brought to the great supper, I honestly thought there had been a huge mistake!"

"I don't think anyone is an 'expert' in following the Way that Jesus taught," mused Sylvia. "Often it's about 'unknowingly' showing love, rather than 'knowing' how things should be."

"Intuition over knowledge?" suggested Greg.

"Yes, and trust over certainty," added Tolu.

"Relationship over systems," said Yvonne.

A thoughtful but happy quiet descended on the camp as the stars continued to twinkle above them.

*

As dawn appeared the friends stirred as the sky began its daily dance of colours - a pastel palette of yellow, orange, pink and purple with every shade in between.

The hike back down the mountain range was filled with encounters with strange and wonderful creatures. Herds of grass-eating dinosaurs looked up in unison as the travellers passed by. A pack of wild dogs ran alongside them and enjoyed being tickled behind their ears.

The group walked down the mountain trail that led into one of the City's more urban neighbourhoods. Tall buildings with crystalline windows for viewing the landscape of the City reflected the pastel shades of the sky. People were already busy about their day with some riding various animals along the tree-lined avenues.

"I suppose many different animals can be used for transport, given that they are all so tame here," said Tolu.

"The teamwork between humans and animals has a deeper synergy here, greater than anything we saw in the Previous Age," explained Greg. "I went to a circus once as a child and there were lions and elephants, but I found out later that they were physically abused to make them obedient. Here, kindness is the basis of the relationship with working animals."

"We became so far removed from nature before the Great Suffering," said Sylvia. "We disregarded the other creatures of the Earth, and we thought so little of them. I am ashamed to think of how arrogant humans were back then."

"It's no surprise to me that animals are so central to life here in the City," said Tolu. "All creatures are loved by the creator, and we are now able to look after them and work with them in a way that reflects *agape love.*"

As the friends continued their journey, they came across many wonderful examples of humans and animals living and working together. Many of the scenes were surprising and joyous enough to make them laugh out loud in wonder. By the end of the afternoon, they had arrived back at their lodgings and were standing outside their rooms.

"Shall we meet up later for a final meal together?" suggested Yvonne, always the most socially-minded.

"I think I will probably enjoy some time on my own just now," said Greg. "I always was a bit on an introvert, and that hasn't changed here on the New Earth."

"Of course, no problem at all," replied Yvonne, sincerely.

"I'd definitely like some down time this afternoon," said Tolu, "but I'd love to meet up with you for supper. We could go to the new Greek restaurant that you mentioned you'd like to try. "

"I'm spending time with an old friend tonight," said Sylvia. "The angel guides knew we had met in the Previous Age, so they arranged for us to have rooms close by one another. But I'm sure the two of you will have a great time."

So the friends retired to their rooms to rest before embarking on their various plans, each one delighting in a deep sense of satisfaction and fulfilment from the amazing sights and experiences they had shared together on their trip.

# Yuri: Frustration Mounts

Thomas, Bull and Cedric the seraph stood back and looked at their day's work. A brand new, spacious wooden cabin now stood on the mountain side. It was shrouded by trees, yet had a clear view of the community below.

"The Hermitage," declared Bull.

"Sort of," chuckled Thomas. "Somewhere to be alone, ponder, pray and rest. It's a way of being that none of the men have ever experienced, but hopefully they might try when they see our example."

"What's the situation down there?" enquired Cedric, who had been helping them with the heavy lifting.

"They're beginning to get organised. They soon realised that fighting was achieving nothing, and they were getting frustrated that nobody was coming out on 'top'," replied Bull.

"They picked the first committee last month. Names out of a hat. The majority are willing to give anything a try just to get some semblance of normality," continued Thomas. "It's dawned on most of them that this is their new reality. They want to eat better and get on with making a life here. And they know it takes organisation for that to happen."

"They were all leading criminal gangs in the Previous Age, weren't they?" asked Cedric.

"Yes, so they know the importance of being organised, though this time it won't be for crime. It'll be for harvesting crops, processing grain, baking bread, fetching and distributing water," said Bull.

Thomas smiled. "Jesus knew the right mix of personalities to put together. He knew their aggression was likely to burn out once they realised it didn't achieve anything. These are tough but pragmatic types. They understand the importance of teamwork."

Cedric nodded. "There are some communities that are only a handful of people, but whatever their size, the personality mix is always arranged by Jesus so that each person has the best opportunity to mature. People begin to see themselves more clearly when they see their attitudes from the Previous Age mirrored in others. My seraph brothers and sisters are always on hand to step in if necessary, but we usually find that people either begin relating better or they withdraw into a highly solitary existence. But even if they cut themselves off from others, God can use their flashbacks and memories to shine his loving light on what they need to address."

"We've certainly seen how important the right composition of people is in all the communities here," said Thomas. "And I can't think of anyone apart from Jesus who would be able to get it so right!"

\*

Yuri arrived at the field where he had been sent by the committee. Owl was already there.

"You're late," he said without looking at Yuri.

"And?" growled Yuri, defensively.

"You know the only difference between chaos and order is commitment to a plan."

"Alright, alright," mumbled Yuri, as he began to attack the ground with a hoe. "I'm here now."

Scattered over the field were several men digging up root vegetables. Their rather unkempt appearance and mud-splattered clothes made them look more like peasants than former gang masters. Some of the men relished the physical labour and feeling the strength in their new bodies being put to good use gave them a sense of oneness with the earth. Others, like Yuri, struggled to get used to a committee telling them what to do.

By the end of the day the men had brought in several large wheelbarrows full of turnips, parsnips, potatoes and carrots to the warehouse that stood on the edge of the settlement. There the crops would be sorted into various storerooms, with some being sent directly to the kitchen department. It was not unusual for the men to attempt to take the best items from the harvest back to their dwellings, with each vegetable smuggled out representing something of a victory over the committee.

Most evenings the men would gather in the central square, where food would be served, card games would be played and songs sung, often those they remembered from the Previous Age.

This evening Owl was sitting with three other men around one of the tables dealing out a hand of cards.

"You've stacked them in your favour," said one of the men, leaning over his drink.

Owl looked over the table at him. "No, Raul. You should know by now I am no cheat."

Gripes such as these could sometimes end up in an argument.

Raul clenched his jaw and sniffed indignantly.

"Come on, let's just play the game," urged Owl. "If you have a complaint, bring it up at the committee."

One of the other players groaned.

"Committees, arguments, work and pissy weak beer. Day after day. The same people and the same place. I'm bored as hell."

"Nothing ever happens," added the other player in the circle. "If Jesus thinks this is how to punish us, maybe he's not as stupid as he seemed."

"Look on the bright side," said Owl, shuffling the deck again. "We've stopped brawling. Hard work and discipline are the only way that things are going to get better."

"Fighting became boring. It didn't get us anywhere. And now everything is boring!"

"But there is order," said Owl, bluntly. "We may have taken a while to settle into this, but look - we all know what we have to do. Most of us work hard, and then we get a decent meal and a game of cards."

"What about them?" asked one of the men, motioning with his head towards Thomas and Bull, who were sitting motionless with eyes closed and legs crossed in the shade of a tree at the edge of the square. They had been doing this for several months now, and after drawing some incredulous comments and insults, the other men had become used to seeing them meditate twice a day. Some had even been up to visit the Hermitage and had begun learning about prayer, contemplation and listening to Ruach.

"They're just lazy," snapped Owl, though he knew it was a lie.

"No Owl, they're not," said another of the card players. "You know they work as hard as any of us in the fields."

"Well, what do they think they are achieving just sitting there? It's pathetic." Owl angrily shuffled the deck once again.

\*

"Stan is still refusing to do his shift in the fields and is now in solitary confinement," reported Yuri to Owl the next day. "It's a clear case of insubordination."

Owl pursed his lips. The way that Yuri seemed to enjoy punishing people bothered him.

"We can afford to keep him in for a good while," continued Yuri. "We have to make him see that disobeying the committee won't be tolerated. I still think we should hurt him properly."

"Well, we could starve him," Owl suggested, trying to find a compromise. "We know he won't die, but he will become hungry and thirsty and that can be his punishment."

"I say we hurt him properly," insisted Yuri.

"And what would that achieve, Yuri?"

"I always laid down the law and no one crossed me in my organisation. But now, if we beat him up, we know he'll just recover. We've seen how bodies just heal themselves in this place. But we can still inflict pain. Place his knees in a vice and tighten it every so often. That will teach him to obey orders," Yuri replied without emotion.

"No. For now, we will keep him in solitary but deprive him of food and water," Owl commanded. He was glad to have the opportunity to rein in Yuri's sadistic streak, but he was interested to see what would happen to New Earth bodies under such conditions.

\*

Yuri slid open the wooden slat that formed a peep-hole in the prison door. In the dank darkness he could make out the figure of a man lying on the ground.

"Get up!" Yuri ordered.

Stan slowly stood up and smiled.

"Day 39." Yuri turned to Owl standing next to him. "Stan is physically just as healthy as when we put him in there."

The two men stood next to the prison hut, discussing their options.

"I'm beginning to wonder whether we should keep him locked up at all. All we're doing is making work for ourselves and the others guarding him," said Owl.

"Letting him out would set a bad example. The others will complain when he continues to refuse to work his shifts and maybe they'll decide to stop working too. You can't afford to look soft as a leader so you know what I'd do. A few hours of agony and he'd soon be begging you to let him work in the fields."

"There is another option," said Owl. "We could banish him from the community, take him somewhere else and insist he doesn't come back. I'll need to run that past the rest of the committee but I can't imagine any objections."

"Ok. That's one way to get rid of him," agreed Yuri, "If they agree, we'll meet here tomorrow morning and take him to another community."

Next morning Yuri and Owl bound the prisoner's hands behind his back and forced him to walk with them away from the community. After several hours, they came to the banks of a stream, which looked like a good place to rest, when they were suddenly confronted by a winged creature that towered over them more than double their height.

Although Owl had arrived at the community on Cedric's back, there was no longer anything approachable or friendly in the seraph's eyes. Instead they seemed to glow with anger. He could pin all three men to the ground with one taloned foot if he so wished, and they knew it.

Dust flew into the air as Cedric took one step forward. Owl closed his eyes, anticipating violence, but Yuri stood his ground and glared at the creature.

"You can have your fistfights and lash out at each other from time to time, but no one gets to leave the community," boomed Cedric with a voice like thunder. "And you, Yuri, must know once and for all that no one gets to torture or inflict constant pain on any living thing here on the New Earth."

"So this is where God finally intervenes?" scoffed Yuri.

"I am not God," roared the seraph. "I act on the boundaries that Jesus has set. Nothing on the New Earth is without its boundaries."

Cedric reached out his paw towards Stan, who hesitatingly stepped forward.

"Turn around," Cedric commanded.

Stan obeyed, and the rope that bound his hands fell to the ground, sliced through at one stroke by the seraph.

"Give this man food and water," Cedric ordered.

After hastily giving Stan some of the supplies they had brought with them on their journey, Owl summoned up the courage to speak.

"But what about our freewill?"

"Freewill is yours, but always within boundaries," replied the seraph.

"Where were those boundaries in the Previous Age?" retorted Yuri. "I never came across any."

"Death was the ultimate boundary," said Cedric. "The worst you could do in the Previous Age was to take another person's life, but that just sent them here. People can't die here on the New Earth, but neither can anyone escape the process they need to experience."

"So have I understood this correctly? The likes of you will stop us every time we overstep the boundaries?" asked Owl.

"Yes, we see and hear it all. Do you think God is unaware of what you are doing? Do you think you are abandoned here? You are not. You are here to learn the futility of your violent ways."

"What's to stop them shutting me away again?" asked Stan, swallowing down a mouthful of bread.

"Nothing, but I will ensure that they do not torture you and that you all stay in the community," boomed Cedric.

With that, the seraph spread his huge wings and ascended into the sky, leaving the three men in the swirling clouds of dust created by his wingbeats.

\*

A few days later Owl walked past several dwellings as he made his way to the square. Glancing through windows, he was surprised to see some of the men sitting or kneeling on their floors, eyes closed. This troubled him. It reminded him of what had happened in the years after Thomas and his group had arrived at his community of survivors in the Previous Age. Owl had prided himself in creating and looking after that enclave of refugees from the Great Suffering, and it was there that he had witnessed his regime of law and order succumb to what he considered to be the weakness of friendship and care.

Passing by another dwelling, through the curtains he saw a man sitting quietly, eyes closed, with the trace of a smile on his face.

Owl pushed open the door to the dwelling and the man leapt to his feet in surprise.

"Committee inspection! What do you think you're doing?" demanded Owl.

"Get out of my hut!" the man yelled angrily, pushing Owl in the chest and trying to shut the door.

"You were meditating, weren't you?" shouted Owl.

"What if I was?" the man said, blocking his doorway with his body.

"Make sure you're at the next meeting and you'll find out," Owl replied, a plan forming in his mind as he continued on his way to meet Yuri.

*

"Yuri, we've been through all this before," Owl said with exasperation.

"But do you really think we've tried everything?" asked Yuri, frustrated. "There must be more we can do!"

"Sit down, and listen to me," instructed Owl. "We have tried violence, but physical bodies just heal quickly here. We have tried starvation, but people don't need food and water to live. We have tried solitary confinement, but that doesn't change people. There doesn't seem to be any way that we can control or force our will on other people here."

"So what do you suggest?" asked Yuri in frustration. "We just let them make us look foolish?"

"No, we can't allow that," replied Owl. "Give me more time and I will think of something."

Yuri clenched his jaw. He felt a familiar hot anger erupt like flames inside his chest.

"For fuck's sake!" he yelled as he jumped up, throwing a chair across the food hall with a clatter. He stormed out, shoving tables and chairs as he went. He cursed over and over under his breath until he was outside. Raising his eyes in the bright daylight, he saw a thin whisp of smoke rising from Thomas and Bull's cabin, just visible through the trees on the steep hillside.

\*

Bull heard the snap of twigs outside the cabin.

"Someone's here," he said, shooting a glance at Thomas, who was sanding down an axe handle.

The door was already open and a moment later Yuri appeared, filling the frame. He was breathing heavily, not from the hike, but from his anger.

"You two need to tell me how I can get out of here... you need to tell me now!"

Bull stood up and motioned toward a chair, but Yuri didn't move. Thomas put down the axe handle and sandpaper.

"What's going on?" he asked calmly.

"I hate this place and everyone here," barked Yuri. "I'm sick of it all. I want to destroy the whole place and wring everyone's neck!"

Thomas filled a cup with apple juice.

"Come and have a drink with us?"

Yuri ignored the invitation and remained standing.

"Nothing works here. You can't make people do what's required," Yuri exclaimed.

"What's the problem?" Bull asked.

"Stan still refuses to do his shifts. He won't cooperate with the rota set up by the committee."

"What have you tried?" asked Thomas.

"Everything. We've beaten him black and blue, starved him and shut him in solitary. Nothing changes his mind."

"Have you tried compassion? Have you spent time with him and attempted to discover why he is not obeying?" asked Bull.

"That's so pathetic!" Yuri sneered. "I want to kick your heads in. Both of you. But if I do, you'll be fine. Nothing works here. Nothing is the way it should be."

Yuri began furiously punching the wooden door frame and soon blood was running down his knuckles. He paused and looked at his hand, which stopped bleeding almost immediately. He stared as within a silent minute the skin had repaired itself and was just as before. He stood there, his shoulders still heaving, but slower now.

"What are you thinking, Yuri?" asked Bull.

Yuri turned and looked at him in silence. A moment later he was gone.

*

The next evening saw the weekly gathering in the square. Some of the men appeared to be in particularly good humour, laughing and joking with each other.

"Why so happy?" Yuri leaned over and asked the man sitting next to him.

"You'll find out when supper is served after the meeting. Make sure to try the chilli sauce. I reckon we've perfected it."

Yuri folded his arms and looked away, making a show of his disinterest.

Owl stood up and clapped his hands three times to signal the start of the meeting.

"It's time to draw names for the next committee, but before we do that, I think it's right to recognise the progress that's been made these last few months. We are beginning to reap the rewards of hard work and discipline and we need to keep heading in the right direction. However, one thing concerns me. I've noticed that some of you have started aping Thomas and Bull and their so-called 'meditation'. I reckon it's best called time-wasting and daydreaming. I hereby put forward a motion to ban any such practices, and I call on everyone who wants to preserve the gains we've made to support me."

A murmur of discontent rippled across the gathering. Picking up on it, Owl doubled down.

"So you think you're like Buddha now? You're all enlightened, are you?"

The man Owl had confronted the previous evening stood up.

"Look, don't knock what you haven't tried. You need to loosen up, Owl. Live and let live!"

The man sitting next to Yuri stood up.

"I know it seems crazy, but a few of us have been working on a chilli sauce to liven up our meals, and it was only after one of us meditated that we knew what we needed to do. You can judge for yourself at supper this evening. It's not the nonsense you think it is, Owl. It's a way of thinking more clearly and focusing on what is good."

Owl shook his head and surveyed the gathering with a look of undisguised contempt.

"Fine! It's your choice. Do what you like. I'm done with the committee anyway."

He sat down with his arms folded tightly over his chest.

Someone stepped forward with a wooden box covered in black cloth with a slit in the top, reached into it and began to call out the names for the next committee.

# Adilah: Animals and Laughter

The scream echoed around the cabins, and everyone stopped what they were doing.

Adilah came running from the trees, fear on her face.

"What's the matter?" called Harmony, brushing dirt from her hands and standing upright in the vegetable patch.

"Snake!" yelled Adilah.

Harmony's heart leapt into her mouth for a split second.

"Wait, Adilah! Wait!"

Adilah turned, continuing to stamp her feet and waving her hands as though trying to shake off an invisible assailant.

Harmony approached her with hands held out. She very gently touched Adilah's elbows, bringing her to a breathless pause.

"Adilah, no animal will attack you here. They no longer need to kill other things in order to eat and protect themselves. It's ok... It's ok."

Adilah looked at Harmony, wide-eyed.

"It was a big one!"

Harmony led Adilah to her cabin, where she was soon sunk deep in her favourite armchair, gratefully sipping a hot cup of cocoa. "I have a question, Harmony, but it's ok if you don't know the answer."

"Sure thing, honey. Ask away," said Harmony, who was sitting next to her, sewing a colourful quilt.

"Animals. Why was it that so many animals would kill and eat one another in the Previous Age? And some would kill humans too. Why was nature so violent if God made it all and God is love?"

"Gosh, that's a big one, Addy! I'll try and answer from what I've understood so far. Basically, everything in the Previous Age was designed to ensure the increase of sentient beings, as Papa wants to have a relationship with as wide a variety of beings as possible. However, it's possible for a species to multiply beyond the ability of its habitat to support it, and that's why he created predators to keep the balance of nature in place. He knew that he would resurrect the essence in each sentient creature, so that's why he accepted this design compromise. Things are different on the New Earth, as populations don't increase through reproduction any more, only resurrection. So God can ensure that the essential balance required in each ecosystem here is maintained, without the design compromise of animals killing each other."

"Where I come from, we had to be so careful. Snakes, scorpions, spiders - they could all kill you."

"Wow, yes. I remember reading about those. America had some dangerous wildlife too, but not as much as Africa. I believe that each species was designed to fit within its local ecosystem, where it was provided with ways to obtain food and protect itself and its kind. There was no evil in this, only a natural desire to survive. God has now removed those previous desires and established different ways of ensuring that the ecosystem on the New Earth can be sustained for eternity."

"I still don't understand why death had to be in the process at all," said Adilah thoughtfully.

"On the Old Earth, death was essential to preserve the balance of populations. Local environments would soon have become overloaded if numbers had increased without a corresponding decrease due to death. Death was an essential part of that stage in God's overall plan. It also marked the transition from one age to another. It looked very frightening from the perspective of a creature in the Previous Age, as most hadn't learnt to trust in their creator to hold them through the transition and they didn't know what lay beyond it. Now, can I ask you something about your own experience?"

"Yes," replied Adilah, with her beautiful shy smile.

"When you died, did you feel frightened?"

Adilah thought for a moment.

"When I was in the flames the pain was so bad that I couldn't think clearly, but, yes, I was frightened. I survived for about a week but I knew that my body had begun to shut down. My hair had all been burned off and my face disfigured, but somehow underneath all the pain and suffering, I had peace. I knew that Friend was with me. In the last two days I felt no pain and I was in some kind of a strange sleep. I didn't dream but I did know that someone was with me and that I was happy to leave my suffering behind. Friend gave me the feeling that I was going to be ok. I can't tell you exactly when I died. At some point I was in a vast space moving toward a beautiful light. I don't know if I was dreaming or whether my body had given up by then. The next thing I knew I woke up in Jesus' home and ... here I am."

"Yes, Ruach, the Holy Spirit, the one you call 'Friend', helps every living being in those final moments to let go. Most people do not recognise her, but she works with each person and creature at those times. Even those who die suddenly and unexpectedly, she comforts during their transition. It seems our spirit leaves our bodies and is then re-homed in our resurrection bodies. We become whole again; mind, body and spirit."

"So, every animal is raised as well?"

"Not every individual creature, but the life force that was hosted by a particular body returns to Papa and it can be re-assigned. All life comes from God. All life is Papa sharing consciousness with creation."

"So, creation is God?"

"All creatures live and move and have their being in God. They are each an embodiment of the divine life, but not the totality of it. Nothing exists apart from Papa."

"Is that why you and Jesus call God 'Papa'?"

"Yes, Jesus is the great example of the character of God. He is a human being just like us but has the full nature of God, so he shows us our maximum divine potential. And he shows us how we can relate to God - the ground of all being, the source of all, the one Jesus calls Papa - as a parent. That's why we can call God Papa - or Mama, it makes no difference. God is love, and love is the reason for everything. It's the heart of the whole process and where all things are heading - even snakes!"

"These thoughts are so big!" gasped Adilah and laughed.

"They certainly are," chuckled Harmony, "but everyone has *ages* to explore them."

*

Evenings, when several of the women in the community would gather in one of the cabins to sing, were Adilah's favourite time of day. Communal singing was the warmest memory from her childhood. She loved the sound of female voices rising and falling in unison, and she took pride in her ability to harmonise.

"Given my name, this should be something I'm good at," joked Harmony one evening.

This amused Adilah so greatly that she was unable to stifle her laughter even after the singing began. It eventually sent the others off into contagious giggles until everyone in the cabin was laughing so hard that Margot, hearing the cacophony from the other side of the camp, dropped her knife and fork and came running to see what was wrong. Bursting in to Adilah's cabin and finding women strewn about the main living room in stages of incapacity, Margot was soon leaning on Harmony, infected with laughter too. Before long the remaining women in the settlement were caught up in the firestorm of mirth that echoed through the trees.

In the coming days Harmony was amused by how funny her simple pun had seemed to Adilah, but she was also aware how the outbreak of laughter had released something in the community. Humour had begun to become part of everyday interaction.

"This has begun to happen in our settlement, too," Anne said to Harmony as they compared notes on an evening walk. "And it seems to me that the women are more easily able to access their full range of emotions because of it."

"Yes, it's as though laughter has helped to break down the dam that was holding back all kinds of emotions. And tears of sadness can flow more easily too," agreed Harmony. The two friends continued their walk and returned home full of thankfulness for the ways in which Papa God's purposes were so clearly being worked out amongst the women, whom they had grown to know and hold very dear.

# Jubilee Changeover

Many years later, Anne and Harmony were again enjoying an evening walk when they noticed a distinctively tall figure clothed in radiant colours moving at pace towards them.

"An angel!" gasped Anne.

"Hello Anne. Howdy Harmony. I've got some news for you. Jesus is giving notice that the first jubilee period is nearly complete. Your team will gather in the City in one month's time. Start preparing your community for transition."

"Thank you. We understand," said Harmony, and then turning to Anne, "This means we will be moving on from here. It's the end of the first fifty-year jubilee period."

"I imagine some of the women will be really upset to have to part with their friends," replied Anne, "but we know it's for their long-term good."

"Change brings new challenges," agreed the angel. "The process is designed to bring growth for everyone. I must go to give the news to Sylvia and Carlos now. Good to see you."

"Send our love," called Harmony as the angel headed off down the road.

"Well, there we go!" said Harmony. "Can you believe it's already fifty years since we came to these villages? It seems to have passed so quickly, don't you think?"

"For us it did," replied Anne. "I'm not sure some of the women feel the same, but it'll be interesting to see how they respond."

The two friends headed back to their cabins in their respective clearings in the forest, both pondering the task that lay ahead of them but also looking forward to the gathering in the City.

\*

Despite having lived for years in their shared home, Carlos and Sylvia were unused to anyone knocking on their door late in the evening. Carlos got up from the table where he had been absorbed in recreating some of the sights of the Eternal City using watercolours in his sketchbook. Opening the door, he was overjoyed to be greeted by an angel.

"Time to get ready," said the angel. "Jesus has called a meeting for Team Thomas in the City in a month's time. The first jubilee transition is coming!"

"So, we're moving on?" said Sylvia, turning to Carlos.

The angel explained a few more details before heading onwards. Sylvia and Carlos sat down together in their front room and began discussing what the jubilee might mean for some of the villagers.

"If Imelda and Dawn are separated, that will put an end to their clothing enterprises," reflected Sylvia.

"I wonder if Fran and Kelly will end up in the same place?" mused Carlos. "Hard to know which would be better for them?"

"I'm glad we can leave it up to Jesus. Together with Ruach, they will have the best idea of where each person should go next."

\*

"Where's Yan?" asked the angel. "I have something to tell you both."

"He'll be meditating about now," said Yvonne. "He lives just round the corner. Let's go and find him."

Yan came to his door in a toga looking calm and serene, but his face lit up when he saw the angel, who proceeded to explain the impending transition to them both.

Waving the angel off, the two friends began to marvel at how the time had passed. They had watched Gerty, Eric and the other children grow into wise young people, and they had rejoiced at the progress Johan and Ebo had made in letting go of their prejudices and finding a path towards full reconciliation.

"We're going to miss everyone, aren't we?" said Yan, thoughtfully

Yvonne paused before replying, as tears began to well up in her eyes.

"Oh yes, we will. The love we have for these people is deep, but I believe that, in time, we will be seeing them again."

"I don't doubt it," said Yan gently, also visibly emotional.

*

"How do you feel?" asked the angel.

"Well, I'll be glad to see the team," replied Bull.

"Are you finding it hard here, guys?"

"It's been challenging," said Thomas. "Sometimes it's been hard to remain patient and kind, but we've tried to keep the big picture in mind and that's helped us to endure the process."

The angel looked around their cabin. "You really have a welcoming home. Do any of the men come and visit you here?"

"We began to get some visitors and some took a few steps forward, but then they'd usually take a few steps back, which is what we expected knowing the type of people that are here. Progress is slow and there is much to work through."

The angel nodded. "As you know, *agape love* never insists on its own way. There's no use in trying to force anything. I'd best be off. I've seen all of Team Thomas now, so I'll head back to the City and tell Jesus that you have all been notified."

"Am I allowed to feel excited about the end of this first period?" asked Bull after the angel had left.

Thomas took a deep breath and exhaled slowly. He approached his friend and wrapped his arms around him.

"I love you, brother," Thomas said gently. "I'm glad you've been with me."

Bull loved a hug and squeezed Thomas back, "I love you too, mate. I wonder what's next for us?"

They stood shoulder to shoulder and looked out of the window down the valley towards the camp.

"This is going to be interesting," said Thomas.

*

"That's right, it's meant to feel different," said Jesus, handing Yvonne the drink he had just made for her. "Kairos time works much better for humans than chronos time. Kairos is about quality, whereas chronos is about quantity - seconds, minutes, hours. In kairos time, you don't think about how it's measured, you are just in the moment."

"Ok, I think we're all here," he said looking around as he made his way to a large table.

Yvonne followed, grateful for the answer to her question about why the fifty years had not felt like a long time.

The team took their places around the table as it was time for the review of the first jubilee.

"Friends, I'm so excited to hear about your first jubilee period!" Jesus was animated and his pleasure at seeing Thomas' whole team again was clear.

"Thomas and Bull, let's hear from you."

"Our community is situated a long way from the City," began Bull. "We always felt reassured knowing Cedric, our watchful seraph, was on hand nearby. It's made up of a couple of hundred tough men from gangs around the world, all of whom have been hardened by their experiences in the Previous Age. Initially they fought amongst themselves to see who would come out on top.

There were regular brawls in the town square, but they soon realised it wasn't getting them anywhere.

In the end, they decided to create temporary committees by drawing names at random. It worked, as none of them wanted to be held responsible for long and it meant everyone got a chance to make their mark. At times things got brutal, and Cedric had to intervene when they tried to expel one of the men from the community. Order seemed to settle after some time, but then the main challenge they faced was boredom. The majority of the men were unwilling to find beauty in each other and their everyday life, which meant they got desperately frustrated."

"Quite early on, we built a place outside of the settlement so that we could meditate in peace and demonstrate the technique to others," continued Thomas. "A few of the men were interested in what we were doing and began meditating privately. We've begun to see a noticeable maturing in some of the men, and they've been sharing with others about how it's helped them come up with new ideas and get more out of their lives."

Jesus nodded. "It's certainly been a challenging assignment for you. These were men with hard hearts. You have set them a good example and modelled *agape love* in that place. Several in your community have made progress."

Jesus now turned to Carlos and Sylvia. "And in your village?"

"Life there has mostly reached a stalemate," began Sylvia. "The past fifty years has seen people start to take small steps towards relationships with one another, but mostly for selfish reasons."

"Their compulsion to be 'right' keeps them from finding deeper connection with each other. They want to constantly impress, which remains the driving force in their everyday lives," said Carlos. "The only sign of community co-operation has been swapping food items with one another to create more variety in their diets."

"Working relationships have been established," added Sylvia. "Some of the women have made use of each other's talents to set themselves up in business, but the motivation has always been self-serving."

"The one exception has been Kelly. She has often opened up to us, and she's made some progress," concluded Carlos.

"I understand," said Jesus. "Most of these people will need a similar community for the next jubilee period. Only by consistently reaping the consequences of their self-centred attitudes will they come to recognise their need for change. Kelly will go to a more supportive environment. Her heart is clearly softening."

Jesus looked around the table. "All of you will be moving to new regions, and you will mostly have new members in your communities. The kindness you show them will keep drawing them to make better choices."

"And how have the children come on?" he asked, turning to Yvonne and Yan.

"Well, it's been an amazing fifty years," enthused Yvonne. "We've watched the children grow up and flourish in the community."

"Thank you for providing the school and community environment that has allowed each of these children to grow into adults," said Jesus. "They didn't get the chance to acquire the skills and the knowledge needed to live as an individual in the Previous Age, but we love to see them mature on the New Earth."

"It was a privilege to help," continued Yvonne. "We developed a curriculum that ensured they all made progress in reading, writing and arithmetic, so that they could then go on and research anything that interested them. We also made sure they learnt practical skills for cooking, making clothes, and taking care of their homes and their environment. And it often surprised us that they seemed to know *agape love* naturally without being taught."

"Indeed," said Yan. "They were often the ones who took the lead in the learning process for the adults."

"It's the great gift of childhood," said Jesus with a twinkle in his eye. "Children carry innocence and wisdom into the world and help those who are older discover them again."

"Many of the adults had carried over various deep-seated issues from their experiences in their Previous Age, and on many occasions it was the children who helped identify these and initiate some of the healing."

"Yes," said Yan. "As time went on, many of the adults were able to open up and talk with us, and we have been so pleased to see much progress in their journeys."

"And people have generally found their work enjoyable and satisfying," said Yvonne. "Especially once they realised that the New Earth yields abundant crops without the backbreaking work of the Previous Age."

Jesus leaned back in his chair. "Yes, working to bring in the harvest for everyone is a great joy."

"Yes, even in our community and despite all its problems, the fields have yielded an abundance of crops," said Bull.

"The New Earth is able to yield the same in all of its many regions," Jesus explained. "The providence of *agape love* makes sure that no one need go hungry. This was how things were in the Previous Age before some people's greed and desire for resources left others with too little. And how have things been in the villages of Beulah, Anne and Harmony?"

"At the beginning, the women were in a very fragile and vulnerable state," said Harmony. "It's taken many years for trust to be built, but we understand that the traumas they experienced will only be healed with patient loving kindness."

"Some seem to be in an ongoing state of victimhood," continued Anne. "We recognise they are victims, of course, but we are looking for their identity to be rooted in who they are as whole people now, not as who they once were."

"Yes, this needs great sensitivity," agreed Jesus. "Seeing oneself as a victim is deeply connected to shame and hurt, but it can also be linked with pride. It takes humility to release oneself from the need to always identify as a victim. It takes time to believe in a deeper identity, separate from whatever happened in the past."

"This is the process we are currently in," continued Harmony. "Some of the women are finding their new sense of self in what they can contribute to the community."

"I think this is progress," said Anne, "although it can sometimes seem like avoiding the issues."

"The lines in our hearts are blurred, but given time, the confidence gained from helping in the community can often help to heal deep issues," said Jesus "Do you feel any of them are ready to spend time in mixed company yet?"

"I would say that by the end of the next jubilee some of them may be," replied Harmony.

"Alright, we will place each of them in communities with just women again," said Jesus. "As for Johan and those in his community, they will be placed in communities appropriate to their current level of maturity."

Jesus looked around the table once again, taking a moment to look in each person's eyes.

"And how are you feeling in yourselves? You're not expected to be superheroes. What are you seeing and learning?"

Harmony checked around the table before speaking first.

"I'm aware of just how different my background is to most of the women I'm working with," she said thoughtfully. "I'm learning not to assume that anything about my upbringing or education is the same as theirs. I feel that I'm constantly having to check my assumptions."

"That's good, Harmony. People's personalities and past experiences are so varied. The process of learning about others never comes to an end," said Jesus.

"I've felt tested at times," said Bull. "In the early days I got physically beaten up, and then it moved on to criticism, accusations and all kinds of verbal attacks."

"I know exactly how that feels," said Jesus.

"I know you do, and that's what's kept Thomas and I going in the darkest times. You didn't choose sides. You stayed true to the way of *agape love* - and you were killed for it."

Jesus nodded slowly. "It's the price we pay for following the path of *agape love* and refusing to take part in the power games of the world. When we choose to lay down our power, others may take advantage of us. The authorities crucified me although I had shown unfailing love to them all."

Bull sighed. "When I think back to all I've done and seen, I can see that the way of *agape love* doesn't need to punish or seek revenge. Experiencing the consequences of one's own actions can produce lasting transformation. I must admit at times, though, it has seemed that the men in our community would *never* change."

"How are you feeling about it, Thomas?" asked Jesus, turning to his old friend.

"I trust and believe in the process, but it can sometimes feel like there is no kairos time for the men, only chronos time, which can seem to drag. The days can feel very slow, but Bull and I can always find Ruach's presence with us as we pause and focus. Bull and I seek her in the mornings and in the evenings, and she has never, ever failed to comfort us. She lifts us up and gives us the energy to face the harder days. Our respite periods in the City have always been a joy too. We have never burned out or lost the plot, because we are so deeply refreshed here. The angels know what we need."

Jesus laughed "Yes, they are certainly wonderful like that!"

"I'm struck by how deep the trauma of war is," said Yan. "We all suffered, but we also remember better days. Some of the men in our village died young and violently. They experienced years of war and military training, and so they remember very little else."

"Many who became soldiers saw things that can shake the soul to its very foundation," said Jesus. "The young men who died in uniform need much love and understanding, and that's why I'm so glad you have been there with them, Yan."

"Are some of them placed in communities with other men who have committed violence, even though they had no choice in being co-opted to fight and obey orders?" asked Yan.

"A few are," said Jesus. "We understand that many had no choice about what they were made to do. But for some, war created the opportunity for them to satisfy their worst desires, and so we have to be very firm to help them clearly see the consequences of their actions and the suffering they caused."

"In our village we have seen a lot of pride and bitterness," said Carlos, "but we have found that this only serves to inspire us to continue living in a different way. Sylvia and I have been very happy in the home we built, and it was really good to involve some of the men from my end of the settlement in the building project. Working together meant that they actually started to communicate with each other after decades of stubborn silence."

"Whereas the women were arguing and gossiping throughout!" added Sylvia.

"Of course, not all women are like that," Anne commented. "We found that many in our community kept themselves to themselves for a very long time."

"Anyone else had people still believing themselves to be addicted to things from the Previous Age?" asked Carlos. "We've had trouble from some people demanding all sorts of things and turning the place upside down trying to find cigarettes, alcohol and drugs."

"Yes, we've experienced that too. And we've also had folk who find it hard to accept that there's no sexual desire on the New Earth," added Yan.

"Their minds are still psychologically programmed to *think* that they want these things," explained Jesus. "This won't change until they are able to fully embrace the present moment and become completely in tune with their resurrection bodies. Then they will see that they are truly free of sexual desire and any previous addictions."

"So, is it just an illusion that they need these things?" asked Harmony.

"Yes and no," replied Jesus, "If they are craving something, the craving is real. They just haven't realised where that craving comes from and that it's not a genuine physical need. The brain in resurrected bodies is completely new, so these desires are not coming from the brain. They are coming from the *mind*, which is much more than simply the brain. These are psychological crutches that they believe are part of who they are, but it's not the truth."

"One lady in our village tried to smoke leaves from some of the trees in the forest," remembered Sylvia, "but she soon gave up when she realised it wasn't giving her any kind of chemical high."

"It often takes unpleasant experiences for people to understand what is and isn't good for them," said Jesus. "Those outside of the Eternal City are in environments that encourage such experiences. It will take some a long time to leave their former behaviours and beliefs behind. They are still perfectly free in their agency to choose for themselves as we do not coerce anyone. It's possible that in the coming jubilee period some will dig themselves into deeper and darker holes, but we know that others will begin to make much healthier and constructive choices."

"Will mixing up their communities and locations help them?" asked Anne.

"Moving to a new community every fifty years is good for everyone. It allows each person to 'restart' their lives unencumbered by any previous choices they may have made in order to fit in with their neighbours. Sometimes a person desires to change but feels unable to because of the expectations of the people around them. Moving everyone into a new community allows each individual to change the persona they present to others, if they wish to do so.

Some need a new environment to explore their attitude to people they won't have previously encountered. Despite having made significant progress on one issue, they may have much to learn about another. As people experience different communities, they will learn deep and lasting lessons.

*Agape love* chooses to see the best in other people - not just your 'favourite' people, but everyone. As you know, once you begin to think in this way, you can live anywhere without discriminating, judging or looking down on your neighbour. You have already learned this lesson because you've listened to Ruach, who shows you the true value in each person."

"So, it may take several jubilee periods for people to make progress?" asked Bull.

"I cannot predict how long it will take. However, I'm often surprised by people's ability to change and grow. For some, it may only take a few jubilee periods to reach the level of understanding and maturity that means they can be welcomed into the Eternal City."

After the meeting drew to a close, they all helped Jesus clear the table and wash up. There was much laughter and everyone was thrilled to have a week in the City to visit friends and be refreshed, ready for the challenge of a second jubilee period in a new location and a new community.

As Jesus waved them off, he prayed silently. "I am so proud of them, Papa. Nothing of this was predetermined, but they have all overcome so much. They carry our heart so beautifully."

He watched as they descended the steps and headed out into the evening. Soft warm light could be seen in the windows of the dwellings and in the distance steam was rising from the hot springs that provided energy for the City and all its inhabitants, while shades of blue, mauve and purple ranged across the sky.

Jesus stood, looking over the heavenly scene before him. A moment later he was joined by Ruach.

"I stand in awe of what these people have gone through," said Jesus quietly. "When we created humanity, we understood the risk that they would choose their independence forever and never want to come to us."

"They are our children," Ruach replied. "They will all come home eventually."

"Sometimes, I wish I could just go and gather them all up and have them here with us now," said Jesus.

"I know. All in the fullness."

# Johan: Enemies?

Johan's eyelids flickered as the soft light of early morning illuminated the room. The pillow under his head felt pleasantly cool as he stretched his body beneath the bedcovers.

Opening his eyes, it took a few seconds for Johan to register that he was in a new environment. Gone were the familiar log walls, and instead he was surrounded by honey-coloured stone.

Now fully awake, he eased himself out of bed. New clothes were hung neatly in a wardrobe and he could see homely furniture in the next room.

Looking out of the window, he could see several stone buildings with wildflowers and tall grass growing around the base of their walls. There were no trees, and the ground appeared level, which confirmed that he was no longer in his mountainside village.

Despite all the changes, Johan felt peaceful. It was the same feeling as when he had first been raised and had met Jesus and Ruach all those years previously. He was thankful for the month of preparation everyone had been given when the angel had brought news of the jubilee transition.

Johan took his time to look around his new dwelling before making his way outside. The day was warm and the fragrance of the wildflowers filled the air. To Johan's great joy, a familiar face came strolling around the corner of a nearby barn.

"Yan!" called Johan excitedly.

Yan came to him and the friends embraced.

"So, the next jubilee period has begun," said Yan, smiling. "Here's our new situation."

"Many new people to meet and get to know," said Johan quietly. "I must admit I am a little nervous."

Yan nodded and smiled. "You'll need to do some exploring, so I'll see you again later."

Johan did as Yan suggested and set out to get his bearings. As well as the stone cottages, there were other buildings that Johan presumed were for agricultural use and creative enterprises. A few other people were also walking around. There were polite exchanges of greetings, but nobody seemed ready for longer conversations.

Johan noticed large trees laden with fruit and an area of land marked out in a distinctive way. He guessed that was where they would be planting their crops.

The grassland that surrounded the settlement stretched out in all directions. After years of living enclosed on all sides by tall pine trees, Johan couldn't help but feel exposed, but he also appreciated being able to see for miles around. On the horizon were purple mountains, some too far away to make out clearly, but in one direction they were closer and he could see hedgerows and clumps of trees in the undulating foothills. The sky felt vaster than before, encircling the whole scene with its multi-coloured display of light playing out on the clouds.

Johan stood for some time, taking in the new landscape. He wished that his sister, Gerty, was by his side and that he could share it with her.

Yan sought him out again after visiting some of the other new residents and placed a caring hand on his shoulder.

"How are you feeling? I know you will miss your sister greatly until you are able to see her again, but she needs to establish herself and her own independence. She will be safe and well in her new community, I can promise you that. In the fullness of time, everyone will be able to see one another whenever they please, but not until all of us have learned to fully live in *agape love*. Until then, we may have to live with some loss and heartache, but that will only make our joy more complete when the full reconciliation takes place."

Johan stared toward the purple mountains. "We all went to sleep one night, and we've all woken up in new places. We knew it was coming, but it's still hard. I don't know how I'm going to manage without her."

"I know it's not easy."

"Yan, you are always smiling, but I know you have a family too."

"Yes, I haven't yet seen my family. I would love to see my Ma and Pa again and be reconciled with my brothers, my cousins and my friends. I have longings and miss them sometimes, but I know that Jesus will ensure that all will be well in the end. There will come a time on the New Earth when we will all be able to see those we love, and even those we hated, in the fullness and completeness of who we really are in the image of God. But first we must all go through the process so that we are ready for that day."

"I'm sorry, Yan. I think sometimes we all forgot that both you and Yvonne were missing loved ones too. Of course, you want to see them again. Knowing it's the same for you helps me trust what you say about the bigger picture."

"We can all feel impatient sometimes, and that's ok. Our longing and yearning are signs that love is alive and at work inside us. That love wants to flow out of us and embrace those who are dear to us."

"Maybe we need to think about those feelings as a kind of hope then?" said Johan thoughtfully.

"Yes, that's a good way to think of it. These feelings, although they aren't comfortable, are a good thing. When we grieved and mourned in the Previous Age, it was because we thought our love could no longer reach those we loved. For many, death meant despair because it seemed like final and permanent separation. But now we know that death will not keep us from one another, so our grief can be turned into hope and longing - longing that will one day be fulfilled."

Encouraged by his talk with Yan, Johan continued to explore the village, determined to make a positive start and to begin to get to know his new neighbours.

*

"I'm just saying, I wish all this was a lot less like the Previous Age. I mean, I'm all for things being familiar, but don't you wish we could all fly, or become invisible or something like that?"

Johan turned to look at the man talking to him. He was fair-haired and had piercing blue eyes which disappeared when he smiled. The two were seated on the grassy hillside they had climbed to get a better idea of the geography of their new environment.

"I'll be honest with you," said Johan, "my Previous Age was awful. I'm just glad I'm not hungry, crawling through mud, or being shot at."

"Soldier?" said the man with interest. "When and where?"

Johan looked at his expression, trying to guess whether to open up or not.

"Apparently they called it World War Two," he said reluctantly. "But I died before it ended."

"Were you killed in battle?" the man asked.

"Yes, shelled in a dugout with my friends. Never knew a thing about it. What about you? What did you do?"

"I'm Chester by the way," said the young man, offering him his hand. "Canadian Air Corps, also World War Two."

"And I'm… Johan." He hesitated and glanced at his companion to gauge his reaction.

"Well," said Chester, immediately withdrawing his hand and looking him up and down with obvious contempt, "I thought I recognised your accent. That makes us enemies."

"So did you die in combat, too?" asked Johan, trying to find common ground.

"No, I never even saw action. I joined up in early '45 and it was all over before we were deployed. So, no. I didn't get the chance to kick your German ass."

"So, what happened? Since being raised, I haven't met any other servicemen, yet alone from the same time as me."

"You don't know?" Chester raised his eyebrows and let out a mocking laugh.

"No, I only know they called it World War Two" said Johan and then quickly raised his hands. "Actually stop. I don't want to know. I don't need to know. It won't help either of us to dig all of that up. We are here and we're not at war. That's enough for me."

"Well, I think you need to know that you lost and lost big time. You Nazi bastards got what was coming to you. You should be ashamed of..."

Johan interrupted with a scowl. "For fuck's sake, I said I didn't want to know!"

"Well, listen up, buddy. You need to know," spat Chester. "You need to know that you caused a war that killed millions of people. And I guess you're going to tell me that you thought those camps where all the Jews were murdered were just holiday camps? "

Chester's anger grew as he stood up and towered over Johan.

"You Nazi scum! You know what? I'm glad my friends bombed your cities and killed your friends and family. I'm glad you fucking died in that dugout. You deserved it."

Chester spat on the ground next to Johan and headed off down the hill towards the village, only turning around to put up a middle finger.

Johan felt as though he had been punched in the stomach. He didn't know if he should run after Chester and try and explain that he'd never been a member of the Nazi party and that he'd been conscripted into the army straight from school. There were so many questions racing through his mind about the war and about Hitler having lost and cities being bombed. And what had Chester meant about camps and Jews being murdered? Johan sat there and hung his head, feeling desperately alone.

Hours went by under the changing sky, and when Johan finally raised his head he saw smoke rising from the chimneys of his new settlement, which meant food was being prepared. He stood motionless for a while before turning and heading further into the hills and away from the village.

*

Yan plumped up his pillow and placed it on his bed, feeling a sense of satisfaction as he put the final touches to making his cottage feel like home. As he looked around, he felt a familiar stirring in his heart and Johan's face came into his mind. Yan went outside and, finding Johan's cottage empty, began looking for him.

"Have you seen the man who lives in that cottage over there?" he asked a group of men, who were standing together around a roaring fire. "He's called Johan."

"You mean the Nazi?" asked one of them.

"Oh come on, he's better than a Nazi," added another. "He's a dead Nazi."

The men laughed loudly.

"I left him in the foothills," said Chester, who was whittling a stick. "If he's got any sense, he'll stay there."

Yan moved quickly, heading toward the hills. They were growing darker every minute as the daylight died away.

# Adilah: Friends with Everyone?

Adilah was pleased to find that she was surrounded by trees again. She always felt safe in their shelter. Her new settlement was deep in a rainforest where the dwellings were built into the trees. They were connected by elevated walkways, above which the treetop canopy echoed with the calls of birds, monkeys and other creatures that she could not identify. Moving on from the familiarity of her previous village was an ordeal for Adilah, as apart from Harmony, Anne and her sister Eshe everyone was new to her. There were more skin tones than she knew existed, and although it was still an all-female community, the unknowns felt overwhelming.

"Live with me?" Adilah had asked Eshe when they had awoken on their first morning.

Eshe had nodded vigorously, and they had soon begun to feel more confident as they investigated what had been provided for them and set about making their treetop house feel like a home.

There was a knock at the door.

"Only us!" called out Harmony.

Adilah opened the door and her two friends stepped inside.

"Aren't these houses just amazing?" exclaimed Harmony with her typical enthusiasm.

"They make me a little nervous," laughed Anne. "I don't like heights."

"Are you allowed to be scared?" asked Eshe.

"It's a leftover from the Previous Age," said Anne. "I completely understand that I'm safe here, but if I were to fall, it would hurt for a few days, and that's never pleasant."

"Everything new is an unknown, and it's normal to feel unsure. That's why we keep reminding ourselves about *agape love*," said Harmony. "That's why we spend time thinking upon all that is good and beautiful around us."

"We aren't expected to be able to work out everything at once," said Anne kindly. "This process is long and deep. It's not good to say that things should be like *this* or like *that*. Being honest with ourselves and with each other is the path forward."

"Where are these women from?" asked Eshe, looking out of the window at the hubbub of activity as people crossed the walkways and began exploring their new surroundings.

"From all over the Earth and across history. You will get to know them in time, but they are all women who have been through difficult circumstances in the Previous Age, just as in your previous community. In order to keep growing, Jesus knows that we need to learn to relate to more people - to understand them and have them understand us. This group of women is just right for where you are on your journey."

"I'm willing to trust that," said Adilah with conviction.

Anne looked her in the eye and smiled kindly. "This is the way forward for all of us - choosing to trust, come what may. It won't always be easy, but if we trust in the bigger picture of growing to live through *agape love*, then we can get through anything."

Eshe remained silent, still feeling overwhelmed by the move, but she was glad to see her sister's resolve.

Just at that moment she caught sight of a pair of round orange eyes looking at her from outside the window. She put a hand on her beating heart and then laughed.

"Look!" she cried. "A bush baby! Can I touch him?"

"It's not up to us," laughed Anne. "Why don't you approach him and try? Animals here aren't afraid of humans."

Eshe tiptoed across the room to the open window until she was a couple of feet away from the small creature, which had its arms wrapped around a branch.

Reaching out a careful hand, Eshe lightly stroked the bush baby's soft grey fluffy back. It didn't move and continued to look up at her.

"Oh, you are such a darling!" she whispered with delight.

Her friends smiled, as they too were looking forward to getting to know their friendly animal neighbours.

*

Adilah was used to living near a jungle, but only at ground level. She found being up in the trees exciting but also a little nerve-racking. It was on the elevated walkways that she felt most tentative, but after a few days she began to trust the wood and rope structures that held everything together.

The climate was wetter than at their last settlement, with regular downpours of warm, fragrant rain that made the rich green leaves sparkle in the sunshine that always followed on close behind. The dwellings were made from bamboo and so perfectly designed that it was sometimes hard to see where the trees stopped and the structures began. Huge bromeliads and orchids hung from the branches, creating a wonderful aroma and a few hundred metres away a crystal-clear stream ran gurgling over rocks. The atmosphere was balmy, but Adilah was delighted to discover that up in the treetops cool refreshing breezes still found their way through the leaves.

It didn't take long for the village to organise rotas for cooking and collecting water. Practical problems were soon addressed and this pleased Adilah greatly as organisation was important to her. She even found that several of the women deferred to her on decisions, which made her feel useful and respected. However,

Adilah was aware that one woman seemed to be constantly challenging her ideas and suggestions.

Mahala was a Native American from the Iroquois tribal region in northeastern America. Her older sister had married a settler, a man of English heritage, and she had learned English while caring for their children. Mahala was a strong and determined woman with a direct way of talking that many found rude.

"Ha! Adilah! You walk like a giraffe - so proud and upright."

Adilah turned around to see Mahala standing by a tree, watching her. Unsure of how to take her comment, Adilah nodded in greeting and carried on.

"You *are* a giraffe!" Mahala called after her.

Adilah put down her basket of guava and put her hands on her hips, unsure of how to reply.

"I don't know why you say this to me. Why am I a giraffe?"

"You are tall and graceful," said Mahala, drawing near to her.

Adilah could not read anything in Mahala's facial expression. She had thought she was being mocked, but now she was not so sure.

"Well, thank you... I think."

"You always avoid me, Adilah. Why?"

Adilah found Mahala's direct manner confrontational but decided a peace offering would be the wisest move.

"You are like a mother bear," she replied. "You are strong and fierce."

A faint smile crossed Mahala's face.

"You make me want to stay out of your way," Adilah continued, grateful for the chance to clear the air between them.

"But we are here together, and we are equal," Mahala continued. "Why do you think yourself unworthy?"

Adilah was brought up short by the personal nature of the question.

"Unworthy of what? Unworthy of being friends with you?" she asked, unable to conceal her indignation.

"No, not just that. But in many ways. You don't know how strong you are."

Adilah felt both energised and confused by the strange mix of questions and observations coming from this woman with jet-black hair and reddish-brown skin. It made Adilah want to push back, like for like.

"And you don't know how rude you sound," she replied with firmness in her voice but with an accepting smile.

The two women stood looking at each other, unsure of whether the conversation was a face-off or an opportunity to bond.

Without saying another word, Mahala turned and walked away until she was swallowed up in the thick vegetation.

Adilah stood for a moment before picking up her basket and continuing back to the settlement, all the while wondering what to make of this curious woman.

*

"It's ok not to be friends with everyone," said Anne as she worked with Adilah on constructing a bedside table out of bamboo for her new home.

"I know, I only have a few people that I'm sure are my real friends, but…" Adilah paused as if trying to find the words, "I think she is a good person. She is so different from me, but some of her words today showed kindness."

"That's a great place to start," said Anne. "Harmony is very different to me in every way, yet we have become like sisters."

"Sisters don't always get on either," observed Adilah.

"That's true," laughed Anne, remembering the times that she and Harmony had disagreed with one another. "Opposites attract, but very different ways of seeing, doing and being can mean that relating together is a challenge."

"But why are we made to live with people who are so different? What if we never become friends?"

"Nobody should feel they have to be friends with everyone - it's impossible anyway. But *agape love* is very different from friendship. Jesus taught us to love our neighbour, not the whole world. Eventually the whole world will feel loved because everyone will have learnt to love their neighbour and want the best for those around them, no matter who they are."

"So loving my neighbour doesn't mean that they have to be my best friend?"

"No, it's important to make that distinction. *Agape love* is something much bigger than friendship. It may include liking someone and being their friend, but you can love someone without necessarily liking them that much."

"Well, that's a liberating thought," said Adilah. "I'd never really seen it that way before, but I'll make sure to keep it in mind when I next see Mahala."

The two women continued their work, enjoying the companionship and easy conversation that flows in a friendship where loving and liking are intertwined.

# Yuri: Surprising Gifts

Yuri stroked Gulag's head and looked out of the window over the misty marshland. He could just make out the roofs of round huts and a scattering of trees through the gloom. He had awoken a few moments earlier, relieved to find Gulag by his side. His previous community suddenly seemed a long way away and a long time ago. Yuri wondered if he would feel more at home in this new environment.

The silence was eerie, and only Gulag's panting could be heard in the stillness. There was no birdsong, not even the sound of a breeze, just a damp and muffled quiet. The temperature was cool and Yuri guessed that it must be early morning.

Yuri couldn't be sure how long he sat staring through the window. Initially he felt euphoria at being somewhere new but this was soon been replaced with growing frustration at the prospect of starting over.

A knock at the door jolted him out of his thoughts.

"Why am I not surprised to see you?" grunted Yuri, as he opened the door and found Thomas standing there.

"Hello Yuri, and hello Gulag," said Thomas warmly, stooping down to greet the German Shepherd, who was always excited to see him, much to Yuri's annoyance.

"Welcome to your second jubilee period," said Thomas. "Do you have everything you need?"

Thomas knew that Yuri did have everything, but wanted to encourage him to notice the way in which he had been provided for.

Yuri looked around with a token glance.

"Yes, yes, it's all fine. Where are we?"

"That's for us to find out. You're welcome to explore and discover what is here. I don't pretend to know, as Bull and I have only just arrived here too."

"You don't get to see the place before everyone else?" Yuri asked, raising his eyebrows.

"No, we're in the same boat as everyone in the community."

"A bit unfair of your boss not to tell you," said Yuri, disparagingly.

"Well, we don't have an advantage over anyone else here. We're not in control, and we're not in charge. We're discovering the New Earth just like you are, and we're here to work just like everyone else here."

"Ok. Thanks for the speech."

"Alright Yuri, I'll see you soon."

Thomas was used to Yuri's brusque nature. He longed for him to see that he and Bull were on his side and not against him, but Yuri was still clearly determined to hold on to his distrust of people. Thomas returned through the gloom to the hut he shared with Bull. Their new environment seemed damp and colourless and felt like the edge of the known New Earth. There would be fewer men in this new community, and Jesus had explained that relationships would go deeper.

Thomas opened the door to find Bull installing fixtures for candles to give light.

"How many do you think will come?" Bull asked, looking back at Thomas over his shoulder.

"Well, they've all been invited, but I don't think many of them will want to be seen as needing anything. My guess is they'll stay in their huts, eat their provisions and only come out when they are hungry."

A few hours later Thomas and Bull were on the edge of the settlement, waving to signal their position to an angel leading a column of animals across a long causeway.

"Welcome," Thomas called out to the angel, who waved back.

A group of dogs followed immediately behind the angel, wagging their tails. Just behind them trotted a group of cats, followed by an assortment of beasts, including donkeys, horses, sheep and even a pair of Indian elephants.

"These are the presents from Jesus?" laughed Bull.

"Yes," said the angel. "These are the animals that many of the men here cared for in the Previous Age. Jesus has sent them as a gift."

"Just like when he gave Gulag to Yuri," said Bull.

"Jesus knows that these creatures can help soften hearts. Many of the men here bonded more closely with their animals than with other humans."

"So none of the men here ever abused animals or were cruel to them?" asked Bull.

"Correct," replied the angel.

Bull chuckled. "Well, this will certainly make things more interesting for them."

"It's the way of *agape love*," said Thomas. "Jesus has been generous to these men. He doesn't hold their past against them, and he's always looking for ways to encourage them to change their hearts. He gives people opportunities to help them find love in their own lives."

By now a few men from the settlement had appeared and were looking with interest at the menagerie. One suddenly broke into a run and came to where the elephants were drinking from a water channel.

One of the elephants reached out and gently explored the man's face and body with his trunk before wrapping it around him and lifting him off the ground. The man reached out his hands, clearly overcome with emotion, and rubbed the elephant's forehead. The other elephant extended its trunk into the embrace.

"Ramesh raised those elephants," said Bull. "He may have hunted and killed people in the war that divided his country, but he kept a tender heart for animals."

"It will be difficult for him to take care of them here," said Thomas. "He'll have to work hard... but maybe that's all part of Jesus' strategy."

"Yes, Jesus is giving these men more to do in this jubilee period," explained the angel. "It's through working hard and accepting the challenge to co-operate that attitudes will begin to change."

Another man appeared out of the gloom and crouched down near the sheep, which immediately gathered around him.

"Darren was a shepherd," explained Thomas. "He was raised in rural Northern Ireland but was abused by his grandfather as a young boy. He grew up into a violent young man and joined the IRA, but he always felt at peace around his sheep. He was devastated when he found these sheep with their throats cut by rival paramilitaries."

The noise of the animals had brought men out of their huts and reunions were now taking place all around Thomas and Bull. For a while they stood with the angel enjoying watching the men receive their gifts.

Thomas and Bull bade the angel farewell but stayed outside until the fog began to roll in from the marshes. Gradually the men returned to their huts with their animals, and the two friends returned to their new home with a couple of unclaimed cats and a parrot as temporary housemates.

*

"There is no way I can do this on my own," thought Yuri. When it was finished, the barn was going to be big - bigger than any other building he had seen on the New Earth. Three times his height and as wide as four huts. Yuri felt the shame that he experienced whenever he needed to ask for help.

"So, you're going to do it?" called Bull, walking towards him.

"I can do it," replied Yuri stoically. "But I will need other men."

"Are you going to ask around to see who can join you?"

"You ask them," he replied.

"I can say that Yuri needs help, if you like?" said Bull.

"Not '*needs help*'. Wants more men. Say it like that."

"Ok," said Bull. "But why would that motivate anyone to come and work with you? Would you respond to a request like that?"

Too egoistic to turn down the chance to earn admiration, but too proud to recruit help to get the job done, Yuri wavered before breaking.

"Fine, I won't do it. I don't fucking care, anyway."

"So you won't finish the barn?" said Bull.

Yuri hesitated again. He wanted respect and the barn would be a symbol of his authority.

"Ok, I'll do it, but I'll do it myself."

"You do what you feel is best," Bull said patiently.

Bull left Yuri standing near one of the doors, too daunted by the size of the job to look inside again. Yuri knew he would need to fell several trees for timber to build the floor but didn't have much clue how to proceed with the project after that. He'd lied to the other men about his ability, not realising the scale of what was required.

Yuri hadn't been handy with tools in the Previous Age, preferring to use his money to pay people to do things for him. However, he'd always felt there were basic things about saws and hammers that, as a man, he should know. He had already discovered a large storeroom full of all sorts of tools, and he headed there now to see what was available.

He was surprised to find another man already there. The man nodded at him and went back to scanning the walls where the tools were hanging.

Yuri felt self-conscious having company, as he was aware he didn't know what he needed. He was further vexed to see the man reach out and with both hands lift down the biggest saw from the wall.

"You ok?" the man asked Yuri, as he turned to go

"I'm ok," Yuri replied curtly, but then, before he had time to overthink it, he added, "What are you going to use that saw for?"

"Cutting down trees. I'm going to make some furniture."

"Ok, that's… good." Yuri searched for a response, wanting to be agreeable without appearing too interested.

The man smiled.

"I'm Angush," he said and held out a hand.

Yuri swung his hand into the man's and clenched it tight. Angush didn't seek to match his grip, which made Yuri feel rather foolish.

"Would you like a hand with the trees?" Yuri surprised himself with the question.

Angush smiled and made a brief bow. "I would very much appreciate that."

# Fran: New Neighbours

There was nothing to object to, and Fran knew it. The village always looked beautiful, and even though some people let their front gardens become overgrown, the wildflowers and long grass were a mass of fragrant colour that attracted a multitude of bees and butterflies. Yet Fran still felt a grumbling irritation with life and the need to kick against anything she could. Anger and cynicism formed the lens through which she viewed the world, although some days she glimpsed the possibility of a different perspective if she could just bring herself to choose it.

Fran finished her nettle tea and looked down into the mug.

"I just find her rather intimidating."

"How about your other new neighbours? Have you talked to them at all?" replied Carlos from across the kitchen table.

"I haven't. I don't miss the old lot, but I'm not too keen on these new folk either. There are all sorts out there."

"Yes, they come from many different backgrounds and cultures. Why not try just saying hello?"

"Ok," said Fran reluctantly. "Maybe I need to get over how this particular woman looks. It's just that I've never met someone who shaves her head and wears clothes like that. I mean, we had Asians in our neighbourhood, but at least they came from the British Empire. Not that we mixed with them."

"That may be true, but people's appearance is just the surface level."

That evening, after Carlos had left, Fran decided to go for a walk around the village. As she was nearing the end of the row of cottages, she saw the woman with the shaven head and full-length robes collecting apples and plums from the fruit trees. Fran hesitated but decided to approach her. The woman looked up and put down her basket.

"Good evening," she said softly.

"Hello," Fran replied in like manner, remaining at a distance.

"Won't you come and gather with me?" asked the woman.

Fran drew nearer, but stopped after a few steps. She felt apprehensive and somewhat embarrassed.

"My name is Chesa," said the woman, who had not broken eye contact with Fran since noticing her.

"I'm Fran. I live just down… well… of course I live right here… in the village. I was in a similar village before. I'm just… trying to adjust to the new setting.

Fran stopped, realising she was talking too fast.

"I have come from a Buddhist community to this place."

"Oh, I see. Have you met Sylvia and Carlos? They're annoying, but everyone can get on people's nerves sometimes. I mean we're all here and we're never going to die, so I guess we all have to get used to each other sooner or later…"

Fran wanted to kick herself for talking so much.

"How are you feeling?" asked the woman. Fran found her question a little strange.

"I think I'm well, thank you," she said politely. "How are you?"

"I am looking forward to eating these," she replied.

"Of course, that's why you're here in the orchard. It's funny, isn't it? I mean, we don't die if we don't eat, but food here tastes good, so it's like…"

Chesa picked up her basket and beckoned warmly for Fran to follow her.

"And where are you from?"

"I'm from London in England. Twentieth century. How about you?"

"I come from the eighteenth century, from a country you would know as Tibet. We met English missionaries who taught us your language. We welcomed foreigners to our monastery. We learnt many languages from those who stayed with us and much about the different religions."

Fran recalled how she had felt toward 'foreigners' in the Previous Age. A Bangladeshi family had moved in across the road from them in the 1960s, and she felt a sudden rush of shame as she remembered how she had called them names behind their backs and how white children had thrown stones at them.

"Well, it's certainly strange that we're all here together now, isn't it?" she said, trying to change the subject.

"Yes, I wasn't sure what to expect after death, but our traditions taught us to focus on the inner self and to pursue that which is holy and pure. We certainly came to believe that the divine nature was bringing us towards love and light, as we often experienced this in our meditations. How about you? Were you a Christian there in England?"

"Yes of course," replied Fran abruptly. "I was a warden for several years at my church. I did the flowers every other week as well."

"I'm sorry, maybe I asked the question the wrong way," replied Chesa. "Did you follow Jesus there in England?"

"Well, I thought I did. Then I died and met Jesus, and now I'm very confused. I have to admit I don't like him that much after all. Turns out I was rather mistaken with what I thought. That's why I'm here, and I guess that's the same for you."

"Yes, the same. It's the same for all," said Chesa. "There is much to learn. You... me... much to learn."

"Well, do you know what? I'd like to teach God a few things too." Fran gave vent to the feelings of irritation and annoyance that were always simmering below the surface.

Chesa didn't answer, but continued to walk slowly, looking at the ground.

"I've just remembered, I need to go and sort something out at my cottage."

"Yes," said Chesa without looking up.

"Yeah… sorry. Maybe another time?"

"Goodbye, Fran."

Fran pulled away, not looking back to see Chesa wave goodbye.

"Smart-arse!" she muttered to herself. "I don't need another bloody guru."

# Enjoying the Eternal City

A cheer erupted around the stadium.

Bull punched the air with one fist and flung his other arm around Harmony's neck. Harmony had never been to a football game before and wasn't sure of all the rules, but she was revelling in the unbridled enthusiasm on display.

Teams were organised on an ad-hoc basis with those who had signed up choosing a coloured shirt when they arrived. Matches were always enjoyed by both the players and the crowd, many of whom came several nights a week to watch the game and spend time with friends. Women and men played together, their resurrection bodies of equal strength and ability.

Jesus had overseen the development of each village, small town and city area, he had included architectural ideas from the wide range of human civilisations across history. Structures were mainly grouped together with others of a similar style with the natural environment complementing the buildings and often intertwining with them to create unique new dwellings. More akin to a country than a city, the Eternal City sprawled across the New Earth in such a way that no one could quite comprehend its vast expanse.

There were angels everywhere, fun and sometimes mischievous, regularly making people laugh. Unlike the image that had been prevalent in the Previous Age, angels were not always dressed in white robes with feathered wings protruding from their backs. Most usually chose to wear ordinary, practical clothes, but they were identified by a sash across their chests.

Many of the inhabitants of the City had suffered terribly in the Previous Age but had followed Ruach's leading through their trials. Some had been faithful followers of Jesus' teaching as it echoed through the centuries, while others had not heard his name but had responded to the call of *agape love* within their hearts.

Each community in the City contained centres of learning with large and spacious classrooms where people could learn about other cultures, languages and customs. This greatly helped them to serve in the many different communities on the New Earth beyond the City's walls. People from every tribe and nation offered classes where their experience and insights were passed on. Classes were places where friendships and laughter were shared and deeply healing discussions could take place.

Music echoed down many of the streets and could be heard from open doorways, parks and gardens. There was a place for every kind of music to be performed, from Dixieland jazz to chamber string quartets, and from hip-hop beats to Gregorian chants. People played instruments for pleasure in their dwellings, while others danced and moved to the rhythms they could hear.

Culinary aromas wafted along the streets of urban areas. Cuisine from every age and from all around the world was being prepared constantly, but with succulent plant-based versions where meat had once been used. Animals were no longer killed for food, and food was no longer eaten for survival. Eating was for pleasure, social interaction and sheer exploration of flavour.

As a young boy, Bull had once visited a five-star hotel with his grandparents. During their brief stay, he had marvelled at the incredible choice of dishes laid out in the buffet. He had wanted to try everything! His experience of the Eternal City had reignited and enhanced this sense of childish wonder and excitement.

Bull and Harmony were enjoying the buzz created by the sights and smells of the food stalls that lined the street as they walked back to their dwellings after the game had finished.

"Wow, these smell incredible - shall we get some?" Bull suggested as they stopped in front of a stall where steaming hot food was being prepared.

"Jerk wrap? Burritos?" asked the man behind the stall.

"Oh, I love that jerk marinade. Want one, Harmony?"

"I've never tried it, but I'll give it a go."

"How much?" asked Bull.

"One talent each," said the man with a sunny grin. "Best jerk in the City!"

With experienced hands, the man assembled two jerk wraps and handed them to Bull and Harmony, wrapped in large green leaves.

"Probably the only jerk in the City, right?" asked Bull.

"No. There's a brother the other side of the river with a jerk stall. He's amazing, but I like to think my recipe has just the edge," the man said proudly, handing Bull and Harmony some napkins.

"Thanks, mate," said Bull. "Where are you from?"

"Trinidad, twenty-first century. I came to the Eternal City at the beginning of this jubilee."

"Welcome home!" said Harmony.

"Sure is home! Jesus said I was ready and I'm so happy to be here."

"Where were you before? Which community?"

The man smiled. "When I was resurrected Jesus placed me in a community of former street children, all from the West Indies. We all knew how tough it was to grow up fending for ourselves."

"And you got here after just one jubilee?"

"Yes. As soon as I was raised, I knew Ruach was asking me to serve my new community by cooking for them. Back in Trinidad I'd used chicken and pork, but I discovered new plant-based recipes and opened a kitchen where I could train other people too."

"That's beautiful to hear, and this is truly delicious," said Harmony.

"I knew Ruach when I was on the streets in the Previous Age. I knew her as a warming presence in my chest that I could feel but couldn't see. Sometimes she felt like a strong emotion, and other times like an idea in my mind that somehow seemed to light up the way ahead. I knew she kept me from taking the wrong path and from doing harm to others, even though violence sometimes looked like the easiest way to get through."

"So, you could feel her guidance?" asked Bull.

"Yeah, I sure did. Every day. My mother told me about her and how I should listen to her voice before she died when I was seven."

"What's your name?" asked Harmony.

"Eddie," replied the man with a broad grin.

"Great to meet you, Eddie," said Harmony. "You've given us much hope for those in our communities today."

"It's so good to be reminded that there are people who are ready to enter the City, even after just one jubilee," said Bull as he and Harmony continued along the street, finishing off their tasty snack. "By the way, what time are we meeting Yvonne?"

"Oh, that's right. There's a composer giving a recital of a new work that Yvonne wanted to hear."

The two friends made their way through the City, taking time to enjoy and take in the various sights with dancing water features, huge rockeries full of flowers in bloom and avenues of ornamental trees. The atmosphere was peaceful in one area and full of mirth and merriment in another, yet everywhere felt friendly and welcoming.

\*

The recital ended in a thrilling crescendo of sound. The audience sat for a moment, enraptured, before everyone rose to their feet and applauded with huge enthusiasm.

"I've never heard anything like that before," said Bull, shaking his head in wonder.

"It's certainly been worth the long wait for a new work," said Yvonne, beaming at him as they continued to applaud the composer, who was gesturing for his orchestra to stand once again, showing them off with pride to the auditorium.

"One day I'll take you to hear some rock and roll," said Harmony. "You'll love Elvis!"

"Oh, I do love Elvis!" shouted Bull over the thunderous applause. "My dad used to play Elvis in the car when I was a boy. I wonder if he's here yet?"

"One day everyone will be here," laughed Harmony.

After the concert, the three of them walked back to their rooms animatedly discussing the genres of music they each preferred and making the very most of their last evening in the City before returning to their communities.

# Johan: Confrontation

Night was different on the New Earth. Colours still appeared and slowly evolved in the sky, but they were darker tones of purple and blue. The air was still, and Johan was glad that the temperature always remained at a comfortable level, even at night. Far off, unknown lights twinkled, but Johan felt completely alone.

He wasn't scared, as he knew the New Earth was safe, but there was a bleakness in his heart. Chester's words echoed in his mind as he strode out over rocks and heather in the half light. He felt shame and confusion over what he had learned from the Canadian, and he struggled to understand why Jesus would allow people who had been at war with one another in the Previous Age to be in the same community.

He cast his mind back to when billowing scarlet flags had hung from every house, a black swastika within a white circle adorning each one. As a boy, the swastika had reminded him of a squashed spider, and it had struck him as oddly fitting now that he knew that the twisted Nazi fantasy had been stamped out by the boots of the Allies. He remembered his Uncle Werner, a fanatical Nazi supporter, and how he had encouraged Johan to look up to the Fuhrer and, when he was old enough, to go and fight for the Reich.

He recalled the many nights he had spent in barracks, trenches and under canvas. He would lie awake listening to the other men talking, thinking about Uncle Werner and hoping he would be proud of his soldier nephew. Johan's mind would often turn to his

198

own father, a very different man of quiet thought, who only spoke when he had something to say. Johan's father had fought in the Great War twenty years earlier and had seen action on the Western Front. Johan adored his papa very much and when he was small had loved to sit on his lap and trace his fingers along the strange pink scars on his arm that were a permanent reminder of the shrapnel that had torn his flesh.

Johan longed for his papa to come and find him now. Looking out from a hilltop over the landscape, he felt as if he was the only person in existence. But at that moment a movement in the heather behind him made him swing around, and in the low light he could just make out the figure of a man with long white hair and a beard in a pale robe that reached to the ground. The man was looking at Johan and holding up both hands as if in surrender.

Johan's heart pounded at the shock of being disturbed, yet there was a reassuring warmth that radiated from the man's presence as he stood there, his hands now held out in front of him, as if he was offering Johan something.

"Hello?" said Johan, wondering if this was an appropriate greeting.

"Johan," replied the man.

"Do I know you?" asked Johan in surprise.

"You do... and you don't. I am here to assure you that you are never alone. You miss your father, and you mourn your life prior to coming here. In fact, you are ashamed of what took place."

Johan nodded but was perplexed by the stranger's knowledge.

"I am here to tell you that you are not to blame, and that you are loved and cherished."

"Cherished?" asked Johan, somewhat bemused. "Surely you have to be with the ones who love you to be cherished."

"You are with ones who love you. People who see the goodness within you."

Johan thought of Yan, Yvonne, and the friends he'd made like Ebo, Jemila and Eric.

"And you will see your parents again. You will see your army comrades and your uncle too. Everything will happen in its right time."

Johan felt a surge of love towards this kind old man who had come to him with these words of comfort.

"But how did you find me? And who are you?"

"I am a friend. I've known you for some time."

"But you are not Jesus?"

The old man smiled. "No, I lived on earth many years before Jesus was born. You may call me Mel."

"Mel?"

"Melchizedek, but I prefer Mel."

"What do you do? Do you go looking for people who are lost?"

"I meet people where they are," said Mel. "I love to wander the highways and byways of the New Earth encouraging those I find."

"How do you know these things about my life?" asked Johan.

"Ruach tells me anything I need to know. You might know her as 'the Holy Ghost'."

"I have heard of 'the Holy Ghost', and I met Ruach when Jesus resurrected me. Do you see her when you talk together?"

"She is with us all. She is spirit and so is everywhere. If you ask her, she will speak to you, too. It's as though we carry an invisible part of her within us; we just have to learn to hear her voice and use the gifts she gives."

"You make it sound easy," said Johan with a slight chuckle.

"Well, it starts with 'Hello', and you've proved you're good at that!"

Johan laughed. This unexpected encounter and the man's wisdom had lightened the darkness that had weighed on his heart and restored his sense of hope and belief that all would be well. As the man raised his hand in farewell, Johan knew that he must return to his community.

\*

Yan never rushed. Time has a very different quality when there is always another day. Remembering the constant worry of being caught by the secret police in the Previous Age, Yan compared his state of mind then with now. He had always been anxious, afraid not only for his own safety but of giving away information that might endanger his friends and family. Now he moved with confidence and intent. Johan was out there, and Yan's focus was to locate him and reassure him.

As the light began to change and evening fell, Yan felt an increasing sense of peace that Ruach was leading him to entrust Johan to her purposes and that he should end his search. Instead, Yan decided to use this opportunity to walk in the night air and draw near to Ruach in meditation.

A familiar warmth began to grow as he turned his full attention to the divine flame within him. Ruach was the essence of God that Yan related to the most. He had great reverence and affection for Jesus, but it was Ruach who had drawn alongside Yan when he had been imprisoned and tortured for his beliefs in the Previous Age.

During many dark nights in prison cells, her flame had burned, and he had experienced heavenly ecstasy as she poured love into his heart. Sometimes he had wondered if he could take any more of her glorious presence, and he had been known to break out into dancing, singing and shouting for joy, even in the midst of the dirt and stench of the prison.

\*

"Oh, you're back are you, Nazi?" sneered Chester, as he saw Johan next morning sitting at a table carving some wood with Yvonne

"Chester, I'd like to talk with you. Would you sit with me?"

"Fuck you!" came the response, as Chester spat and went on his way.

Johan looked helplessly at Yvonne, who gave him an empathetic smile. Some minutes went by as they continued their work, but despite his previous resolve, Johan could contain his frustration no longer.

"What am I supposed to do? I didn't start the war! And I didn't kill his friends! I lost my life in it, for Christ's sake. I'm more of a victim than *he* is!"

Johan threw down his tools and stormed off. Seeing Chester coiling some rope in the distance, Johan strode towards him, still seething. The closer he got, the more he was consumed by the injustice of the situation.

"Chester!"

Chester turned around, surprised.

"Don't you see? I'm a victim of that war even more than you are. You have no idea..."

Chester dropped the rope and stepped towards Johan.

"No, you bastard, *you* have no idea. Millions of people killed in your death camps?"

Johan felt winded.

"But I didn't know!" he protested.

"You disgust me."

"What do you want from me? To hear me say that I'm sorry? Well, I *am* sorry. I'm sorry for the whole damned lot of it. I'm sorry that I died, and that I was on the wrong side of it. Don't you think you were just lucky? I mean, you could just as easily have been born where I was, and I might just as easily have been born where you were."

Chester threw out his arms. "Look at all this? Don't you believe in God now? Don't you think it's clear that God made us and put us where he wanted us on the Earth?"

"Yes, but I don't think God made me to be caught up in the Third Reich. And I don't think God determined that I should die in a war. What kind of God would make that happen?"

"A sovereign one," retorted Chester.

"So sovereign that all kinds of evil happen all the time?" asked Johan, becoming emotional.

"If that is God's will."

"And yet here we are now. You believe certain things and I don't - but we've both ended up together in the same place."

Chester hesitated. "Yeah, but I'm here and not in the Eternal City because of the things I did wrong, so you must be too."

"So, the things you did wrong must be as bad as me being a Nazi?"

Chester looked flummoxed.

"According to your logic, I'm evil and guilty of genocide, and somehow you're better than me. Yet here we both are - in the same place. So, what did you do that was as bad as being a Nazi?"

Chester made no reply.

"Come on, Chester. Let's at least talk this through together?"

"Not interested," said Chester with a shrug of his shoulders. He picked up the rope and began coiling it again.

Johan's hands fell to his sides in exasperation. He turned and walked away.

*

A few days later Johan was thumbing through the first few pages of the thick tome that Yan had presented him with. His forehead was furrowed as he skim-read the text.

Yan stood leaning on a chair on the other side of the table.

"Who wrote this?" asked Johan.

"Angelic observers. They have written accounts of human history since the beginning. This one details Europe in the first half of the twentieth century."

"Why? Didn't God see what was happening?"

"It's not for God's use. It's so that people can learn about the Previous Age. It's for moments like this one. It's simply a report from an objective and unbiased viewpoint of what happened. Jesus trusts that this can bring insight and understanding to those with open hearts"

Johan closed the book and sat back, taking a deep breath.

Yan came around the table.

"I know it will be a hard read, but just remember that every life that was lost is being raised to an abundant future. No one is lost forever."

"But that doesn't take away the immense suffering, does it?"

"No, but we have the ages ahead of us to heal all the wounds that were sustained in those days. The infinite life ahead of us means that eventually the years spent in the Previous Age will be swallowed up. A tennis ball might feel large in your hand, but next to a planet it doesn't seem so big, does it? And compared with the universe, well, you get the idea. It's the same with eternity and all the ages to come. It will put everything into perspective."

"I guess my task is to try and understand and move forward?"

"As you progress and immerse yourself in new experiences, you will be able to see the past in a new light. It takes time to trust the vantage point from which we can now view the Previous Age. Don't worry, Johan, just trust the process."

Johan nodded and re-opened the book.

*

Months turned into years. As Johan studied, he became deeply familiar with twentieth-century history. The knowledge he acquired gave him the tools to better understand his own story, as well as the experience and attitudes of others who lived through those tumultuous decades.

For a long time, Chester resisted the invitations that Johan gave him to come and discuss these matters. However, one day as the wind was blowing across the grassy plains, Johan glanced up from his book to see Chester's face looking in through his window.

Johan smiled and gestured for Chester to enter. Chester opened the door and stood at the threshold.

"Ok, Johan. We need to talk."

"You are welcome, Chester. Come in and take a seat," said Johan, motioning toward the chair next to him.

Chester hesitated but slowly made his way across the room to the chair.

"Are you ok?" asked Johan, noting his reticence.

"I think you will understand what I have to say."

Johan was struck by the change in Chester's demeanour. It was the first time he had shown any sign of vulnerability. In fact, his face betrayed such a clear sense of discomfort that he appeared to be in physical pain.

Chester sat down stiffly.

"Recently I asked an angel to supply me with one of their observation books. I got a book on the history of Canada. It seems... it was not what I was expecting. I knew about the wars between the British and the French in Canada but we weren't taught at school about the indigenous peoples and how we took their land so that many of them died from disease and starvation. And it wasn't just what happened a long time ago. During my grandparents' and my parents' generations, children were taken from their families and sent to boarding schools where they weren't allowed to speak their own language or learn anything about their own culture. Dreadful things happened to them in some of those places. And Johan, it was still going on when I was alive... and I didn't know about it."

Johan closed the book he had been reading and the two began to talk. Over the next few hours tears were shed. After they had shared a simple supper Chester had no hesitation in accepting Johan's invitation to stay the night. He felt totally understood, humbled and welcomed. The two men slept more soundly than they had done for a long while.

# Fran: Trying Harder

Fran sat with her arms folded tightly over her chest. Nothing about her posture was relaxed.

"There's really no other way," said Sylvia as gently as she could.

"Right, I see. Well, obviously I must try harder then!"

With that, Fran stood up and walked out of the room.

Sylvia turned to Carlos and said nothing, her caring expression needed no words.

"If that's her approach, it will only set her back. She'll be further from the Eternal City than ever," sighed Carlos. "You can't just *try harder* there."

"Yes, loving others takes effort and determination, but it also needs a change of heart. It can't just be a performance to tick the right boxes. Anyway, let's wait and see what happens. It may be that Ruach can use Fran's mixed motives for her good."

"Ruach does that a lot," Carlos agreed. "We've explained to Fran many times that love is the only way to the City, so let's hope she can begin to grasp what that means in this new situation."

*

On the way back to her cottage, Fran took a moment to stand with her hands on her hips. Feeling young again was still a delight, and she regularly paused during the day to feel the power in her resurrected body. She thought about her conversation with Sylvia and Carlos and mulled over the idea of 'love' as she surveyed her

207

new community. She cast her mind back to the Previous Age and remembered how she had sometimes dropped a few coins into the collections taken by the Salvation Army for their work with the homeless. They had been kindly folk in uniforms who had stood shaking a bucket in her local high street as the brass band played. That seemed to Fran like a great way to show love. Maybe she could do something similar?

Feeling pleased with her new idea, Fran returned home and sat at her table with a notepad determined to make a plan. She found it surprisingly difficult to think of many needs here on the New Earth, since there was no more death or disease, disability or depravation. But then her thoughts turned to Chesa, the Buddhist lady who collected fruit in a small wicker basket. If she had a more efficient way of transporting her foraging, maybe Chesa could start a business and trade her fruit on a much greater scale? Suddenly she pictured a wheelbarrow. Maybe someone in the village who was good at woodwork could be commissioned to make one. What a perfect solution for the Buddhist and so much better than her small basket!

For the rest of the morning, Fran was happily engrossed in making a large banner using lots of bright colours. "Wheelbarrows for Buddhists!' it read. She could already picture herself as the centre of attention at the next weekly market, and imagining how grateful and loved Chesa would feel gave her a warm, fuzzy feeling inside.

A few days later, Fran hung up her banner at the market and stood under it, excited to drum up support for her charitable endeavour. It didn't take long for a small group of people to gather.

"What on the New Earth is this?" one laughed.

"It's my new charity. Some of us are more caring than others," replied Fran smugly.

"'Wheelbarrows for Buddhists'? That's the worst cause I've ever heard of in this age or the previous one! Why do Buddhists need wheelbarrows? And why should you be the one to get them for them?"

"Well, you may not have noticed, but Chesa goes out collecting fruit and she only has a basket. It takes love to notice people's needs, I'll have you know!"

"Ha!" scoffed another woman. "I'm going to enjoy watching this disaster unfold."

"If you're not interested in helping, then I suggest you move along and make room for those who understand what it means to love their neighbour," snapped Fran.

The onlookers shook their heads and wandered away. Fran cleared her throat self-consciously and continued standing under her banner, a notebook at the ready to take down the details of anyone who wished to join her cause.

Chesa was busy swapping fruit and vegetables at various stalls and other women were helping to find and pass the items used in the exchanges. As she worked her way along the row of stalls towards where Fran was standing, she looked up and was bemused to read Fran's banner.

Chesa calmly approached Fran, one eyebrow raised and smiling.

"Hello Fran. How are you?"

Fran grinned back. "Oh, I am just *fine,* thank you, Chesa. I see you have noticed my new charity?"

"Well, yes I have. Can you tell me what it's about? I see you have mentioned Buddhists?"

"Well yes, of course. This charity is to help you!" beamed Fran.

"Well, I am touched, so tell me more about it."

"You only have a basket, right? Imagine how much more fruit you could collect if you had a wheelbarrow. It would make life much easier for you and you could even set up a proper business. My charity is here to help you, so don't worry, you don't need to do a thing. We'll get you a wheelbarrow without you needing to give anything in exchange."

Chesa was taken aback but managed not to show her surprise.

"Right, I see. That's a very kind thought."

"Oh, you're welcome. I know that some of our technology in the West might be new to you, but in England we always use wheelbarrows for gardening and transporting all kinds of things."

"No, it's not new to me," replied Chesa, unable to suppress her laughter. "I don't mean to be rude or ungrateful, Fran, but I don't need your help, thank you. I use a simple basket because I don't want to take more than my fair share of what is growing on the trees as it belongs to everyone in the community. Besides, I think my next-door neighbour already has a wheelbarrow in her garden. I'm sure I could borrow it if I really needed one."

Fran suddenly felt very foolish. With an angry red blush on her cheeks, she turned around, tore down the banner and stuffed it into her bag.

"You should be grateful," she muttered under her breath.

Chesa heard her and put a hand gently on Fran's shoulder. Fran shrugged it off and stormed off home.

"Told you!" shouted one of the women who had watched the whole exchange.

Fran felt both crushed and ashamed. Slamming the door behind her, she slumped into a chair. "God, I hate it here!" she cried as the tears rolled down her cheeks.

*

Fran remained in an angry mood for several months. Chesa smiled and tried to make conversation whenever they met around the village, but Fran did her best to avoid everyone, feeling embarrassed and resentful at the "Wheelbarrows for Buddhists" episode.

One afternoon Fran felt so desperate that she decided to visit Sylvia.

"Is there really no way to get out of here?" she asked belligerently. "What if I just kept walking? Where would I get to?"

Sylvia looked thoughtfully at Fran's strained and angry face before replying.

"Every person on the New Earth is assigned a place to live in each jubilee. There are no spare dwellings for you to move to. But you will be in a different community in the next jubilee period."

Fran thought for a minute.

"The next jubilee is years away. What if I could find out where my daughter and my son are living? Could I move in with one of them?"

"That's a lovely thought, but I don't know if your children have been raised yet, and even if they have, there's no way of knowing where on the New Earth they might be."

"Well then, I'll ask Jesus!" snapped Fran. "If he's my personal Saviour, shouldn't I be able to make an appointment with him?"

"I take your point," said Sylvia, "but I'm afraid it doesn't work quite like that. You see, Jesus has many people to care for, and he is busy welcoming more people to the New Earth and determining the populations of the next communities. But I'm sure you will see him again at some point. Jesus is just one man and can only be in one place at a time."

"Pah! But he's 'God', isn't he?"

"Yes, but he is also a man and can't be everywhere," explained Sylvia gently. "But you know you can always talk to Ruach, don't you?"

Fran suddenly became very still. A new and troubling thought had crossed her mind.

"Hang on," she said, with trepidation in her voice. "My son and my daughter... what if they are in a place worse than here? They didn't reckon much to churchgoing in the Previous Age, so what if they are in a proper hell? Maybe even in a lake of fire?"

Sylvia put a comforting hand on Fran's forearm.

"No one is in a lake of fire, Fran. You're remembering language from the Bible that was always meant to be symbolic, not literal. But it's true that people experience fiery trials to help them mature and prepare them for life in the Eternal City."

"Oh yes," sighed Fran, suddenly sounding weary and deflated. "I sometimes forget that this really is it. *This* is the afterlife and I am stuck here. There may not be actual flames, but ..."

"Fran, what would you say are the fiery trials you are facing at the moment?" asked Sylvia gently.

"Well, my neighbour is a real bitch and thinks she's better than I am in every conceivable way. And that bloody Buddhist! She's the most patronising, condescending person I've ever met. I hate this community. I'm bored of the food. Basically, I'm fed up with everything."

"I see."

Fran was annoyed by Sylvia's seeming ambivalence.

"You just don't care!" she muttered.

"I do care and I am listening," said Sylvia. "I'm here with you, and you can tell me anything."

"Well, it's alright for you, isn't it? You love it here!"

"You're right, I do. I love this village and I love being with everyone here."

"So you don't have any of these trials you've been talking about?"

"I do, and I have done," said Sylvia, in such a firm tone that Fran was a little surprised.

"So why aren't you as pissed off as I am?"

"Honestly? I think it's about attitude," Sylvia replied. "I trust that all will be well. Everything that isn't ok just hasn't got there yet."

Fran looked at Sylvia in disbelief.

"Oh, come on!" she groaned. "It cannot be that simple."

"Well, I think it is. You see, I have experienced what *agape love* can do. I've seen how it heals and transforms. Trust me, I suffered in the Previous Age, and I wasn't always like this. But I have seen how love can make everything beautiful."

"Ok, but right now, I have all this stuff going on that is such a pain in the neck."

"So, what can you do?" asked Sylvia.

"What can *I* do?"

"Yes, what can you do?"

"What *can* I do?" retorted Fran. "What can I *do*?"

It was this question that Fran continued to roll around in her mind, placing the emphasis on each word in turn, as she walked home after having vented more of her frustrations on Sylvia.

Later that evening, as Fran sat in her living room, practicing some calligraphy, it seemed to her that she somehow felt calmer and not quite so resentful. Carefully placing her ink pen in its holder, she sat back and folded her arms over her chest. It began to dawn on her that maybe she had more power to choose her attitude in life than she had previously realised. She thought back to her meeting with Jesus and all the talks she had had with Sylvia and Carlos. Maybe they weren't just trying to coerce her into behaving a certain way but were trying to show her that she had all the means within herself to love herself and others. She began to imagine how life might be if she was no longer imprisoned within her own defensiveness and resentment.

The next morning, she felt lighter inside and realised that she didn't want to continue avoiding people. She decided to head out in search of company and conversation.

*

Fran spotted Chesa in her bright orange robes on the far side of a nearby lake. She waved a few times to try and attract her attention, but she was too engrossed in picking elderflowers to notice.

Fran looked at the water. It was a warm day and it looked cool and inviting. The thought of popping up on the far shore and surprising Chesa filled her with a childlike sense of mischief. Why not? She felt a surge of exhilaration as she entered the water and felt the power of her body propelling her forwards with strong strokes. After several minutes, her feet touched the shingle of the lake bed and she strode out onto the shore.

Hearing the splashes, Chesa turned to see Fran laughing and giggling as she waded out of the water, fully clothed and dripping from head to toe.

Chesa came towards her, as surprised by Fran's smiling face as by her watery appearance.

"You funny girl!" she exclaimed. "What are you doing?"

"Well, I saw you on the other side of the lake and wanted to say hello, but you didn't notice me. So… here I am!" Fran laughed.

Chesa put her arm around Fran's soaking wet shoulders. "It's good to see you laugh and smile. Would you like to come and join me? I'm going to make elderflower cordial and we can find you some dry clothes."

"Thank you," Fran replied with a smile. "I'd like that."

# Adilah: Do I Have to Like Them?

Adilah and Anne had become the primary woodworkers for their community. Every evening they spent time making chairs, tables and shelving.

"There was a time I would have thought that only men could do this kind of thing," said Adilah, blowing away wood-dust from the plank she was sanding. "We weren't allowed to touch any tools, other than the things we needed for cooking. I guess the militia were worried we might use them to attack them."

Anne nodded but kept her eyes on the table leg she was nailing into place. "I had to learn some of these skills when I was a little girl, but I never got to use them much once I became a wife. But here we are, and we can make so many things."

Anne hammered home the last nail and turned the table over.

"There, that looks good to me," she said with a sense of satisfaction.

She glanced up and immediately recognised the expression on Adilah's face.

"Are you ok?"

"It's just... whenever something sparks a memory of those men, the militia, I feel so many things. I feel angry, and worried. I know in my head they aren't here and that I'm safe, but I feel they don't deserve to be raised and live again... at all."

"I can understand that, Adilah, and the important thing is that you are honest. As you know, I was killed by a mob of men in the Previous Age. When I was raised, I had to learn to trust again. It was difficult, but I knew it was something I had to do."

"Were you able to forgive those men who killed you?" asked Adilah.

"I think there are levels of forgiveness. First, there is the decision not to hate, and then there is the decision to let go of any desire for revenge. Both of those stages took a long time and many tears as I gradually allowed *agape love* to change my heart. It was only then that I felt ready and able to connect with those who had hurt me - reconciliation, I guess. In my experience, forgiveness is one of the hardest but also one of the most divinely inspired things we can learn."

"I am not there yet," said Adilah quietly. "Whenever I see their faces in my mind, I still want to hurt them. I want them to feel the fear we felt."

"Well, at least you are able to identify where you are on the journey, and that's really positive. And you know, you don't ever have to like them."

"But... I thought I had to love them?"

"Forgiveness is part of *agape love* - it flows from it. But that's not the same as having a personal friendship with someone. No one is asking you to be friends with everyone in the world. We will always have a circle of people we are close to and feel comfortable with. But with more than a hundred billion people coming to live on the New Earth, it will be impossible to be close friends with everyone. But it will be possible to treat everyone we come across with an attitude of *agape love.*"

"You know, Anne, that makes sense and it makes me feel better about it."

"Yes, it's good to know that no one is expecting us to 'cuddle up' to those who abused and hurt us. When we are all together in the

Eternal City, you may never even see them. But, if you do, you will be ready and you'll know what to do. Ruach, the one you call 'Friend', will guide you."

"Well, I want to be ready, but I don't want to pretend."

"That's good," Anne reassured her. "We certainly cannot trick Jesus or Ruach. They know when we are ready to be invited, and it will take just the right amount of time for each person. A heart that wants to progress and desires to be in the Eternal City has much to gain. It's just that Ruach can see if someone is genuinely wanting to live by *agape love* or if they are seeking rewards for themselves."

"I know I can't trick Ruach. She searches my heart for truth," agreed Adilah.

"Ruach is always working from and towards *agape love*. That is the very essence of God. Papa God, Jesus and Ruach cannot be or do anything else."

"But I feel we have the choice of whether we follow their way or not. We know the way they want us to go, but they don't demand it, do they?"

"Indeed, that's why it's always an *invitation*. Nothing is forced, nothing is coerced. *Agape love* is like an open door and we can choose to go through it or not, but the more we act in love, the more natural it becomes for us. Like anything, it takes time to learn and practice. You may find regular meditation helps - thirty minutes each day just being quiet and still."

Adilah looked over to where Eshe was building the fire with some of the other women.

"My sister," said Adilah, nodding in Eshe's direction, "she taught me to how to love, even in the darkest place."

"Sometimes that's where love shines the brightest, isn't it? Love can exist in the most dreadful suffering and bring meaning and hope. There have been countless attempts to stamp love out, but it has never worked. Love is strong, even though it can appear weak."

Adilah nodded, still looking at Eshe. "We were weak, we had no power, and we were captives. But we could still love each other."

Eshe noticed Adilah looking at her and waved at her sister. She crossed her eyes, poked out her tongue and laughed.

\*

It had not taken long at the beginning of the new jubilee period for the community to settle into a regular routine with the women initially gravitating towards the jobs they knew well and felt confident doing. As the months and years went by, many of the women took on the challenge of different tasks and began to learn new skills, partly for the sake of variety in their daily lives, but also from the desire to get to know others in the community through working together.

The tree-top houses were comfortable homes, and many of the friendliest animals came to share these dwellings with the women. Bush babies, koalas, pandas, sloths and all kinds of birds became part of everyday life, bringing much delight to the community.

"The bush babies are overeating," remarked Eshe to Adilah one morning.

"How do you know?" asked Adilah.

"Look at their poo. Their tummies are upset. I think we should ask everyone to stop giving them treats from the food that we eat," continued Eshe, her hands on her hips.

Later, Adilah spoke to Anne.

"We love our animal neighbours and don't want to do anything to harm them, but we've got to learn what is best for them," explained Adilah.

Anne nodded. "Yes, we need to be good stewards of creation even here on the New Earth. There may no longer by any disease or death, but we still have a duty of care towards all the living things around us."

"That was always our job, wasn't it?"

"It was meant to be. But in the Previous Age we forgot that caring for the Earth is one of the ways that we look after ourselves. We now know that we need Ruach's guidance to care for creation in the best possible way."

"And animals care for us in their own way, too," Adilah remarked.

"Yes, they do. They bring their special wonder to creation, and they bring us comfort and delight and help us in our work."

"It's best when we can work together with them to look after our world," said Adilah.

"That is certainly the most beautiful way for us to be with our animal friends," agreed Anne.

Eshe approached them, drying her hands with a cloth. "I've looked into it and I reckon we've been giving them too many sugary things from the food we make."

From then on, everyone in the community was careful not to give the bush babies snacks meant for human stomachs. Instead, some of the women spent time developing a range of new snacks based on the bush babies' natural diet so that everyone could still enjoy giving them the occasional treat.

# Yuri: Rage and Disgust

Angush was clearly an experienced carpenter. Yuri watched him closely, mentally noting how he used the tools. Over the course of the morning, Angush and Yuri had felled two big pine trees. Yuri was used to physical work, but the constant sawing to clear the branches from the trunk was tiring, even for a resurrected body. The two men worked in silence, content not to talk but to focus on the work in hand. After several hours Angush looked up and Yuri met his eye. They seemed to have had the same thought at the same moment.

With a smile, Angush put down his end of the two-man saw, and Yuri followed suit.

"Let's take a break."

Yuri suspected that Angush was hoping to gain the upper hand by being the one to make the suggestion.

"Ok, this way," gestured Yuri, trying to assert himself.

Angush shrugged and followed Yuri below the tree line and across a small field to a spring. Both men drank from cupped hands and splashed their faces with the cold water that bubbled up from the ground.

"Tell me about yourself," suggested Angush as he sat on the mossy bank.

Yuri immediately felt uncomfortable.

"I don't know what to tell you," Yuri replied, concealing his embarrassment.

"Well, where are you from?"

"Russia. Twenty-first century."

"What did you do?"

Yuri felt, for the first time, a twinge deep down in his stomach. It was a strange, knotted feeling. How could he describe what he had done? He didn't want to go into details and tell this new acquaintance about his past.

"I did a lot of things. I did what it took to survive."

"I see."

"And you?" said Yuri, hoping to deflect the conversation.

"I sold the best quality opium in the world," replied Angush without a moment's hesitation, making an 'ok' sign with both his hands.

"Yeah?" Yuri was suddenly interested.

"Yes. Pakistan, Afghanistan, India."

"But you've got skills, and I reckon you've been educated too."

"That's true. But I saw an opportunity. My family were rich from the weapons trade. I just saw a way to make even more money. I was able to pay private security to protect me and the trade routes."

"We sold heroin and cocaine across Eastern Europe, and we sold girls too." said Yuri, still feeling uncomfortable but not wishing to be outdone.

"Just girls?" asked Angush with a slightly raised eyebrow.

"Sometimes boys."

"Yes, there was good money to be made from children. We sold some to pimps in Thailand. War orphans. Easy."

Yuri hadn't thought about the children he had sold into sexual slavery for a long time. He felt suddenly hot and nauseous as he remembered how they had cried when they were bundled off and sold to strangers.

"Heroin to the West was the best money though," continued Angush, who seemed almost wistful as he talked about his previous life. "America wasn't so easy for me, but Europe? No problem."

Yuri tried to converse with similar ease, but he was surprised at how much he didn't want to think about his life in the Previous Age.

"I bet you've got some stories to tell, seeing as you're here?" smirked Angush.

"I saw things. I did things. That's all." Yuri felt any energy for the conversation draining away as in his mind he saw the faces of frightened children being loaded into lorries bound for brothels in nearby cities.

"I enjoyed the money and I lived a long and happy life," mused Angush. "And it's not so bad being here. I like being alive again. Jesus was rather underwhelming though, wasn't he? Pathetic really."

Unexpectedly, Yuri found these words jarring. Despite walking out on Jesus, thinking of him now made Yuri feel strangely emotional.

"Underwhelming? How so?"

"Well, he welcomed me and wasn't unpleasant, but he was - I don't know... I couldn't get him to laugh with me, you know?"

"I don't think I tried," murmured Yuri, without irony.

"I like to laugh. It feels good not to have a care in the world."

Yuri was disturbed by Angush. Despite everything Yuri had done, he had never thought of his dealings as amusing. There had been very little happiness in his life and any pleasure had been fleeting and empty. All the suffering he had seen and inflicted on others had been rooted in misery. It was all he knew and looking back now, he realised that he hated his life. But here was a man who seemed to feel no disgust or shame for what he had done. Yuri felt as though a mirror had been held up, and for the first time he genuinely felt hatred for what he saw. Gone was

222

the numbness that had enveloped him in the first jubilee. Here was something new and visceral.

Angush continued. "Isn't it good to feel so free? Jesus makes everyone alive again, so all's well that ends well, isn't that what they say? Turns out it didn't matter what happened to those snotty-nosed kids, not that it bothered me anyway."

Yuri felt rage this time - rage toward Angush and a new, searing hatred toward himself. There were images of children in Yuri's head that made him want to vomit.

"You're very quiet, Yuri?"

"Well, we weren't all born with a fucking silver spoon in our mouths. I haven't felt happy for a single day of my life. I don't know how you can laugh things off like that. You must be some kind of psychopath."

Angush laughed in Yuri's face. "Oh, I'm so sorry. I think you're jealous because I don't give a fuck!"

Something in Yuri snapped. The machete that he had used for hacking branches lay on the ground beside him. He grabbed it and before Angush could defend himself, swung the blade into the left side of his head. Angush stumbled to his feet but a forceful push from Yuri sent him backwards into the stream where he lay writhing in the water, his hands clutching at his head.

Yuri turned his back and walked away, his whole body shaking with hatred and revulsion for Angush - and himself.

"Fuck you, Angush, fuck you," he hissed under his breath, over and over.

Arriving back at his dwelling, Yuri slumped in the chair. His fists were still balled tight and his whole body was tensed. Blood had soaked into his shirt in dark crimson blotches.

'I'm not like him. I'm better than he is. I'm going to make sure he knows it,' Yuri thought as he skulked in the growing gloom of the day.

Eventually he became aware of a commotion somewhere not far away. He heard shouts and banging on doors. The sounds drew closer until fists were beating on Yuri's door. Taking the machete in his hand again, Yuri pulled the door open roughly.

A man stood there. It was clear it was not Angush.

"Let me inside," he hissed urgently.

Yuri looked the man up and down. "No, get out of my doorway!"

"I think you'll want to hear what I have to say. I'm not here for Angush."

Yuri hesitated but then flicked his head and the man followed him inside, keeping a wary eye on the weapon in Yuri's hand.

"Listen, I know what you did to Angush today. I'm glad about it. I've also felt I'd like to kill that man."

"Why?"

"Angush isn't like the rest of us. He never had to fight for survival like we did. He boasts about the pain he caused and he doesn't play fair."

"It's true," said Yuri. "He's just another rich boy who spent his life playing with his daddy's money."

"Many of us here hate him," said the man, "but no one apart from you has done anything about it. Angush needs to know that we don't respect his type here. We'll follow you, Yuri. You just need to say when and where."

Yuri felt a glow of pride and vindication. "Sit down and tell me your name," he said, motioning toward a chair.

# The Second Jubilee Reviewed

"You're a talented chef," said Jesus, picking up the last dish from the draining board. "Thank you for cooking for us, Bull."

"Excellent meal," agreed Sylvia. "We'll leave you guys to it."

Jesus nodded, smiling warmly at Thomas' team who had come back together for the end-of-jubilee feast. The others headed out to enjoy a walk around the local area, leaving Thomas and Bull with Jesus for an evaluation of the last fifty years. Jesus poured some fresh lemonade into glasses on a tray.

"Let's go into the sitting room," he said. Bull and Thomas put the last of the clean crockery away and followed him.

"Tell me, Jesus, what was your thinking behind placing Angush in the same community as Yuri and the others?" asked Bull. "I must admit I'm still rather perplexed after living the last fifty years with them."

Jesus smiled and handed the glasses to the two men as they took their seats. "Angush had a heart that was still immersed in evil. He needed to be confronted by his peers – men who came from a similarly violent background. In the first jubilee, it was clear that Yuri was still attached to violence and delighted in the suffering of others. Do you remember when Cedric had to intervene?"

Thomas and Bull nodded.

"The only way Yuri could come to recognise the darkness in his own heart was to meet someone even more attached to evil and violence than himself. Through meeting and talking with Angush, Yuri realised that deep down he was disgusted by what Angush had done in the Previous Age and his lack of remorse. This was the starting point that enabled him to see himself differently and to see who he could be."

"And Angush?" asked Bull.

"Angush had never once been challenged about what he had done. After Yuri began to stand up to him, he began to deconstruct the narrative he had created for himself. He was used to being liked by others and making people laugh along with him."

"I see," said Bull. "So when the other men began to call out his attitude and the laughter stopped, he had to ask himself who he really was and what his life was about. He became very withdrawn and quiet when people in the community turned against him, and it's been sad to see how he's become increasingly embittered and lonely as the years have gone by."

Jesus nodded. "Yes, but it's often the case that when someone doubles down, they go on to experience a breakthrough in their next environment. Angush must understand that his inability to recognise the suffering of others stems from his upbringing and the culture of his family. As a young child, he was taught that the only things that mattered were wealth and power, and that anyone outside the family was there to be exploited. Emotions were seen as weakness and crying was met with physical punishment. In such an environment, it's not surprising that he grew up emotionally detached and without empathy for those living beyond the walls of the family compound.

Angush has now discovered that people find his behaviour and attitudes repulsive, because, unlike them, he wasn't driven by the need to survive. He's now experiencing the pain of rejection and loneliness. He will have to learn to accept these feelings before he can begin to appreciate that other people also have feelings and can suffer. It may be that he comes running to the open arms of love faster than others because, scratching around in the dust of his former value system, he discovers he has nothing left of any worth. Sometimes in our loneliness, when there are no other voices, one can sense Ruach's whisper more clearly.

In this past jubilee period, Angush and Yuri have been a mirror to each another. I didn't plan the exact course of events that occurred, but when mirrors are held up, there is often confrontation. Angush will spend the next jubilee period in a small group with other men who perpetrated the sexual abuse of children. They cannot yet recognise their actions as abuse because they refuse to feel what their victims felt. Eventually, these mirrors and flashbacks will begin to break down their defences. But tell me more about Yuri. How is he now?"

"Yuri was uncomfortable with being hailed a hero by most of the other men," Thomas reported. "He had attacked Angush out of pure disgust, which was how many others in the community felt about him and his boasting about trafficking children. They wanted to make Yuri the leader of their community, but Yuri suggested the committee system that he had seen at work in the first jubilee and instead kept his head down and focused on working on the new buildings. After a while he came to us to talk about the turmoil that was going on inside him. He regretted attacking Angush, but that encounter caused him to rethink his entire life in the Previous Age. He has realised that what *he* did stemmed from an inbuilt desire to survive. Yes, it was an extremely twisted desire that meant killing and exploiting anyone who posed a threat, but he now has some self-understanding and is questioning his previous ideas of justice and what is right and wrong. He's still stubborn, but I do believe he's turned a corner."

"Yes," added Bull, "he took his turn when his name was picked for the committee and he did his best to help the other men care for their animals. Because he'd been one of the first to be given a resurrected companion, he felt healthy pride in helping the other men care for theirs."

"Gulag was always going to be one of the keys to unlocking Yuri," said Jesus with a smile. "Yuri's next environment is one in which he will be faced with issues of justice and what he thinks is fair and unfair – and he couldn't have begun to understand these things without having met Angush."

The friends continued to discuss other people and matters from the community before Thomas and Bull bade Jesus farewell and headed out to enjoy the rest of their day in the City.

*

Next into the sitting room were Yvonne and Yan. Jesus fetched them drinks and suggested they move out to sit on the balcony where they could enjoy the view that stretched out far across the landscape of the City. In the near distance, clusters of buildings interspersed with lush vegetation basked in the bright colours of the sky and birdsong provided a perfect background to the scene.

They settled down in comfortable chairs around a small table and began their review.

"Johan has made huge progress in understanding how he was indoctrinated by the fascist regime he grew up under," began Yvonne. "He's been able to see that many of his attitudes and prejudices were the result of his schooling and his experience in the army. In turn, he's been courageous in confronting prejudice when it was directed at him. He was able to show love and compassion toward his 'accuser', Chester, and helped him to see that he needed to let go of his own deeply ingrained prejudices."

"Johan has always had a sweet and tender heart, just like many of those caught up in the horrors of war," said Jesus. "War can crush tenderness and harden hearts, but witnessing the destruction brought about when human desires become twisted and unchecked can also create the desire to embrace reconciliation and peace in this age. When so much is so wrong, it produces a hunger and thirst for what is good and right. It means that the suffering created by war is not without its redemptive qualities."

Yan leaned forward. "There is one thing I am concerned about for Johan though. He and Chester are always immersed in their history books and are rarely seen in the community. When they do appear, they can rather overwhelm people with their knowledge. It feels like we've lost them to their studying."

"The most important thing is that they've let go of their hate towards themselves, their experiences and each other though, isn't it?" asked Yvonne.

"That's true," Jesus agreed. "But when you discover something that has great importance for your life, it can sometimes lead to a judgemental attitude toward those who don't share the same approach. It's likely they will be taken up with their studies for a while longer yet. That is due to their personalities and their calling. As they mature and progress, they have the potential to become fine teachers for many others.

Too much time in books and the pursuit of knowledge can lead people away from listening to Ruach, so it's important to encourage them in their meditation and contemplation. The pursuit and exchange of knowledge is a wonderful thing, but it only brings revelation to the human heart when it is rooted in *agape love*. So have patience with them over the next few jubilees, and I believe they will both bear much fruit as the age unfolds."

\*

It was now Harmony and Anne's turn to talk with Jesus.

"I fancy a walk," said Jesus. "Shall we go down to see the flamingos?"

They set off down the gentle incline to the lake, a profusion of fragrant flowers lining their path.

"I'm buzzing with excitement when I think of Adilah and Eshe," said Harmony. "Those two are just so amazing!"

"They certainly are," laughed Jesus. "What are your thoughts on their journey?"

"We have seen many moments of healing and the restoration of trust. Sometimes there have been obvious breakthroughs, and sometimes they would have been imperceptible without Ruach's guidance," Harmony began.

"Our women have found much comfort and understanding through sharing their stories and their lives with one another," said Anne. "The mix of different cultures and personalities brought new challenges, but these women already possessed much empathy and with some gentle guidance soon found connection with one another.

Towards the end of the jubilee, Adilah shared with us that she felt ready to spend time with men again in her next community. We had encouraged her to connect with memories of her father, who was a kind and gentle man, and this had helped her realise that not all men are violent and abusive."

"One of the major breakthroughs for Adilah came when she realised that physical harm is something that can no longer threaten your life or even your wellbeing," continued Harmony. "There was a day when she was carrying a pile of clothes on one of the elevated walkways in the trees and tripped. She fell to the ground, far enough below to break both of her arms and shatter a knee. She was in pain for only a few minutes, as her resurrection body soon repaired itself. That was a huge boost to her confidence, knowing that nothing on the New Earth could permanently hurt her and that all injuries would be healed."

"Yes, she seemed much more adventurous and open to new experiences when I next saw her," agreed Anne. "And the same has been true for many of the other women in the community."

"This is one of the greatest freedoms that people experience here on the New Earth," Jesus replied with a broad smile. "Papa has ensured that we will always have agile and resilient bodies throughout the ages to come. I well remember the joy of this freedom when I was raised from death."

"I have a question about Adilah," said Anne. "Might it be possible for her to meet her father when she joins her next community?"

"Tell me what you think first," Jesus replied.

"Well, I know she would love to be reunited with her father, but I can see how easy it would be for her to depend on him and not learn to trust other men."

"Yes," agreed Jesus, "it's easy for people to default to a childlike connection with parents, especially if they lost them at a young age. Adilah needs to experience equal relationships with men, where she is neither a daughter nor a victim. For her, and for many like her, relating to men needs careful reconstruction."

"But something tells me it won't be long until she sees her parents again," said Harmony with a smile.

"I think you're right," Jesus replied. "Her circumstances in the next jubilee should prepare her very well for that reunion. I have always said that those like Adilah who were seen as *last* in the Previous Age would be *first* in the kingdom."

"But I feel that she may need some time away from Eshe," Harmony added. "It seems harsh, but they need to be separate for a while in order to establish and strengthen their own individual identities."

"I agree," said Jesus. "Adilah needed to spend the first two jubilees with her sister, but now that they are both growing in confidence, they must discover life apart. No one in the Eternal City is dependent on anyone else in any way. They will understand that they will see each other again soon. Thank you for your care and patience with both of these precious women."

"And Adilah was patient with me, too," said Harmony.

"I know," said Jesus with a wink.

By now the friends had reached the wide, shallow lake, where scores of flamingos were standing in the water, their forms perfectly reflected in its calm surface. They stayed for a while, savouring the moment of profound peace, before heading back to Jesus' house discussing other matters from the community.

\*

"Sylvia and Carlos! Come in!"

The two hugged Jesus and sat down while he poured some fresh tea.

"I'm so happy to know that Fran is learning to let go," said Jesus, kicking off the discussion. "Jumping into the river like that tells me that she's beginning to allow herself to have fun."

"She is one of the few," said Sylvia. "Many of the other women are still clinging on to past resentments and sabotaging their own progress."

"Resentment is a deep-seated vicious circle in the human heart and it produces nothing but misery," sighed Jesus. "People are resentful that they feel resentful, and so it goes on. It needs great courage to break that circle and choose a different response, but it can take just one moment of connection, laughter and joy. It seems that by jumping in the river, Fran chose that moment in connecting with Chesa. But I hear things have not progressed smoothly since then."

"No, sadly they haven't," replied Sylvia. "Fran felt that she had made a new 'best friend' and was too demanding of their relationship. She wanted to talk with Chesa every day and do everything together, but it was too much pressure and Chesa ended up backing off and avoiding her. When Fran realised what was happening, she felt rejected and reverted to her default mode of resentment and hatred. She feels that this episode with Chesa makes a mockery of her life on the New Earth."

"I see," said Jesus. "It shows why the course of jubilees must run for as long as it takes for lessons to be learned. It's sad that Fran focused all her attention on one person and didn't try to make wider friendships, but in a community full of women who are used to being isolated and bitter, it's not so straightforward."

"But Chesa did learn from this experience with Fran," said Carlos, continuing the story. "She realised that she couldn't continue to live as a self-sufficient island but also that a single friendship can easily become too intense. So she began to be more friendly and forthcoming with some of the other women. She was initially unsure about making friendships with non-Buddhists, especially after what had happened with Fran, but she came to see that taking time every day to greet her neighbours and making the effort to initiate conversations helped build trust. It was less intense than with Fran and more effective in the longer term."

"Trust takes time," agreed Jesus. "People are complex, and when someone moves too fast, it can be too much."

"I can imagine that Chesa will continue to grow in openness with others in her next community," said Carlos. "But what's next for Fran?"

"Fran will be placed in another village with opportunities for friendship. It's my hope that she will develop greater self-awareness in this next jubilee period, but no one can force her to relinquish her certainty that she is *right* and that everyone else is *wrong*. Those from the affluent West often struggle to recognise that love is not a transaction whereby we give in order to receive. Agape love is an active choice that desires the best for another person without demanding anything in return. But take heart, everyone recognises their need for *agape love* eventually."

As Sylvia and Carlos continued to review various aspects of life in the village, evening drew on and the rest of the team returned to Jesus' house for another meal and time together. They stayed in the City for several days, resting, meeting up with friends and having fun in preparation for their next jubilee assignments.

# The Third Jubilee

Anne squeezed Harmony's hand. Harmony squeezed back in an unspoken understanding that they were both anxious but excited. Adilah walked a few paces in front of them. The woodland path gradually opened out to reveal a spacious clearing.

"Here we are," said Harmony, gently.

In the middle of the clearing was a fireplace. Three figures sat around it talking quietly. As the three women approached, one of the figures turned and stood up. Adilah hesitated.

"It's a man," said Adilah under her breath, but loud enough for the group to hear.

"Yes, it is," said Anne. "This is our friend Simon."

Simon waved with both hands. They were now close enough to see the broad smile on his face.

"Welcome," he said as the women approached. "Come, would you like some soup?"

The other two figures now stood up, awkwardly.

"You must be Adilah?" said Simon. "Come and meet Tunde and Kanu."

Adilah took a deep breath and held out her hand to Simon. Simon shook her hand very gently. "It's so very good to meet you," he said warmly.

They all greeted one another and sat down on the hay bales around the fire. After some initial pleasantries, they began to share their stories. Both Tunde and Kanu had been abducted into slavery, just like Adilah, and had been forced to work in diamond mines. They had experienced much hardship and also great cruelty at the hands of their captors. Both had been killed when a mine shaft collapsed. They had heard the voice of one of the militia men calling for help and had turned back to try to rescue him instead of fleeing. Ruach had seen this act of extraordinary *agape love* and Jesus had placed them both in similar communities to Adilah upon their resurrection.

As the women walked back through the woodland to their cabins after the meeting, Adilah shared her impressions. "I felt nervous but Simon's warm welcome made me feel safe. And it was so good to meet Tunde and Kanu - men who could understand my journey so well. I knew in my head that not all men were like the militia, but now I know it in my heart."

*

Harmony took a sip of water. "And that is how Adilah began to overcome her fear of men."

A murmur of approval went around the table, each member of Thomas' team talking quietly with those seated next to them. The third jubilee period had ended, and they were relishing every second of being together again. For this meeting, Jesus had taken them to one of his favourite restaurants in the City.

"Tunde and Kanu are just two of the many men in Simon's community. They had been denied any contact with women during their years of enslavement, but Simon had felt they were ready to take this new step," said Jesus. "That meeting brought healing for everyone."

"Yes, it took place about fifteen years into the jubilee," said Anne. "After initial meetings in small groups like this one, the men and women from the two communities began to socialise and learn how to be around each other."

"Do you think Adilah is ready to live in a mixed community in the next jubilee?" asked Jesus.

"The remaining years of this jubilee have been peaceful and she has continued to grow in confidence. I would say that she is ready," replied Harmony. "She has also worked out that choosing forgiveness for her captors will be a path to further healing, but she is not truly at peace with this yet. Through her conversations with Tunde and Kanu, she has realised that this is a conscious choice she will have to continually make."

"Forgiveness is an attitude that is at the heart of *agape love*," agreed Jesus. "It is an ongoing attitude, which is maintained through understanding that love does not hold anything against anyone."

Harmony furrowed her brow slightly. "Many in our community, like Adilah, are aware of this but are finding it difficult. They don't know how to think about those who abused them and still hope that in some way they will face justice and suffer like they did."

"*Agape love* still pursues justice, and the justice of God includes correction," Jesus replied. "For those who perpetrated evil and caused others to suffer, it is in facing up to their wrongdoing that is a suffering in its own right. Recognising what they have done becomes its own punishment, just as love is its own reward. This is the spiritual law of the heart. Their suffering is not inflicted by Papa God, but it is a necessary part of the process toward maturity in this age."

"So their captors are in environments like Yuri," observed Bull. "He inflicted horrific pain and suffering during the Previous Age, but during the past three jubilees he has experienced the futility of violence, power and abuse. It has been an assault on his ego and his pride."

"Tell me more about his third jubilee," asked Jesus.

"Well, Yuri adapted really well to being in a rural farming community," Thomas began his report. "He was relieved to be in a completely new environment with new people and decided right from the start to have a different attitude, being quicker to smile and more open to making friends. But this change of heart didn't last throughout the whole jubilee as he often became discouraged when friendships didn't mean he always got his way. He tried meditating, but this often led to devastating flashbacks to his violent life in the Previous Age."

"Yuri didn't have any true friendships in the Previous Age," added Bull. "Not since he was a child. But there came a time in this jubilee when he realised that he wanted a friend."

*

It was a still day with no breeze, deep into the third jubilee. Yuri was walking Gulag in the woods when he came across two men.

"Timothy!" shouted Paul. "We have a guest... sorry... guests," he added, seeing the large dog by Yuri's side.

Timothy appeared from inside a large canvas tent. "Great! The mushroom soup is almost ready. I just need to add some more seasoning. Come and sit down. I'm sure we can find an extra bowl for your four-legged friend."

Yuri, who had been standing at an awkward distance, came and sat down on the grass at the tent entrance with Gulag settling at his feet

"Let me ask you something," said Paul. "Have you ever had strong flashbacks to your life in the Previous Age?"

Yuri inwardly flinched at such a direct question from a stranger.

"Have *you*?" Yuri retorted with sincere interest, though he sounded defensive.

"I had them after I was blinded in the Previous Age. They were extremely powerful, almost like reliving scenes from my own life again."

"How did you become blind?" asked Yuri.

"I met Jesus and his presence was so bright. But you know, I needed to have my sight taken away so that I could focus on my inner life and experience those flashbacks."

Yuri was intrigued.

"Mind you, you had been involved in some seriously destructive ways, hadn't you?" Timothy pitched in, still stirring the soup.

"What did you do?" asked Yuri. He was now listening intently and had moved closer to Paul.

"I was extremely religious and wanted to be the most zealous and pious Jew who had ever lived. It disgusted me that some of our faith were claiming that the one true God, the God of Israel, had become a man - Jesus of Nazareth. It was an appalling idea to me and filled me with hatred. I took it upon myself to hunt down any of his followers. I thought of them as vermin, as blasphemers who deserved God's punishment."

"I understand," said Yuri, nodding.

"If we found any followers of Jesus, we'd drag them out of their homes and throw them into prison. I'd stir up the crowds and even bribe people to act as false witnesses against them, so they didn't stand a chance when they were tried by our Jewish leaders. Some were beaten but many were stoned to death, and all the while I stood there and gave it my stamp of approval."

"I guess you had to do what you had to do," said Yuri.

"The thing is, I didn't *have* to do any of it," said Paul, stony-faced. "Yes, I thought I was right, but it was my pride and my twisted sense of importance that meant I took pleasure in it all. One day it was the turn of a man called Stephen to be brought to trial. He stood in front of us with such dignity and spoke about his faith in God and Jesus. I can still remember the light that seemed to shine from his face. The mob was baying for blood and he was dragged out of the city and stoned..."

Paul stopped and hung his head and drew a quivering breath.

"He didn't once try to fight back and as he died, battered and covered in blood, he prayed that God would forgive us. It wasn't long afterwards that I met Jesus for myself, and my eyes stopped seeing. I had flashbacks and relived Stephen's death and others like it, over and over, but from a new perspective. It was like being in my own personal hell. I cried out to Jesus to help me, and Ruach came to me in such power. Once I accepted that I had been wrong, so totally, totally lacking in love and that all my zeal had been based on a desire for spiritual superiority, my eyes began to work again and the flashbacks stopped."

"So let me ask you again," continued Paul. "Do you have flashbacks?"

Yuri didn't want to answer, but Paul gently pressed him further.

"If you do, think about what triggers them."

Timothy handed a bowl of soup to Yuri and placed another on the ground for Gulag.

Yuri looked at the soup and at his dog and remembered the time Jesus had slid him that shot of vodka. What was it about these people that bothered him so much?

*

"The flashbacks have been very disturbing for him," said Bull. "He's beginning to experience what he did in the Previous Age with understanding, and it's causing him much distress. The memories come in waves and are sometimes so overwhelming he can cope with little but the basics of everyday life."

"This is the process that leads to empathy and the desire to turn away from hurting others," said Jesus. "The suffering that he is experiencing will ultimately lead him to seek forgiveness and reconciliation. *Agape love* is the reason for the process and lies at its heart. The distress and regret that Yuri is currently experiencing are like the outermost twigs of a tree, but they are still connected to its core. In the next jubilee period Yuri may continue to suffer, but he will also have the opportunity to make new friends. Tell me, Sylvia, how are things now with Fran?"

"When Fran entered her third jubilee, like Yuri she decided early on to try and have a new attitude in her new environment.

She felt that she had failed in her friendship with Chesa, so she decided to take on the role of organising rotas and schedules so that she could feel like she was being helpful."

"But, as you can imagine, she soon alienated people in her new community because her actions stemmed from her own need to be in charge," continued Carlos. "Other people in the community were also trying to find ways of being in control, so there were many arguments and upsets that caused resentment, grudges and suspicion. Fran's biggest obstacle is her inability to humble herself and trust that she is likeable for who she is, and not because of what she owns or what she can do. It seems that she cannot understand *agape love* yet, because she still sees everything as a transaction."

"All this stems from her low self-worth," said Jesus sadly. "Fran and others in her community try to feel better about themselves by putting people down. But true self-esteem grows when people know they are loved and choose to become loving and kind. Fran will be placed in a smaller community for the next jubilee. It will be harder at first, because they will be more dependent on each other. But it creates the potential for individual contributions to be more highly valued, and that will help to boost each person's self-esteem."

"Johan also hasn't made progress in this jubilee," said Yvonne. "He didn't know anyone in his new community, so he chose to withdraw into books rather than making new relationships."

"It's like he doesn't know who to be outside of his experiences in the Previous Age," Yan remarked. "He's read history books for a long time, but when we tried to interest him in some lighter material, he rejected it all."

"Johan did well at making friends when the stakes were high," said Jesus. "But recently he has based his identity on his study. Books are helpful for understanding the Previous Age, but they can't heal the heart."

"Only discovering who we are according to *agape love* can do that," agreed Yan. "For a long time I saw myself as a martyr first and a much-loved son of Papa God second. My identity was based on what I had done and what had happened to me, rather than in the present moment."

"It's something of an irony that it takes time to awaken to the present moment," said Jesus with a little chuckle. "The past can be a useful guide for our current actions, but Johan needs to learn to enjoy life and show *agape love* in the 'now'. Johan misses his former friends and family, and so he has shut down his emotions rather than exploring relationships with those around him. The next jubilee period will give him the opportunity to do that, so let's hope he takes it."

"Yes, many people are still overwhelmed by what is missing," said Yan with a sigh. "I wish they would focus more on what is present."

"As you know, Yan, it is only *agape love* that makes that possible. All of you here have come to see the people you are with, in the Eternal City and in your communities, in the light of *agape love*, and therefore you are always more mindful of those you are with than those who are absent."

Thomas' team continued to talk with Jesus well into the evening until it was time for them to retire to their dwellings in the City for more rest before the start of the next jubilee period.

# Adilah Enters the Eternal City

Two people sat near a small fire in the middle of a circle of cabins. Their fourth jubilee was nearing its end and they had enjoyed several decades of living in peaceful friendship with one another. Differences and disagreements had been overcome quickly, as each person was prepared to accept loving correction through patient discussion. The community had learned to listen to each other, seeking to understand and honour each person.

"He was my brother, in the same way that every man was somebody's brother, son and father."

Adilah nodded slowly. She knew what this meant. The logic was clear, but she knew that allowing it to enter her heart could mean only one thing: forgiveness.

The man sitting opposite her wiped tears from his cheeks. "It still hurts to think of him, because I haven't yet seen him again here on the New Earth."

"When was the last time you saw him?" asked Adilah. Somehow this conversation felt acutely intimate and important. Over the last few decades, she had grown to understand that the men in her community did not pose a threat to her safety. Though tentative at first, she made the effort to spend time with them. She had listened and opened her heart to them and the men had reciprocated.

"He climbed on to the back of a jeep and they drove away. What hurt the most was that he looked at me with defiance, as if to say he had done nothing wrong. Maybe it was because he'd spared my life, but I wished he hadn't. He killed my wife and my two children – his own nephew and niece – just because they belonged to the wrong tribe."

"Even we heard about the Rwandan genocide," said Adilah. "The militia talked about it sometimes."

The two sat in silence for a long time.

"Do you want to see him again?" Adilah asked.

"Sometimes I do," said the man. "But sometimes I do not. I know my heart is set and that I have chosen to forgive. I see what Jesus is doing here, and I understand that the only way for all things to be reconciled is to set my heart on *agape love*."

The fire continued to crackle, as owls called to each other in the distant treetops.

"Do you think about where he might be?"

"I assume that he will be raised and will have to face up to what he did. I know that Jesus will have designed a process that will help him and ultimately save him. I am sure that he will experience both the chastisement and the loving kindness of Papa God. The two are really the same, but it takes time to see it, doesn't it?"

"It does," Adilah nodded in agreement. "Throughout these jubilee periods, I have been challenged to think of myself as more than just a victim. My body no longer bears the scars of the Previous Age, but it took me a long time to understand how those experiences had scarred my identity."

Adilah became quiet as she stared into the fire. She reached up a hand and ran it over her hair, where once she had been burned.

"And I know what I must do to finally defeat my victim mindset."

The man searched Adilah's face, willing her to take the next vital step.

"So right now, I choose to forgive."

Adilah's head dropped to her chest and she closed her eyes tight.

"I forgive all those who hurt me and my sister," she sobbed. "I recognise they were people just like me."

The man bowed his head, recognising the power of this moment, as Adilah allowed her tears to flow. She called to mind the faces of her captors, one by one, and visualised herself telling them that they were forgiven. As she did so, she felt an energy welling up within her, like a volcano on the point of erupting.

"Thank you, friend," she cried through her tears. Ruach had been with her from childhood and throughout everything she had experienced - her death, her resurrection and this process - leading her all the way to this moment.

*

"Weeks and months went by from that evening around the fire," said Harmony. "Adilah sometimes felt flashes of her previous anger and resentment towards those who had caused so much suffering in the Previous Age, but she consistently focused her mind on her decision to forgive. Sometimes she felt disappointed, because it didn't feel easy, but at other times she experienced a deep joy and freedom like never before."

"Ruach saw her determination to keep actively choosing forgiveness, and that's how we knew that this day had come," said Jesus with delight. "Come on, let's go to her!"

*

Adilah was singing to herself as she sat on her small veranda polishing a saucepan. The sound of birdsong in the evening never failed to elevate her spirits, and she loved to sit outside as the colours changed around her. Hearing footsteps on the path, she looked up and gasped as she recognised Jesus walking toward her with Anne and Harmony.

Jesus held out his arms and Adilah ran towards him. He wrapped her in a long embrace with her head nestled under his chin. Anne and Harmony both beamed with anticipation.

"Adilah," said Jesus, holding her gently by the shoulders and looking deep into her eyes. "Ruach, Harmony and Anne have seen your heart. You have chosen to clothe yourself in *agape love* and have decided to love those who hurt you. You have come to see yourself as you truly are - a cherished daughter of Papa God. You are ready to enter the Eternal City."

Adilah covered her face with her hands for a few seconds and then opened them to reveal her radiant smile. She heard Jesus' words but was unsure what they fully meant.

"Come with us," beckoned Jesus. "You remember Cynthia?"

The seraph turned and bowed low. The four friends climbed onto her broad back and were soon soaring over the meadows of Beulah toward the Eternal City.

They landed in a square where tables and chairs were set out, like an Italian piazza. Sliding to the ground, Adilah looked around, overwhelmed by the many things she'd never seen before. The piazza lay at the foot of mountainous crags, the tops of which were hidden in rosy-hued clouds. Dwellings of various colours were built into the rock faces with flowers blooming on the balconies and on the thick outcrops between the buildings. Adilah turned around slowly, trying to take it all in.

Jesus, Harmony and Anne stood back, enjoying the look of wonder on Adilah's face. Jesus reached out and took her hand. She looked up at him and silently mouthed the word "Thank you."

Jesus motioned for her to turn around. Standing a few feet away were a man and a woman, arm in arm.

Adilah's hands returned to her face for a few seconds before she lowered them, looked again, and then ran towards the couple crying "Mama, Papa!"

Adilah's parents held her tight, and they wept together in a moment that seemed to be suspended in time. Adilah knew that she was finally home and that all her suffering, her resilience and her patience had been leading to this.

Soon they were sitting in the comfortable living room of one of Jesus' homes. The breeze gently moved the curtains as the reunited family told each other of their journeys through the Previous Age and the New Earth. As they laughed and cried together, Jesus took great pleasure in serving them food and drinks.

"What of Eshe?" Adilah looked up and asked Jesus.

"Everyone has their own day for entering the Eternal City," he replied, "much as when you were raised to the New Earth. Today is about you. You can trust me with your sister, and all the others that you love."

"And not just those I love," replied Adilah, with a directness and confidence that made Jesus put down the tray of drinks.

"No," he said gently. "Not just those you love."

"When?" asked Adilah.

Jesus sat down with the family and turned to Adilah.

"You must remember that you have the strength to meet anyone here in the City. And by the same token, anyone here in the City is ready to meet you. Will it be easy? Not necessarily. Will it be awkward? Yes, possibly. But you have clothed yourself in *agape love*, and you can be confident that you will know how to interact with anyone you meet here. Some people deliberately ask for a reconciliation meeting. If that is what you wish, we will arrange it. Others prefer to leave it to happenstance, trusting that the timing and the circumstances will flow naturally, which of course they will. Your spirit is one with Ruach, your friend. You are mature in our everlasting love."

"What would you like to do, my daughter?" asked Adilah's mother.

"I think... I would like this to happen... as and when," said Adilah. "Jesus, I trust you and I trust myself."

"Right, that is how it will be. And now," said Jesus breaking out into a broad smile, "you are free to explore and experience the wonders of the City in your own time. Your time for rest has come."

*

"Can we join in?"

Adilah turned around and lowered her bat. "For sure," she smiled. "You two, do you want to join the fielding team, and…"

She stopped. Her hand fell to her side as she looked hard at one of the two men who had approached them on the baseball pitch.

He looked back with the same sense of recognition on his face. Sensing what was happening, the others made space for them and moved quietly aside.

"Adilah?" asked the man.

"Yes," she replied. She felt her stomach tense with nerves but at the same time a calm clarity of mind.

"Come," said Adilah, "Let's walk together."

The man nodded and the pair walked off the field in silence, watched by those remaining, who sent love and support in their hearts to both individuals. They understood that these moments could arise, often with no introduction.

"I know a place nearby where we can talk," said the man.

"Okay. What is your name?" she asked.

"My name is Bem, but you knew me as 'Knife'." His voice wavered and he cleared his throat.

They sat on a bench overlooking a neighbourhood in a suburban district of the City.

"Adilah, I know you have come here because you are ready in your heart, but I still need to say this to you."

Bem knelt before Adilah and looked up at her.

"I am sorry for what I did to you and so many others in the Previous Age. I acknowledge the pain and suffering you endured. I know what I did, and I understand why I did those things."

Adilah looked down at him and her forehead furrowed slightly. She could still remember the screams as he sliced the flesh of her sister to mark her as the property of the militia. But she could also see the humanity that she shared with him in his eyes. "Bem," she said, "sit with me and tell me about your life in the Previous Age." She leaned down and took his face in her hands. "Tell me about your journey on the New Earth and how you came into the City. I want to know, I want to understand everything."

Adilah and Bem sat together on the bench for a long time, and then they moved on to a quiet restaurant. They talked with no concept of time. As they explained their stories, their hearts made room to accommodate each other.

Listening became learning; learning became understanding; understanding became empathy, and empathy became total acceptance that they were brother and sister within God's family.

# Johan Enters the Eternal City

"Johan continued to be thirsty for facts and context throughout the fourth jubilee and the start of this one too," Yvonne reported as Team Thomas gathered once again with Jesus to review the past jubilee period. "The angelic records describe much that is destructive and ugly, but they also note many accounts of *agape love* breaking through the sufferings of the Previous Age. Johan ignored these at first, but the more he read, the more he became inspired by the stories recording human kindness and empathy."

"Inspiration is one of my favourite influences on the human heart," said Jesus. "I felt so glad when my words inspired the people I met in my Previous Age. It's a wonderful thing when inspiration becomes motivation."

"It was early in his fifth jubilee when Johan's reading inspired him to desire relationships," said Yan. "He became convinced that the point of existence is *agape love*, and eventually he found the perfect opportunity to rejoin the community and put that into practice."

\*

Johan looked out of the window with a furrowed brow. It was unusual to hear any activity outside of his dwelling, let alone the clinking of metal spades. He placed the bookmark in the page he had been reading and closed the book. As he opened his door, a man approached him, smiling.

"Hello!" he said cheerfully, holding out a hand. Johan hadn't spoken to anyone for a long while, and so he blinked at the man a couple of times before accepting the handshake.

"Hello," said Johan quietly.

"Sorry friend, did we disturb you?"

"It's ok," replied Johan.

"We're digging an irrigation channel. I'm Frazer, by the way."

"Hello, I'm Johan."

"I haven't seen you around much," said Frazer.

Johan cleared his throat self-consciously and looked at the ground. "No. I haven't been out much."

"We could do with some help. Would you be willing to join us?"

Johan felt a knot of anxiety forming in his stomach at the thought of being around new people.

"Once we get the channel to the top of the hill it will connect to a spring, and water will flow down to a new vegetable garden we've created over there."

Johan felt a little guilty that he enjoyed the benefit of freshly grown food at the market each week but did so little to contribute to its production.

"Yes, I am willing to help," he replied.

"That's great! If you put on your oldest work clothes, I'll introduce you to the rest of the group."

Frazer led Johan over to where the men were digging. The sound of spades slicing through soil triggered a rush of memories of digging foxholes with his comrades in the Previous Age. Johan felt himself overcome with a sadness that he hadn't experienced for a long time. One of the men looked up at Johan.

"Hey, mate, are you alright?" he asked.

Frazer looked at Johan's troubled face and put an arm around his shoulder. Johan was deeply touched by the concern shown by these men he'd only just met.

The whole team put down their spades, and before he knew it, Johan was seated on the grass surrounded by six new friends.

"I haven't been in company for so long," he said in a small voice.

"I was nervous of meeting people, too," said one of men. "When this jubilee began, I decided that I just wanted to paint in my garden. Didn't feel I wanted to get to know new people after I was parted from my friends in the last jubilee. Didn't see the point of making new friends if we kept getting split up."

Johan nodded. "I miss my sister, and my friends - not to mention those I haven't seen since the Previous Age. I just want to read all the time and not talk to anyone."

"Many of us have been on the same journey," said another, kindly. "We're all here together because we're all learning how to heal from our wounds. Were you a soldier in the Previous?"

"How did you guess?" laughed Johan, though tears were now quietly flowing as he made himself vulnerable.

"I somehow felt that the sound of digging might have triggered memories from army life," the man replied.

"But... how?" asked Johan.

"You remember Ruach? Well, we sit and allow her to meet with us," said Frazer. The other men nodded.

"We make time to be still and listen to her each day," said one of the men. "You would be welcome to join us."

"I find it easier to read," replied Johan, feeling a little uncomfortable at the idea. But seeing the friendly faces that surrounded him, he continued, "But I am interested. Maybe I could join you tomorrow and at least give it a go? And for now, let me help you."

"I'll fetch you a spade," grinned Frazer. "Many hands make light work!"

251

As he settled into the rhythm of digging, Johan felt a wave of satisfaction. For the first time in many years, he felt connected to people again.

The men talked as they worked, cracking jokes and reminiscing about their lives in the Previous Age and the jubilee periods they'd experienced so far. The atmosphere was more friendly and jovial than Johan had ever known with other men. As the hours went by, swift progress was made forming a channel down to the level ground where the new vegetable beds had been prepared.

"Johan, you should be the one to break the barrier at the top of the hill," suggested one of the men.

"But I joined the work last," Johan protested. "It shouldn't be me."

"You're the newest member of the team, and this is your welcome," said Frazer.

"Why don't we all break the barrier together?" suggested Johan, smiling at his companions. "Come on, let's go up, all of us."

The seven men walked back up the hill, following the line of the irrigation channel until they reached the place where a short span of earth kept the spring pool from flowing freely down the new waterway. The men each began to remove the earth, a spadeful at a time.

"Here it goes!" shouted Johan as the last slithers of earth fell away.

The men cheered and laughed as the crystalline water cascaded down the channel. Some began to run, trying to keep pace with the water, and the others followed suit, until they were all at the vegetable beds, joyfully watching the water flow.

\*

Johan had found a way back to community and connection with other people. He was delighted to learn from Frazer that there were women and children living in the village, as well as entire families who had died together in various wars. Using his experience with Gerty from his first jubilee, he threw himself into volunteering at the village school, showing the children the basics of thatching and roof repair.

As the days, weeks and months went by, Johan developed a teaching method that was firm but fair and showed that he expected each child to do their best. Teaching enabled him to practise the skills of patience and empathy that he had read so much about in the angelic records.

He quietly resolved to spend quality one-to-one time with every young child at the school to learn more about their interests. Slowly but surely, Johan came to be liked and trusted by each child in the village, as they realised that this man cared for them deeply. Johan also got to know each of their families and their different stories. He saw the beauty in their journeys and helped them process some of what they had experienced.

One warm evening Johan was putting his thatching tools away when he noticed a man and a woman standing behind a low stone wall looking in his direction. As Johan looked more carefully, he saw that the woman was wiping tears from her cheeks.

"Gerty!" he gasped, rushing towards her and vaulting over the wall. As he enveloped her in his arms, he realised that the man standing next to her with a beaming smile was Jesus. Johan's eyes widened in surprise, and then he reached out an arm and brought him into the embrace.

"Johan, we have come with some news," Jesus told him, as Johan stood back, quite breathless from the surprise.

"We are here to invite you to the Eternal City. Your heart is ready. You have learnt how to give and receive *agape love* and have overcome the temptation to isolate yourself from other people. Ruach has told me how you have been meditating with your friends and letting go of the resentment and bitterness that held you back in the past. You have allowed *agape love* to become your compass and your source of inspiration."

"Come to the City!" said Gerty. "I live there now, and so do Mum and Dad."

Johan hadn't thought about his parents for some time. Life had become sweet in the village, and he realised he had no longer been thinking of the past, nor of the future, but had truly learned to inhabit the present.

Gerty took his arm. "Come and see?"

Johan nodded. "Yes, of course. Mother, Father..."

"And so many friends!" added Gerty with a giggle.

Johan took a deep breath. There was so much to take in, and he could only begin to imagine how he would feel seeing his family reunited again. But at the same time, he knew it meant leaving the people in the village he had come to love and care for so deeply.

"That will be wonderful, Gerty. But I need to say some goodbyes first."

Jesus nodded. "Of course, Johan. We understand. We'll be here and ready when you are."

Johan made his way around the dwellings in his community. He looked each person in the eye as he embraced them. Words of affection and thanks were whispered as adults and children alike wished Johan well for the new chapter that lay ahead. Everyone accompanied him back to his house and waved as he was ushered onto a seraph's back by his excited sister.

A short ride took Jesus, Gerty and Johan to one of the towering open gateways into the City, where they climbed down from the seraph's back just outside the city walls.

The three walked under a colossal arch and into a landscape of fields and lush meadows, interspersed with wooden houses with exposed beams. In the distance there were rolling foothills that led to mountain ranges far away in the distance. A figure, who had been sitting under a large weeping willow, stood up to greet them.

Johan's face broke into a broad grin. "Chester, you're here!"

"Got here yesterday!" said Chester, throwing his arms around Johan.

"Chester has had an interesting journey since you last saw him," said Jesus. "But you will have all the time you need to hear about it."

Gerty grabbed Johan's hand, pulling him along, just as she had done as a little girl. Though she was now a grown woman, she still had the unmistakeable air of someone who had not witnessed the suffering of the Previous Age. There was an unbridled joy and enthusiasm for life that she had never lost, and Johan marvelled at her infectious spirit. But now, at last, Johan felt that nothing was holding him back from embracing life in exactly the same way as she did.

"Let's meet up tomorrow, Chester!" Johan called out as his small party continued along a pathway that led through the fields towards a building that reminded him of the alpine skiing lodges that he had seen in picture books. Chester waved a hand in acknowledgement and entered a nearby house. Johan's heart began to race with anticipation at seeing his parents again.

Gerty let go of Johan's hand and hurried towards the doorway of the house. Before she could knock, the door opened and Johan saw a man and a woman standing in the entrance. They were strangers, and yet instantly familiar. He knew without doubt that these were his parents, but they looked so young and happy.

His mother covered her mouth and his father held out his hands. Johan approached slowly, taking in the fullness of the moment. The four family members held each another for some time, allowing the silence to hold all their emotions.

Jesus had gone through into the kitchen, where he began preparing refreshments. The family began to talk, slowly at first, but soon they were animatedly taking turns to describe their individual journeys in the Previous Age and then on the

New Earth. Laughter and tears flowed as they learnt of the joy and the pain they had each experienced and the events that had created the path leading to this moment.

"Johan, there are loved ones you have yet to meet," his mother said, as they ate the food that Jesus had prepared.

Johan put down his plate.

Johan's father cleared his throat. "There's something that we haven't talked about yet."

Johan looked into his father's eyes and knew immediately what he was going to say.

"Dad, you were gay," Johan smiled.

His father looked much relieved and nodded. "Yes, son. I was."

"Your father loved a man," continued his mother, placing her hand on her husband's arm.

"His name is Gregor," said Gerty.

"It's ok, Papa. I knew you were gay before I died."

"Gregor is here, too," continued Johan's mother. "All of us consider him a dear friend."

"And what of you, Mama?" asked Johan. "Were you lonely in the Previous Life?"

Johan's mother opened her hands. "I knew your father loved me as a wife and that he loved me as much as he could love a woman. We remained married until he died. However, I knew that Gregor gave your father much that I could never give him. I grew to accept that and chose to love who they were together. Eventually we became a secret family, the three of us, and Gregor cared for me after your father died. It wasn't always perfect, and yes, I was sad sometimes."

Johan's father took his mother's hands. "This woman showed Gregor and I what grace looks like."

Jesus stood leaning against the worktop in the kitchen, listening intently. Johan looked up at him enquiringly.

"Yes, Johan, even during the war when your parents lost their daughter and their son, and in the misery of post-war Germany, these three chose goodness and demonstrated love for each other in their intentions and their actions. I condemn no one. And I know when a human heart can understand, accept and demonstrate *agape love* enough to dwell here in the Eternal City."

Johan nodded.

"I think it's fair to say," said Johan's father, "that we all accepted how poor in spirit we were at that time. Your mother, Gregor, myself - we were all humbled by life. All we could do was trust and believe that a better day would come. Of course, we had much to learn and to heal here on the New Earth, but Jesus and his friends never failed to love us."

"Faith, hope and *agape love*," said Jesus. "These are the qualities that remain. These are what were within the three of you when you died and what you awakened to in this age. We just... helped iron out any creases."

"And for those of us who needed more time to reach the City, it was our experiences in communities on the New Earth that made it possible for these qualities to take root in our hearts," added Johan, thoughtfully.

"And now we all have so much of these that we can forever share them with everyone!" laughed Gerty with delight, looking forward to sharing the joys of life in the City with her brother and her reunited family.

# Yuri Enters the Eternal City

Yuri ladled some steaming vegetable stew into the bowl presented by the last person in the line.

"Thank you," said the woman, with a grateful smile.

Yuri returned the smile a little awkwardly. He had never considered how it would feel to be trusted and appreciated until arriving in this community at the start of his seventh jubilee.

Yuri spent a whole day once a week cooking up a vast feast for everyone in his village. The idea had come to him after a neighbour had commented on the delicious smell emanating from his kitchen. Yuri had invited him to share his supper and, discovering that he rather enjoyed the experience, resolved to do it again.

With increasing frequency, he extended the invitation to more of his neighbours, until he had the idea of spending a whole day each week cooking for everyone. On those days, Gulag would lie at his feet and many in the line would stoop down to stroke him as they queued for Yuri's much-loved stew. The whole community, about eighty people, treated those evenings as a weekly celebration and would sit in the open air, eating, laughing and sharing stories.

More than the compliments that people paid him on his culinary skills, it was the openness with which people approached him and their obvious delight in eating his food that caused Yuri to glow with satisfaction. It didn't seem long ago that he had wanted people to fear him, or more recently, to leave him alone. Now he was popular and liked. It had taken a while for Yuri to accept that people could take a gift of food from him and not treat him with suspicion.

Scraping up the last of the stew from one of the large cooking pots, Yuri took his bowl and found a place to settle down on a wooden seat near his cooking station, tired but happy. He noticed that people seated in a group nearby were glancing in his direction as they spoke to one another. Yuri nodded at them and smiled before making a start on his meal.

To his surprise, the people in the group stood up and moved over to where Yuri was sitting and were soon settled around his feet.

"Everything ok?" he asked them.

"Absolutely," said one of them. "We just wanted to be with you. This is our favourite day of the week, thanks to you."

"Will you tell us how you came here?" asked another of them. "We don't know your story. You always seem happier to listen than to talk, but we care about you, Yuri."

Yuri swallowed his mouthful and put down his bowl, rubbing his hands on his apron. He felt touched by their kindness but was still a little embarrassed at finding himself the centre of attention.

"Well…" he began slowly, "my childhood in the Previous Age was tough. I learned quickly that the world owed me nothing, so I took what I could to survive. I used violence to get what I needed, but that soon turned into getting what I *wanted* too. The choices I made hurt people, and I am sorry to say that I killed people, too. I thought the only person I could trust was myself, so I built high walls to keep people out. I had a girlfriend but I knew nothing about love and I destroyed her."

Everyone in the group by now had stopped eating and were listening intently to Yuri's story. Yuri felt a surge of regret and sorrow wash over him.

"The only things I wanted were wealth and power, but these still left me feeling empty. I got into gambling as the high stakes and euphoria of winning at least made me feel alive. Except I lost and got into debt... big time. Some of the people I owed money to attacked me on the street, and that's when it seems my heart failed. I don't think anyone shed a tear for me."

"What did Jesus say when he raised you?" asked one of women in the group.

Yuri paused and felt a tsunami of love so strongly that he thought he might pass out. It was as though a freight train had gone through him, shaking his whole body. It passed, but tears were now streaming down his face.

"He gave me my dog. The only thing I ever truly loved in my life." Yuri looked down at Gulag who returned his gaze.

"Jesus showed me love from the first moment I met him," continued Yuri. "He welcomed me with a shot of vodka and gave me back my best friend. But I didn't know how to receive love, so I pushed him away. I thought he was weak. I had such twisted ideas back then. Jesus put me in a community where I began to learn that violence could no longer be used to control others. In the second jubilee, I found that I had a basic understanding of injustice and that I could feel empathy for those abused by people with power. In my next community, I discovered that I could make friends and that kindness was not weakness. In the jubilees that followed, I learned more about myself and about other people from their stories. I have come to see how wrong my attitude and actions were. I want to do better! And so here I am today. I feel accepted as part of this community and I trust now that Jesus accepts me and that I can trust him."

"Jesus has always put us with people that are best able to help us grow," said one man in the group. "My story is similar. At first, I thought Jesus was punishing me by putting me with people who had come from the same rough background in the Previous Age. They were all just like me, but then I started to see that in such communities we could grow and learn from each other. And the first thing we had to learn was to listen to each other. To see ourselves in each other was the first step."

"And it's not just you men who were violent," said the woman who had been the last in the line to get her food. "I beat and neglected my kids. Lord knows I am sorry for what I did. I took my own life in the Previous Age, because I hated myself and believed I didn't deserve to live. I thought if there was a God that I deserved to be punished, but Jesus and his friends treated me with kindness and respect. That was the start of the healing process. For a long time I felt numb, but I feel things now. I've had so many flashbacks - like a waking nightmare. But I understand that it is my conscience showing me the truth."

"I believe with all my heart that we will all get to say sorry to those we abused," said Yuri. "I know that's what I want to do now."

"Do you remember the people that Jesus placed among us to be an example of love?" asked one of the men seated nearby.

Yuri smiled fondly, thinking of Thomas and Bull. "Man, I gave those guys a hard time!"

Heads nodded.

"All they ever wanted to do was cheer us on towards a better way of living. They really were a gift from God," said another.

"I can't wait to see them again," said Yuri. "And believe me, I never thought I'd say that!"

"And you won't have to wait long."

A voice called out from behind Yuri. He turned and saw a man quietly sitting by the cooking pots.

"Jesus?" said Yuri, in a whisper of disbelief.

Gulag sprang up and bounded over to Jesus, excitedly licking his face. Jesus laughed and stood up.

"I've been listening with such a happy heart," said Jesus. "You are all such a delight to me!"

Gasps and joyful whispers went up as the community realised that Jesus was among them.

"My friends," said Jesus, "I have seen the way your hearts have opened to one another and how, time and time again, you have chosen *agape love*. How I have looked forward to this day!"

Yuri's knees buckled and he found himself kneeling on the grass with Gulag at his side.

Jesus turned to him and put a hand on his shoulder. "Yuri, my brother, you are to come to the Eternal City, to my home. Each of your friends will be coming soon, but today is your day."

Yuri looked up at Jesus and for the first time did not flinch at the fiery love in his eyes. He knew Jesus could see the totality of who he was, but now there was nothing he needed to hide. Yuri stood up and the community burst into spontaneous applause as the two men embraced.

It was then that Yuri noticed Cedric the seraph standing behind Jesus. The creature bowed low in greeting. "Hello, young man," said Cedric warmly. And it was true – Yuri did feel young; younger than he'd ever felt before.

Climbing onto Cedric's broad back, Yuri felt like a little boy. He grinned with anticipation as Jesus climbed on and Gulag leapt up and settled himself between them.

"Hold tight and enjoy the ride!" Jesus called out.

Before long they were soaring through the sky with the landscape of the New Earth beneath them. As Cedric flew lower, Yuri saw that they were heading for a colourful garden of flowers, trees and pools of water. As they dismounted, Yuri stood and breathed in the vibrant scents, while Gulag was soon weaving his way in and out of the greenery.

"Yuri," said Jesus, his voice calm and clear in the perfect stillness of the garden. "This place is a garden of reconciliation. There is someone here I want you to meet."

A lump formed in Yuri's throat.

"I understand," he said, preparing himself for what he knew must take place.

Jesus motioned toward a circular pool of sky-blue water. At the head of the pool was an arch carved into a tall green yew hedge, and at that moment, the person Yuri knew he must meet appeared in the archway.

Helena stood watching Yuri from across the blue pool. Yuri felt the knot in his throat grow harder and he found it difficult to breathe. Jesus stood close by his side as Helena walked slowly, glancing down at the ground and then looking again at Yuri as she approached.

And then she was standing in front of him - the man who had hooked her on drugs, used her for sex and beaten her to death. Yuri trembled and his knees gave way again. He found himself looking up at Helena, one hand holding tight to Jesus' arm beside him.

"Please stand up," said Helena. "I would like you to look me in the eye as an equal."

Yuri was overcome by her dignity and the gentleness in her voice, in which he sensed the presence of grace and *agape love*.

"I... I... can't," Yuri sobbed.

Helena knelt so that her face was opposite Yuri's.

"Then I will come to you," she said.

"Helena, I... I know what I did. I see it now. I know what I did to you."

"I know," she whispered. "You would not be here unless you could see clearly."

Yuri bowed his head, tears falling into the grass.

"Yuri, you need to hear this now..." began Helena.

"No! Wait please, Helena. Let me speak first. I need to. Allow me to say it..."

Helena paused, her face now wrought with emotion as she bit her bottom lip to keep back the tears.

"Helena, I am sorry. I am so sorry. I know what I did. I know what I was. I destroyed you."

"Yes, Yuri, you did. You destroyed me. I suffered at your hands. You disfigured and killed me and degraded yourself in the process."

Once more Yuri saw himself raining his fists down on Helena's swollen body, blood pouring from her nose and lips.

"Lift your head, Yuri. Look me in the eyes."

Yuri looked up. He felt dazzled as though the sun was shining directly behind her, but he could see that her face was perfectly restored. She spoke with such authority and power, Yuri felt totally overwhelmed.

"Yuri, I love you with *agape love*. I forgive you everything. I forgive you for all that you did to me."

Yuri felt a flame pass through his body, his mind and his spirit. In that moment a blazing light penetrated the darkness of his memory, and the image of what he did to Helena was blotted out by its pure brilliance. Now, at last, he knew that he could let go of who he once was and see himself as an entirely new creation.

Helena stood up and held out her hands. Yuri took them and she pulled him up so that they were at an equal height again.

"What bound us together in the past has been the source of our redemption," she said, her voice quiet, yet powerful.

"Yes, Jesus has turned everything that was broken into the very source of our healing." Yuri turned to thank Jesus, but to his surprise found that he was no longer there.

"This is our reality now, and it changes how we view the past, the present and the future," said Helena. "The old has gone and the new is here."

Yuri and Helena walked together into the garden. There was so much to share about their journeys and so much to learn and understand about each other.

Two souls that had been linked in darkness were now born anew in light. The future stretched before them with limitless possibilities.

# Fran Enters the Eternal City

Carlos finished counting out on his fingers. "This is Fran's fourteenth jubilee," he said. Sylvia let out a long sigh.

"Let's recap her journey so far," suggested Jesus.

"Fran's biggest stumbling block to her progression has been her sense of entitlement. She has consistently reverted to her core belief that because she was religious in the Previous Age, she deserves to be rewarded," said Carlos.

"Fran's sense of entitlement also stems from her comfortable life in England during the second half of the twentieth century," continued Sylvia. "Her husband worked hard and she didn't want for much in her life, so she had little empathy with those who found life challenging. She based her identity on what she owned and judged people according to their level of affluence - she was envious of those who had more and looked down on those who had less. And she enjoyed gossiping about people rather than making friends. These were the attitudes that she brought with her to the New Earth, so when friendships didn't work out the way she wanted, she just gave up on them rather than wondering what she could have done differently."

Jesus pursed his lips. "A hard heart can take a long time to soften."

Carlos nodded. "Yes, she has blamed everyone else for her circumstances and for many jubilees has stubbornly refused to look at herself. But this began to change when you placed her in the same community as Imelda again."

"Yes," said Jesus, "I felt at that point that they were finally ready to see each other again. Because they had shared their first jubilee together, I hoped their bond might be the cornerstone for Fran to begin to see the value in people in their own right, rather than just using them or getting them to do what she wanted."

"It was after being placed with Imelda that Fran began to prioritise relationships with others. I think she was desperate not to be lonely anymore, and Imelda had reached the same point too. It was their shared love of The Beatles that gave them something in common to talk joyfully about as soon as they were reunited," said Sylvia, smiling at the memory of hearing them singing together through an open window.

"Discovering the joy of friendship was like the first crack in a dam. One positive emotion led to another, and as the jubilees went by, both women became able to welcome and include more people into their lives and enjoy contributing to their communities," Carlos reported.

"There were numerous setbacks along the way though, and they found that jealousy can easily creep into friendships," Sylvia added. "Fran sometimes got jealous when Imelda expressed affection for anyone else and wanted to spent time with them. This took a long time to overcome, but when they were in their eleventh jubilee, Fran came to understand the beauty of kairos time and realised that in the ages to come she would always have Imelda as a friend and that they would be able spend as much time together as they could ever wish."

*

"Stop!" Fran shouted in between mock screams and breathless laughter. Imelda continued to playfully raise the hosepipe up into the air sending a cold shower down over Fran and three other friends who had been reclining on picnic blankets. They often sat outside together in the evenings and were sometimes joined by other neighbours from their village community in the land of

Beulah, located close to the Eternal City. Imelda giggled with a cheeky final flick of the hosepipe.

"Come on, Imelda, tell us the rest of your story. You were on Top of the Pops, weren't you? Who did you meet?" Fran wiped the water from her hair and the group of friends settled back down on the blanket again.

"Well, we weren't supposed to talk to the stars, but we knew which exit they used, so that's where we used to hang around. It was my lucky day when the pop star Marc Bolan came out and stopped to sign autographs and chat to us. Do you remember his blue eyes and amazing curly hair? Couldn't believe it when just a few years later he was killed in a road accident."

"I was in a community with a pop star that knew him." said Harriet, a recent friend of Fran's. "He said he was a real gentleman and great fun to be around."

"It's funny when you think how long we've been alive on New Earth," said Fran, "and how many people we've spent time with in all our different communities. I often wonder where they all are now."

"It's true," said Imelda. "But I know I've needed this long to begin to change. Do you remember how awful we were to each other in our first community, Fran? And how I made Dawn work so hard in my dressmaking business just so I could impress you and everyone else?"

"Yes, I'll never forget how jealous I was of that purple coat with gold buttons you got her to make for you! Honestly, why didn't we just sit down with a cup of tea and enjoy getting to know each other instead of all that malarkey? But look at us all now. At least we got there in the end."

"You certainly have," came an unexpected voice from behind where they were sitting.

"Jesus!" cried Fran, as they all turned around and sprang to their feet to welcome him.

"Hello gang!" Jesus greeted them with characteristic affection. "Forgive me, but I do enjoy surprising people."

"Oh Jesus," began Fran, "we were just saying how it's taken a while but we can see our progress. It's been such a journey, but now I couldn't be happier."

"I can assure you that you will be happier!" laughed Jesus. "It's your time to come to the Eternal City."

"Really?"

"Yes Fran. You've finally understood what *agape love* is and how to live by it. Just look around." Jesus motioned with his hand to Fran's friends, who were all smiling broadly. "You only have friends here, and in the last few jubilees you've only spoken kindly about other people. People love you, Fran. You serve without reservation, and you've allowed yourself to be loved in equal measure."

"It's true, Jesus, she is wonderful in every way," Imelda said with tears in her eyes. "I am going to miss her."

"Imelda, I'll be back for you and each one of you very soon. Ruach has told me about your life here in the community - your daily acts of kindness and selflessness and how you resolve your differences with respect and grace."

"When we do that, we feel in harmony with all of creation," said Harriet.

"Ah, Harriet, you have always been a poet. What you feel is *shalom*, the peace of God that permeates all of creation. It is the fruit of *agape love*."

Harriet beamed. "*Shalom*. What a beautiful word."

*

Fran had never been much of a dancer in the Previous Age. She could bop along to 'Twist and Shout' but always felt awkward and self-conscious. Later, as a married woman, she would avoid dancing with her husband, ashamed of her weight and the shape of her body.

That evening, Fran and her children had opted for the Jazz Club. In the Previous Age Fran had always been taught that jazz was 'the devil's music', so it was with relish that she now embraced her freedom and began to dance as never before. The jazz band played with rhythms and unpredictable melodies that she had never thought possible, and people danced together, expressing their emotions.

"Mum, you have all the moves!" Louise shouted over the music.

"Looking good, Mum!" called out Terry with a wink, as he held out his hand to twirl his mother.

In the Previous Age, her children had often ridiculed Fran for not dancing and had regularly disobeyed her by sneaking out of the house for a 'night on the tiles'. Fran looked over to see where her friend Kelly was dancing with her arms around her own daughter, Clare. They had been in the same community many jubilee periods ago, but in those days Kelly had been consumed with bitterness and anger after losing her daughter in a road accident and Fran had been too focused on herself to offer friendship or feel any compassion. Kelly looked over her daughter's raven black hair and her eyes met Fran's. A look of pure surprise and joy was exchanged between them as they danced with their children and felt the energy surging through their own youthful bodies.

Fran slept so well that night and was delighted to discover her children at her door the next morning to share breakfast together.

"I was so bitter about life when I got older," she confessed as they sat around the table together. "I was too hard on you because I was jealous of your freedom."

"We thought so too, to be honest, Mum," said Louise, stroking the head of Sammy, the family beagle who had been gifted to Louise on her resurrection.

"And we resented the way that you and Dad didn't try to understand us. You just thought everything we did was sinful," added Terry. "But now we understand you were genuinely worried about what we were doing. It wasn't until I became a father that I understood, but you had already passed away by then. Won't it be great when Dad can join us too?"

"I can't wait to see him and am looking forward to getting to know my grandchildren too," exclaimed Fran with delight as she passed her son the marmalade. "Now each generation can see each other through the eyes of *agape love*, we can understand each other so much better. You *see* me and I *see* you!"

*

"Just look at the colour of those leaves, and can you see those birds perched up there?" Fran said to her daughter, Louise, while out on a walk in the countryside. "Life here is familiar, yet it's always exciting with so much to discover, isn't it?"

"Yes, I don't think we will ever get bored," agreed Louise. "We never imagined that we could be free to enjoy life like this, did we? I think it's because we've learned to be ourselves without hiding behind the masks we *thought* we had to wear."

"I look back and realise how narrow and constrained I used to be," said Fran. "I think it was because deep down I didn't like myself very much that I took such delight in focusing on other people's shortcomings. And I was very controlling, wasn't I? Always wanting people to behave as I thought they should."

"We all make mistakes, Mum, and I guess we all believed the lies our culture and our upbringing told us about ourselves. I know I wasn't the easiest of teenagers, but my journey here on the New Earth has helped me understand that I built up resentment against you and the church because you gave so much time and energy to it, instead of being there for us."

"And for that I am so sorry," said Fran, squeezing her daughter's hand. "I realise now that I was trying to gain approval from my *idea* of God and from the other church folk. I wanted to impress the vicar, and I thought I was only worth something if I kept the rules and looked good in front of others. I tried to love, but I don't think I really understood what love was in those days."

"We've all had to learn to take off the masks we wore," said Louise thoughtfully. "But here is our reward at the end of all the hard learning. We get to be together, forever, and nothing can take away the connection and the love we have for one another."

The two walked arm in arm along a path shaded by tall trees. Butterflies fluttered around them seeking nectar from the wildflowers that bloomed in profusion at their feet, and birds called from the branches above them.

"Hello Fran!" came a voice from behind one of the trees.

Fran stopped dead in her tracks. Yes, there was no mistaking that voice!

Imelda appeared holding a basket of berries and came up to Fran with a warm smile.

"Well, look at us!" she declared, jubilantly. "Through everything, finally here together."

"Oh Imelda, how wonderful to see you! This is my daughter, Louise."

"Great to meet you, Louise. Your mother and I were the best of enemies. It took some time, but now we can't imagine being anything but the best of friends."

"We certainly can't. Come and walk with us a while?" invited Fran.

Imelda opened her arms and Fran hugged her back. Louise stood watching, amazed at the warmth and emotion that flowed so naturally from her mother. Though they had all been through so much, both in the Previous Age and here on the New Earth, it felt as though endless possibilities still lay ahead of them.

# Abundant Life in the Eternal City

A warm, bright light came streaming into the room. Everything was quiet. Johan awoke from a thoroughly refreshing night's sleep and felt so energized that he laughed. He then lay perfectly still, relishing the sense of strength that filled his whole being.

Looking forward to the day ahead, he washed and dressed, making a mental note to collect more water as the jug by his wash bowl was now empty.

He knew he did not need food to stay alive but he still enjoyed the taste of a juicy pear for his breakfast that he had picked the previous day. He sang quietly to himself as he carried out his morning routine of making his bed, sweeping the floor and cleaning his wash bowl and kitchen sink. He smiled as he heard other songs drifting on the breeze through his windows as his neighbours went about their daily chores.

After tidying the house, he took some clothes and his water jug to the stream. There he found his neighbour Harriet and they chatted happily while washing their clothes in the sparkling water.

"What do you have planned for the day?" asked Johan.

"I'm going to my poetry group this morning. We're trying to capture the beauty of the landscape here in words, but so far my efforts don't do it justice. And this afternoon I'm helping Yuri prepare the communal meal for this evening. It's always fun to work with him and we belt out songs together as we stir the pots. What are you up to?"

"I'm playing tennis with Yan this morning, meeting friends for lunch and then working with the maintenance team this afternoon," Johan replied.

After wringing out their clothes and filling their jugs, they walked back and wished each other a good day.

Johan hung his washing on the line and packed his work overalls, a change of clothes, a towel and some swimming trunks into a small rucksack. Picking up his tennis racket and taking twenty talents from the drawer, he set out for the court.

*

Feeling well exercised but determined to improve his game after yet another defeat at the hands of Yan, Johan was walking to his lunch appointment when three men appeared from the side street just ahead of him.

"Hey guys, how good to see you!" exclaimed Johan as he recognised Thomas, Bem and Eric's friendly faces.

Thomas gave Johan a warm hug. "Are you still enjoying your tennis?" he asked.

Johan covered his face with his hands in mock drama.

"I would be if I could beat Yan!" he replied, through his fingers.

The men chuckled.

"Anyway, it's good to see you too, Eric. How's your family?" Johan asked, giving Eric a fist bump.

"Ma and Pa have just been to a gospel choir festival. They loved it. And I've joined a barber-shop quartet. You'll have to come and listen when we give our first performance."

"I surely will," said Johan, who after chatting some more with his friends continued on his way to the *Taverna Yialos*, where Harmony and Fran were already sitting at a table, drinks in hand.

"Hello you two! What have you been up to?" he asked as he joined them.

Harmony looked at Fran and gestured for her to speak first. "I've been attending an art class. I never used to think of myself as creative, so it's been amazing to discover that side of myself. I'm still very much a beginner, but I'm learning lots. Today was still life with a bowl of fruit. You know, I don't think I'd ever stopped to look at things properly before."

"We'd love to see your work, Fran. It's so good to learn new things, isn't it?" agreed Harmony. "I've been learning Greek cooking in my group."

"You'll be able to help the chef here soon," said Johan with a smile.

"Don't you think I have enough to do already?" retorted Harmony, playfully slapping Johan on the arm as Fran looked on and laughed.

"Are you ready to order?" asked Anne coming to the table.

"Hello Anne, we're sorry you're not able to join us this week," said Fran.

"I was asked to do this shift, but I'll be able to join you next week, so we'll be able to debrief about the garden party then. Most of the preparations are complete. Would you like your usual dips and pita bread?"

"You know us well! Yes, that would be great and a jug of water with it please," Johan replied, and Anne moved on to the next table of customers.

The three friends enjoyed catching up with each other over their meal before their afternoon activities.

"I'm tree-pruning this afternoon, and I'm wondering who will be helping me," said Johan. "I have to admit there are a few people who test my patience."

"Personalities can still clash here, can't they?" said Fran. "At least until you really get to know people. It's raspberry jam making for me today. I need to make a few more jars before the market next week."

"And I'm working out a route for a walk I'm organising," said Harmony. "It'll be well away from where most people live and will take most of the day, but there should be great views and lots of wildlife too. Let me know if you're interested and would like to come."

As the group stood up, Anne came over, collected their talents and wished them all the best for the afternoon.

Johan bid his friends farewell and went to meet the pruning team, secretly hoping that a few of them might have forgotten to turn up.

*

It was still pleasantly warm late into the evening and many people were enjoying messing about in the river. Johan changed from his work overalls into his swimming trunks and slipped into the cool water. Feeling refreshed, he swam for a while and then turned on his back and lay still, watching the clouds.

Someone splashing beside him broke his reverie. Sylvia had spotted him and swum over to join him.

"Are you going to the garden party next week?" she asked, breathlessly.

"I wouldn't miss it. I can't wait to catch up with Thomas' team and all the others."

"Yes, I'm looking forward to it too. If you're going to the communal meal this evening, let's go together. I'll race you to the bank," she said, before taking a deep breath and kicking out with strong underwater stokes for where they had left their clothes.

Johan coped well with his second sporting defeat of the day and was surprised to realise after they had finished drying and changing side by side that their nakedness had created no awkwardness or embarrassment. He mulled over how different it was to the way things were in the Previous Age as he walked with Sylvia to the communal meal served up by Yuri and his team of helpers.

After the meal they stayed in the square to hear Helena and Clare performing a selection of songs that had been popular in the Previous Age. One of them reminded Johan of his childhood, and he thought about his parents and Gerty. It had been so good to see them six months ago on his travels through the neighbouring villages. He relished the freedom to travel and keep in touch with everyone, and knowing that they were here in the Eternal City brought such peace to his heart.

Feeling tired but with a deep sense of contentment, Johan made his way back home and was soon sound asleep.

*

The table was set in the middle of a large swathe of lawn surrounded by trees and banks of flowers. Chairs had been arranged around it, each unique and made by skilled artisans. Figures emerged from the house that looked over the garden carrying trays full of glasses.

"Yuri, would you mind grabbing the last tray?" asked Fran. "Adilah and I will set out the glasses at each place."

"I'll start bringing down the jugs," suggested Johan as he placed his tray on one of the tables. "How many do you think we'll need?"

Soon the four friends had finished setting the table and the sound of chatter and laughter signalled the arrival of Thomas and his team. Harmony, Anne, Sylvia and Carlos led the group, with Yan, Bull, Thomas and Yvonne a few steps behind.

Yuri excitedly flung open the garden gate and took each of them in his arms as they entered. Adilah giggled and danced with delight, Johan wore a huge grin and Fran beamed as she led them to where the refreshments were laid out.

"This is such a wonderful idea," said Thomas to Fran as they sat in the bright afternoon light.

277

"Well, it feels rather like a full circle moment, doesn't it?" she said. "It feels right to celebrate. Ah, here come the others!"

Every few minutes, more people appeared and gathered in pairs or small groups near the table. Johan looked around, drinking in the beauty of the scene, but his heart jumped as he recognised a smiling face approaching him. Though no longer wearing his small round spectacles and army uniform, there was no mistaking his friend Wilhelm with his distinctive cheeky grin.

"I was told I could find you here, brother," Wilhelm greeted him warmly as he embraced his former comrade.

For a moment, Johan was lost for words. He hadn't thought about the army and his experience of war for a long time. That period felt unreal, like a bad dream. Yet here stood a man who had shared his foxhole, drunk from the same water bottle and smoked more than his fair share of their cigarettes. Yes, this was a man who had died by his side in their dugout.

"Listen, Johan, I want you to know that I always loved you. But I need to apologise. I took advantage of your kind nature. You were always so patient and generous. You showed me love, even when I didn't deserve it. I now see that you had *agape love* in your heart, even then."

"Wilhelm, my friend, it's so good to see you! Come, let's tell each other our stories."

Yuri smiled as he saw the two men strolling around the garden, arm in arm, as he arranged the bread rolls on the table. Just then, someone cleared their throat behind him. Turning around he saw a tall man with a newly trimmed beard and short black hair. It took Yuri a moment to realise he was looking at Angush.

Angush stood there, clearly nervous, waiting for Yuri to speak. Yuri felt a flush of shame - this was a man he had violently assaulted - and then the thought flashed through his mind that Angush might have come to take revenge. But as Yuri took a deep breath and felt the pure air of the City in his lungs, peace spread through his body.

The moment was awkward; neither man could deny that. They stood, each hesitating to be the first to offer a handshake, but the momentary tension was broken by Johan and Wilhelm's voices and laughter as they walked nearby. Yuri slowly extended his hand and Angush grasped it, letting out a relieved and grateful breath.

"It's all ok, isn't it?" asked Yuri quietly.

Angush let out a deep breath. "Yes, it is. It is."

"You look well," said Yuri.

"Fortunately scars don't remain here in the City," said Angush with a straight face.

Yuri was unsure how to respond, but Angush immediately burst into laughter.

"Don't worry. Everything is ok. I know who I was - or who I thought I was. I'm not that person anymore."

"I can see that, my friend," replied Yuri. It was true. There was no sign of the arrogant smirk that had always been on Angush's face, and no false happiness, no projection of ego.

"I am grateful to you, Yuri. Meeting you in my second jubilee set me on a new course. No one had ever stood up to me before, and no one had ever challenged the way I lived."

"I didn't go about it the right way and I'm sorry for attacking you. I was so full of rage back then. But meeting you helped change my direction, too. For the first time I realised that I believed in some kind of justice and that I had a sense of right and wrong."

Angush nodded. "I think we were a mirror to each other. It began the process of purification and here we are now in the City as new creations. Fully alive and fully human - just as Papa God meant us to be. So why don't I give you a hand with those bread rolls?"

The two former enemies continued to talk as they headed to the kitchen to fetch more bread with the joy and relief of reconciliation filling their hearts.

Fran sent off the next batch of fresh rolls with Yuri and Angush and clapped off some of the flour that was on her hands. She stood on the veranda surveying the scene when she noticed a familiar figure walking purposefully towards her.

"Reverend!" exclaimed Fran.

"Hello Fran. No more of the 'Reverend'! Do call me Brian. I heard that you would be here and wanted to talk with you."

"Well, it's good to see you, Brian. You've probably been here longer than all of us!"

"Now, Fran," said Brian gently, "you know it doesn't work like that. It's been a long journey and I have to admit I've only recently arrived in the Eternal City. Now that I'm here, I want to apologise to you and all my parishioners. I told you that God would only save a few chosen people who believed the right things and that everyone else would be punished for all of eternity. I feel ashamed that my idea of God was so small, so tribal and so vengeful."

"Yes, we thought we had it all worked out, didn't we? We were right and everyone else was wrong. To be honest, I think we rather relished that idea."

Brian nodded. "I think you're right. But I've been humbled. Meeting Jesus and then everything I experienced throughout many jubilees challenged my beliefs. Jesus knew exactly what was needed to free me from my spiritual prison, and look at us all now! God's plan was so much bigger than we could ever have imagined."

"Yes, Jesus has been so patient and kind to us. It took a while but our hearts changed eventually."

"Amen to that!" said Brian with a grin.

Back in the kitchen, Adilah was kneading dough for the final batch of baking with such concentration that she didn't notice a figure appear next to her until another fist was plunged into it.

Adilah looked up and Eshe burst into bright laughter at her expression of surprise.

"Eshe!" Adilah flung her arms around her sister, and they held each other in a tight swaying embrace.

"Let me look at you," Adilah said through tears of joy.

"I've come to find you. Our entire tribe has a place on the plains of the Eternal City. So many have come together there - many who were with the militia, and many who were captives. Oh, Adilah, it is the healing of our nation! You must come and see for yourself."

"Of course, I will come. My heart is so happy it is dancing! But first, stay with me for this meal. Let us celebrate with everyone here, and then I will come with you."

The sisters embraced again and talked of the paths that had brought them to this moment as they worked together on the final preparations for the meal.

Soon it was time for everyone to be seated around the table and the food was served. Stories were shared about the journeys each had been on and how they had learnt the way of *agape love*. Gladness and gratitude flowed through the conversations as the dancing lights of the new heavens illuminated the garden. Across the ages, wherever people have formed communities there have been such gatherings, but here in the Eternal City, with no need to hide behind masks or fear being judged by one's neighbour, they were free to enjoy the fullness of every moment.

As people finished eating, Adilah stood and asked for attention. "Let us raise a glass to Jesus, the overseer of our journeys towards finding *agape love*, to Ruach dwelling within us and to Papa our Father, who, as promised, has given us this abundant life that will only grow richer in the ages ahead."

All stood and raised their glasses. As they looked around at the company gathered there, they were in awe of what *agape love* had achieved, and each renewed their faith in the future that Jesus was masterminding. It was true; there was indeed hope for everyone.

# Afterword

There comes a point when language fails. The tongue falls silent and typing fingers rest. The search for words to articulate feeling ceases and a hushed reverence is the only possible response.

The characters we have followed in this story are, of course, avatars through which we have explored some of our thoughts around the process of reconciliation. They are motifs representing elements within the wide spectrum of humanity.

We leave our characters lost in awe at the magnitude of what *agape love* is doing. They have come to understand a little of the ongoing story of God. We do not know for certain what the future holds for humankind, but we believe we have glimpsed a vision of an unfolding story in which the source of all continues to create and recreate out of the generosity of *agape love*.

If you have read our depiction of a town or village in the Eternal City and feel that you would not wish to live there, do remember that God loves variety. Human history is full of wonderful diversity, and we are sure that will not change in the ages to come. We believe that God will create settings appropriate for each individual once they have matured to live by *agape love*. Humankind will know a freedom to live as never before - to live and move and 'be' in an expansive and totally fulfilling environment.

Have you ever known what it is to be loved? To be held? To be told that everything will be alright? At our core we all need to hear this. It's good news, because so much in our world tells us the opposite.

Many theologians from many faith traditions have expounded the virtues of love. Many believers trust in a God who *is* love. However, not many have attempted a theory of the mechanics of *how* such a God might love creation into eternity - the ages to come - and into individual and collective maturity.

Whoever we are and whatever we have done, we are convinced that we are all included in God's plan for redemption. Nobody has ever burned their bridges to *agape love*, and we believe nobody ever could. As the Apostle Paul wrote, this love 'keeps no record of wrongs... It always protects, always trusts, always hopes, always perseveres.'

The belief that everyone is loved by God gives hope to us all. This vision of the future leaves no one behind and that is why we have called it *Hope for Everyone*. God does not abandon any of us and no one will slip through his fingers into some abyss. To such ideas of eternal loss and punishment we say an emphatic, impassioned and prayerful 'NO!' This story and our accompanying online project, Love Above All Things, aim to encourage a thoughtful and honest exploration of this good news.

Our modus operandi is not to argue or convince, but rather to invite and facilitate investigation into what we believe. We are far from alone in holding such convictions. People of faith throughout the centuries have believed that God will redeem and restore all things (the Greek word for this doctrine is *apokatastasis*). There are myriad books, blogs, talks, essays and histories about these beliefs to discover and explore. Indeed, the best stories inspire us to dream bigger dreams, hope bigger hopes and engage with life in a more energised and positive way.

It is not possible to finish a story that continues into the eternal ages to come. We have explored the process - the *how* of love - and have stopped at a convenient point with our four main characters in the Eternal City. It's difficult, and probably impossible, for us to fully comprehend what the ages ahead would hold for them and for us. Fundamentally, we believe that this strange, wonderful, terrible, beautiful experience we currently find ourselves in is full of meaning. Absolutely nothing is wasted - even our pain and our suffering. All things can, and will, be made new in the fullness of time.

We believe we are all loved and that eventually everyone will love everyone and live an abundant life.

# Author Profiles

David Bell and Dave Griffiths offer their second book 'Hope for Everyone', a sequel to 'Emerging from the Rubble'. It has been created from their joint passion to spread the message that love is above all things and that all will be well eventually.

David Bell spent much of his childhood helping on the family farm. After graduating he earned his living in various IT positions and has now been retired for over fifteen years. He has devoted much of his retirement to an investigation of how the afterlife has been envisioned and theodicy (the problem of evil). He was raised in a Christian family and has attended churches of many denominations. He no longer attends a church but enjoys the company of others in local clubs and societies. David's second wife died of pancreatic cancer. He has three children, two step-children and, so far, five grandchildren.

Dave Griffiths is a musician by night and a Children and Families Minister in his local parish by day. He has released several critically acclaimed albums with his bands Bosh, Chaos Curb and Held by Trees, as well as solo work. He graduated from Moorlands College with a BA in Applied Theology and lives with his wife, Jess, and their three kids, two cats and one dog in Dorset, England.

Milton Keynes UK
Ingram Content Group UK Ltd.
UKHW032131100924
448136UK00001B/33